# BRASS

Cerberus Personal Security Specialists
Book 2

## ELLIE MASTERS

## MASTER OF ROMANTIC SUSPENSE

JEM Publishing

*This book is dedicated to my one and only—my amazing and wonderful husband.*

*Without your care and support, my writing would not have made it this far.*

*You pushed me when I needed to be pushed.*

*You supported me when I felt discouraged.*

*You believed in me when I didn't believe in myself.*

*If it weren't for you, this book never would have come to life.*

*SUGGESTED READING ORDER*

*START HERE*

*Rockstar Romance*

*The Angel Fire Rock Romance Series*

EACH BOOK IN THIS SERIES CAN BE READ AS A STANDALONE AND IS ABOUT A DIFFERENT COUPLE WITH AN **HEA.**

IT IS RECOMMENDED THEY ARE READ IN ORDER.

*Heart's Insanity*

*Ashes to New*

*Heart's Desire*

*Heart's Collide*

*Hearts Divided*

*Hearts Entwined*

*Forest's FALL*

*Hearts The Last Beat*

*CONTINUE HERE…*

*Military Romance*

*Guardian Hostage Rescue Specialists*

*Rescuing Melissa*

**(Get a FREE copy of Rescuing Melissa when you join Ellie's Newsletter)**

*Alpha Team*

*Rescuing Zoe*

*Rescuing Moira*

*Rescuing Eve*

*Rescuing Lily*

*Rescuing Jinx*

*Rescuing Maria*

*Bravo Team*

*Rescuing Angie*

*Rescuing Isabelle*

*Rescuing Carmen*

*Rescuing Rosalie*

*Rescuing Kaye*

*Cara's Protector*

*Rescuing Barbi*

*Charlie Team*

*Rescuing Rebel*

*Rescuing Stitch*

*Rescuing Mia*

*Jenna's Protector*

*Rescuing Sophia*

*Rescuing Malia*

*Rescuing Ally (Part 1)*

*Rescuing Ally (Part 2)*

*Delta Team*

*Rescuing Ember*

*Rescuing Aria*

**STANDALONES IN THE GUARDIAN HOSTAGE RESCUE
SERIES YOU CAN READ ANYTIME**

*Military Romance*

*Guardian Personal Protection Specialists*

*Sybil's Protector*

*Lyra's Protector*

*Angel's Peak Series*

*Steamy Instalove Small Town*

EACH BOOK IN THIS SERIES CAN BE READ AS A STANDALONE AND IS ABOUT A DIFFERENT COUPLE WITH AN HEA.

**Snowed in with the Mountain Doctor**

**Rescued by the Mountain Guide**

**Stranded with the Resort Owner**

**Matched with the Small-Town Chef**

**Trapped with the Forest Ranger**

**Snowbound with the Vineyard Owner**

**Reunited with the Hometown Hero**

**Colliding with the Coffee Shop Owner**

**Falling for the Firefighter**

**Wrecked with the Reclusive Author**

**Tangled with the Single Dad**

**Whirlwinded by the Helicopter Pilot**

**Sheltered by the Veterinarian**

**Bound by the Sheriff**

*The One I Want Series*

*(Small Town, Military Heroes)*

*By Jet & Ellie Masters*

## To My Readers

*This book is a work of fiction. It does not exist in the real world and should not be construed as reality. As in most romantic fiction, I've taken liberties. I've compressed the romance into a sliver of time. I've allowed these characters to develop strong bonds of trust over a matter of days.*

*This does not happen in real life where you, my amazing readers, live. Take more time in your romance and learn who you're giving a piece of your heart to. I urge you to move with caution. Always protect yourself.*

# Grab the First Book in The Guardian Hostage Rescue Specialists Series for Free

**https://elliemasters.com/RescuingMelissa**

ONE

## Celeste

_______________

The alley behind Murphy's Pub reeks of stale beer and cigarettes. Water drips from fire escapes overhead, a steady rhythm against the slick pavement. I check my watch again—8:27 PM. Jared's late.

He's never late.

I hunch deeper into my coat, scanning both ends of the alley. My messenger bag hangs heavy against my hip, laptop and recorder tucked inside. Three months chasing shadows. Three sources gone silent: Quentin Hargrove's "heart attack" at forty-two with no prior health issues, Zara Nouri's single-car accident on a straight dry road, and Lachlan Reeves's "suicide" despite the half-finished wedding invitations on his desk.

And now Jared Caldwell, former data analyst at Northridge Defense Solutions, is the only one still answering my calls. The only one who might know what connects them all.

My phone buzzes. Text from a number I don't recognize: *Change of plans. Come to the Windsor Hotel. Room 512. Walls have ears.*

My stomach knots. This isn't protocol. But Jared's paranoia

has kept him alive this long, so I rush to my car and head across town to the hotel.

The Windsor is all faded elegance—brass fixtures tarnished just enough to suggest character rather than neglect. I take the stairs instead of the elevator, checking over my shoulder at each landing.

Room 512's door stands slightly ajar.

"Jared?" My voice echoes in the empty hallway. I push the door open with my fingertips.

The copper smell hits me first. Metallic. Primal. Wrong.

Jared lies sprawled across the bed. His throat—God, his throat. A red line carved from ear to ear, blood soaking the white hotel sheets. His eyes, fixed and dilated, stare at the ceiling. His laptop is gone.

Bile surges up my throat. I should call the police. Should scream. Should run.

Instead, I move on instinct—a safeguard we swore we'd never need. If it ever comes to this, *check the remote.*

My hands shake as I slide the back panel off the TV remote. Batteries spill onto the carpet. One is hollow, a dummy. The flash drive is taped beneath the cover, exactly where he promised it would be.

For a second, I can't breathe. He knew. He planned for this.

I shove the drive into my pocket.

And then I run.

Now, speeding through D.C.'s rain-slicked streets, every shadow feels like a predator. Every traffic light is a countdown to something terrible. The flash drive burns in my pocket, heavy with whatever secrets cost Jared his life.

And someone is following me.

A black SUV has been in my mirror since the corner of K and 14th. At first, I dismissed it as paranoia—a coincidence, just another vehicle caught in the same downpour. But when I switch lanes? They follow. When I deliberately miss my turn onto Massachusetts? They miss theirs, too.

Another glance in the rearview. The SUV looms larger now. Closer. Too close for coincidence. Its headlights bore through the rain like twin predatory eyes, high beams deliberately switched on to blind me. The windshield wipers can't keep up with the downpour, each swipe buying only a second of clarity before the world blurs again.

I grip the wheel tighter, knuckles whitening. Switch lanes again. Rush through a yellow light. The SUV follows, matching my every move.

Twenty blocks from the hotel, and I'm certain. I'm being hunted.

My heartbeat drowns out the radio. Sweat slicks my palms despite the cold air blasting from the vents. I take a sharp right onto a one-way street, tires skidding slightly on the wet pavement. The SUV hangs back for just a moment—hesitating—then accelerates.

Amateur move on my part. The street narrows. Less traffic. No witnesses.

The black vehicle surges forward. Gains on me. Ten car lengths. Five. Three.

I slam the accelerator to the floor. The engine whines in protest. Not enough.

In the mirror, I catch a glimpse of the driver. A flash of pale skin under the streetlights. No expression. No rage. No hurry. Just cold, calculating eyes locked on my car.

He wears what looks like a comm device in one ear. His mouth moves, speaking to someone I can't see. Not alone then. Coordinated. Professional. He adjusts his grip on the wheel, gloved hands shifting. Our eyes meet in the mirror for a split second. No emotion registers at all. Just the flat, dead gaze of someone doing a job.

This isn't personal. It's worse. It's business.

The SUV kisses my bumper.

"Shit!" White-knuckle grip on the wheel. Heart hammering against my ribs.

A horn blares from somewhere to my left. The SUV taps me again, harder this time. My tires scream across wet asphalt.

I jerk the wheel right, trying to pull away. Slam the brake. Stomp the accelerator. Nothing matters.

They ram me.

Metal crushes against metal. The sound deafens—a terrible screech that vibrates through my bones. My world becomes a violent carousel. The steering wheel rips from my hands as the car spins. My head snaps forward, then back. Streetlights streak across the windshield in dizzy arcs of color.

My body slams against the door. Ribs crack. Air punches from my lungs.

The seatbelt cuts into my chest, burning across my collarbone, the only thing keeping me from becoming a projectile.

Headlights blind me—a taxi swerves, horn blaring, clipping my bumper. The impact sends my car spinning again. Something warm trickles down my temple. Blood or sweat or rain leaking through the fractured window, I can't tell.

The SUV fishtails, regains control, then disappears into traffic. Leaving me. My car sputters, coughs, and dies in the middle of the intersection, steam billowing from the crumpled hood, hissing into the rain. The smell of burned rubber and antifreeze chokes me.

I claw at the seatbelt release. *Click.* Freedom. Pain shoots through my left side. Broken rib, maybe two. My legs tremble as I force the door open and stumble into the downpour.

Glass and plastic crunch beneath my boots. My knee buckles, sending lightning up my thigh. Rain pelts my face, washing away whatever's trickling from my hairline. My wool coat hangs sodden, dragging at my shoulders, weighing me down.

Sirens wail in the distance. Police or ambulance. Questions I can't answer. People who can't protect me.

Across the street—salvation. The Dupont Circle subway entrance, its light spilling out onto the sidewalk like an invitation.

I run. Every step jars my ribs. Every breath burns.

The flash drive knocks against my thigh through my pocket. Worth dying for, Jared thought. Worth killing for, someone else decided.

Down the steps, gripping the handrail to keep from falling. The fluorescent lighting assaults my eyes after the darkness outside. The air down here hangs thick with humanity—stale perfume, wet clothes, the metallic tang of the trains, and beneath it all, the unmistakable reek of urine and mildew clinging to every surface.

My hair clings to my eyes. I swipe it back, wincing as my fingers graze a knot swelling at my temple.

Deeper into the station. Left turn. Another staircase. The rumble of an approaching train vibrates through the concrete. Safety in numbers. That's my plan. Lose myself in the crowd. Catch the Red Line. Get to my apartment. Pack. Run.

I reach the platform.

There is no crowd.

Tuesday night. Late. Rain. Just a few scattered commuters huddled under flickering lights, faces buried in phones, purposefully ignoring each other. Three teenagers sharing earbuds. A homeless man is asleep on a bench. An elderly woman is clutching her purse. No safety in these numbers.

Then I hear it.

Footsteps. Synchronized. Deliberate. Different from the casual shuffle of commuters.

I turn. Cold sweat breaks across my neck despite the chill.

Four men descend the escalator. Dark coats. Identical builds. One adjusts something beneath his jacket—the telltale gesture of checking a weapon. Another lifts his chin, scanning the platform. His eyes lock onto mine.

Recognition flares. Not of me personally, but of a target acquired.

"Fuck." The word escapes as vapor in the cold air.

My heart slams against my broken ribs. I back away, shoes slipping slightly on the wet tile. The train's rumbling grows louder, but it won't arrive in time.

Two of them angle left. The other two cut right. Cutting off escape routes. Herding me.

My back hits the tiled wall. Nowhere to go. The flash drive feels like it's burning through my pocket, branding me. I bring my hands up, remembering fragments from a self-defense class I took after covering a story on campus assaults. Thumbs to eyes. Knee to groin. Scream fire, not rape or help.

None of it will save me from four trained killers.

They close in. Ten feet away. Eight. Five.

A large hand grabs my upper arm. I scream, twisting to fight this new threat from behind.

"Stay behind me."

The voice cuts through my panic. Low. Calm. Absolute authority.

A stranger materializes beside me. Tall—six-three, maybe six-four. Broad shoulders tapering to a narrow waist. Military posture. Close-cropped dark blond hair. A jagged scar beneath his left eye that pulls slightly at the corner.

He steps forward, positioning his body between me and the approaching men. His movements are fluid, calculated. Nothing wasted. I catch the outline of a shoulder holster beneath his jacket.

"You've made a mistake," he calls to them, voice carrying across the platform without shouting. "Walk away."

The four men exchange glances. No hesitation. No fear. The leader, a tight-faced man with cold gray eyes, smirks. "This doesn't concern you."

"It does now." My defender's tone is almost conversational.

I press against the wall, every nerve humming with adrenaline. The approaching train's vibration intensifies beneath my feet, but it's still too far away. The few commuters on the platform have noticed the tension—they edge away, gazes averted, unwilling to become involved.

"Last chance," says Gray Eyes, hand slipping inside his coat.

My protector shifts his weight to the balls of his feet. "Four against one. Not great odds." A beat. "For you."

The first man rushes him.

The stranger moves like water. A sidestep, then a precise strike to the attacker's throat. The man crumples, gasping. Second attacker comes in low—my defender drives a knee up, catches him under the chin. Bone cracks. The man drops.

Gray Eyes pulls a knife. The blade catches the fluorescent light—five inches of serrated steel. He lunges. The stranger deflects, twists, and suddenly the knife is in his hand. He slashes backward, opening a red line across his attacker's chest.

The fourth man has circled behind. He reaches for me. I scream, ducking away. The stranger spins, hurls the knife. It embeds in the wall an inch from the man's ear—a warning.

"Next one goes in your eye," my defender promises.

The train roars into the station, brakes screeching. Doors slide open. The commuters hurry on, desperate to escape the violence.

Gray Eyes clutches his bleeding chest, face contorted with fury. "This isn't over."

"Wrong." My protector growls, low and ominous. "You're outmatched, out-skilled, and half your team is down. Whatever they're paying you, it's not enough."

TWO

# Ryan

---

I CHECK MY WATCH AGAIN. 10:47 PM. TRAIN SHOULD'VE BEEN here seven minutes ago. Typical D.C. inefficiency.

Rain hammers the platform roof, echoing through the station. Four days in the nation's capital is about three and a half too many. Especially when those days revolve around my mother's endless parade of "suitable" women at her Thanksgiving table. Four potential daughters-in-law, each more aggressively cheerful than the last.

*"You could have a normal life, Ryan. A good job. Children. Not running around the world getting shot at for people who don't even know your name."*

My jaw tightens. Twenty years since Dad died, and she still doesn't understand that some men are built for what I do. It's in my DNA, just as it was in my father's.

The platform is sparse for a Tuesday night. Young couple at the far end, wrapped up in each other. Homeless man asleep on a bench. Elderly woman gripping her purse like it contains the nuclear codes. Group of teenagers sharing earbuds. Businessman buried in his phone. Standard nighttime metro crowd.

I roll my shoulders, trying to work the tension out. The briefcase at my feet contains the only decent thing from this visit—Mom's pumpkin bread. Enough to share with the team back at Cerberus. Ghost will appreciate that at least.

Motion catches my eye. A woman practically flies down the escalator, her pace too urgent for casual travel. She's favoring her left side—injured ribs most likely. Blood matting her hair at the temple. Rain-soaked.

Fleeing something.

She's striking—all angles and determination. High cheek-bones, full mouth set in a tight line, dark hair plastered across her shoulders. But it's her eyes that grab me. Wide, wild, pumped full of adrenaline.

Hunted.

My pulse slows. Time dilates. The world crystallizes into data points and threat vectors—a skill honed across three continents and fourteen combat zones.

More movement at the top of the escalator. Four men descending. Not together, but synchronized. Staggered positions. Three-foot spacing. Too perfect to be coincidental.

Details snap into focus with photographic clarity. Then I do what I do best.

I protect.

Motion from the corner of my eye. I turn my head, maintaining peripheral awareness of the neutralized group. Four more men descend the escalator. Same tactical gear. Same purpose. Fresh operators while I'm already engaged.

Reinforcements.

The train approaches, brakes screeching. We need to be on it.

Gray Eyes follows my gaze, sees his backup. A smile spreads across his face despite his injury. "Like I said. Not over."

I evaluate our position. First team: effectively neutralized for now, though Gray Eyes and the fourth man could still engage if pressed. Second team: four fresh operators moving with purpose. The woman behind me is injured, slowing our options. The approaching train won't reach us before the new team does.

Only one viable option.

"Change of plans," I mutter, grabbing her wrist.

"What are you—"

I don't wait for her to finish. I vault over the platform edge, dragging her with me. She lands hard beside me on the tracks, crying out as the impact jars her ribs.

"Are you insane?" she hisses, trying to pull away from me.

"Probably." I pull her down into a service tunnel just as the train barrels past, covering our escape. "But we're still breathing, so there's that."

She struggles against my grip. "Let go of me."

"After I just saved your life?" The tunnel is narrow, pitch-black, except for the emergency lights creating pools of sickly yellow every fifty feet. "Keep moving."

"Who are you? FBI? CIA?"

"Someone who risked his life for yours. Although the better question is: who are you, and why does a professional hit squad want you dead?" I navigate through the darkness, pulling her along.

"I had it under control."

I stop dead in my tracks, spinning to face her. Even in the dim light, defiance blazes in her eyes.

"They were muggers," she says, voice tight with obstinance. "I could have handled it."

"Muggers? Are you fucking kidding me right now?"

"Language—"

"No." I step closer, invading her space. "Muggers don't move in tactical formation. Muggers don't coordinate through comm units. Muggers don't execute professional flanking maneuvers. And you know that."

She lifts her chin defiantly despite being cornered. "You don't know what you saw."

"I know exactly what I saw." My voice drops dangerously low. "I've spent fifteen years watching men like that operate on three continents. That was a professional hit squad with military training."

"You're paranoid," she challenges, but her eyes dart away.

"And you're lying." I press closer, my frustration mounting with every heartbeat. "Why would a team of professional assassins target a random woman for a mugging?"

"I don't know, maybe—"

"Stop." I slam my palm against the tunnel wall beside her head. She flinches but doesn't cower. "Whatever you're involved in has painted a target on your back. Your refusal to acknowledge the danger isn't just stupid—it's going to get you killed."

The tunnel suddenly vibrates, a distant rumble growing louder. Another train approaching.

"I don't need your protection," she hisses, face inches from mine. "And I certainly don't need your lectures. You think I'm supposed to trust a guy who just snapped a man's windpipe like it was nothing?"

"Would you prefer I let him put a bullet in your skull?" I counter, temper flaring. "Because that was the alternative."

"How do I know you're not one of them?" Her eyes flash with fear disguised as anger. "You appeared out of nowhere, killed three men without breaking a sweat—"

"Incapacitated," I correct through gritted teeth. "And a simple 'thank you' wouldn't kill you."

"Thank you?" She shoves against my chest. "For what? Dragging me into a dark tunnel? For all I know, you're worse than they are."

The train's rumble becomes a roar. The tunnel walls tremble.

"If I wanted to hurt you, I wouldn't have saved you." I have to shout over the growing noise. My patience unravels with each word. "Jesus Christ, woman, are you always this stubborn, or is it just when someone's trying to keep you alive?"

"I don't need a man to save me." Her voice trembles despite her bravado. "I've handled worse."

"Clearly not, or you wouldn't have blood in your hair and men with military training hunting you." I lean closer, can almost taste the defiance radiating off her. "Because from where I was standing, you had about ten seconds before those men put a bullet in your head and dumped your body on the tracks."

"You don't know anything about me or my situation." Fear breaks through her voice now—real, raw fear.

The train's rumble becomes a deafening roar.

"I know enough." I shout over the noise. "You're in over your head. Those weren't ordinary criminals. And if you keep running without help, you'll be dead before morning."

Her jaw clenches. "I've never trusted anyone in my life, and I'm not about to start with some—some violent stranger who appears from nowhere."

The approaching train's headlight illuminates the tunnel, casting harsh shadows across her face. In seconds, tons of metal will hurtle past inches from where we stand.

"Trust this then." I grab her shoulders and press her against the wall, shielding her body with mine as the train barrels toward us.

She gasps, hands instinctively gripping my arms. I flatten myself against her, pressing us both into the shallow alcove in the tunnel wall. Her breath comes in sharp bursts against my neck.

The train thunders past. Deafening. Violent. The wind it generates tears at my clothes, threatens to suck us into its path. I brace one arm above her head, the other wrapped around her waist, holding her secure against the wall, against me.

Chest to chest. Hip to hip. Her heartbeat hammers against mine.

Her face turns, cheek brushing mine, lips nearly touching my ear so I can hear her through the chaos. "This doesn't mean I trust you."

Something electric passes between us. Anger, fear, adrenaline —and something else entirely. Something dangerous.

The train passes, leaving us in near darkness, still pressed together. I should step back. I don't.

"Doesn't mean you don't need me either," I respond, voice rough. "Whatever mess you're in, whoever those men are, they're professionals. You can't handle this alone."

"I've always handled everything alone," she whispers, but there's less conviction now.

For three heartbeats, we stay locked together, breathing each other's air. Her defiance making my blood run hot. Her vulnerability making my grip tighten. Both making my focus slip—a cardinal sin in my line of work.

I force myself to release her, creating distance. "We need to move."

"Why should I go anywhere with you?" But she doesn't back away.

"Because right now, I'm the only thing standing between you and whatever storm you've kicked up." I check my watch. "We have about three minutes before they find the service entrance and come looking. So make your choice. Trust issues or survival?"

Her eyes search mine, looking for deception. "How do I know you won't kill me yourself once we're alone?"

"If that was my plan, I wouldn't have bothered with the dramatic rescue." I can't keep the edge from my voice. "Contrary to what you might think, I don't make a habit of saving women from professional killers for the exercise."

For a moment, I think she might actually walk away. Then her shoulders slump, just slightly.

"Fine." She swallows hard. "Where are we going?"

"Somewhere safe." I take her elbow, gentler this time. "But first, I need to know: what's your name, and why are there professional hit teams trying to kill you?"

She hesitates, calculating. Finally: "Celeste. Celeste Hart."

"Well, Celeste Hart, I'm Ryan Ellis. And you've just made my already shitty week a whole lot more interesting."

THREE

## Ryan

I lead Celeste Hart deeper into the maintenance tunnel, my fingers locked around her slender wrist. Her pulse hammers against my thumb—rapid, erratic. Afraid, but moving. Good enough for now.

Water drips from rusted pipes overhead, each droplet striking concrete with metronomic precision.

The rhythm marks our progress—thirty drops, forty feet gained. Sixty drops, another junction cleared.

The emergency lights flicker at irregular intervals, casting our shadows into grotesque, elongated versions of ourselves that dance along mildew-stained walls. The air hangs thick with decay and ozone, coating the back of my throat with each breath.

"How far?" Her voice barely rises above a whisper.

"Far enough that they lose our trail." I don't slow our pace.

Three minutes and twenty-seven seconds since we entered the service tunnel. The hit team will have regrouped by now. The two I incapacitated won't be mobile, but the others—including the reinforcements—will have established a search grid. Standard procedure after losing a target: secure all known exits, then sweep inward. They'll find the maintenance door we used in approximately ninety seconds.

I map our position in my head. These tunnels were part of my mental geography during my last D.C. deployment—six years, two months ago. A habit from training: memorize escape routes, alternative paths, choke points. Three service tunnels intersect seventeen yards ahead. Left leads to the Red Line, populated areas. Right stretches deeper into the maintenance network. Straight continues parallel to the main line.

I choose right. Deeper is safer. Less predictable.

Her breathing grows shallower and more labored by the second. Contusion on her temple. Favoring her left knee. Factoring her injuries, I estimate we can maintain this pace for another six minutes before she falters. Not enough to reach the Georgetown access point I'm aiming for.

"Slow down," she hisses, tugging against my grip.

I don't. "They're behind us."

"You don't know that."

"I do."

She keeps glancing over her shoulder, flinching at shadows, eyes wide and darting. A woman involved in something deadly enough to warrant a professional hit is afraid of the dark.

Ironic.

I guide her around a corner where the tunnel narrows, the ceiling dropping lower. To our right, a junction box hums with electrical current. The vibration through the concrete signals an approaching train somewhere above—Red Line, based on the timing pattern.

The floor changes from smooth concrete to uneven brick, with sections crumbling from decades of moisture damage. Maintenance crews don't prioritize areas passengers never see.

She stumbles, foot catching on exposed rebar. Her body pitches forward. I release her wrist, pivoting to catch her before she hits the ground. My arms wrap around her waist, pulling her hard against my chest. The impact forces a small gasp from her lips.

For one suspended moment, we freeze. Her body flush against mine, soft curves pressed into hard angles. Her breath warm against my throat. The scent of her hair—citrus shampoo and rain—cuts through the tunnel's mustiness. Even in the dim emergency lighting, I can count her eyelashes, see the tiny flecks of gold in her brown eyes as they widen, registering our sudden proximity.

Something electric passes between us. A current more dangerous than the humming junction box.

My hands should move. They don't.

Her palms rest against my chest, neither pushing away nor pulling closer. Her heartbeat accelerates where our bodies connect—no longer from fear alone.

"I—" she starts.

The distant clang of metal against concrete freezes us both. The service door—forced open with what sounds like a breaching tool. Professional equipment. Professional team. Of course.

"What was that?" Her voice pitches higher, echoing slightly in the confined space.

I press my index finger against my lips. "They found our entry point."

Voices bounce off concrete walls. Flashlight beams slice through the darkness behind us, sweeping methodical patterns across tunnel walls. Tactical search formation. They're being thorough.

"Move," I whisper, releasing her but maintaining contact. A tactical mistake. Less control, more connection. I do it anyway.

Sixty seconds until they reach our position. No time to outrun them.

I scan our surroundings. Twenty feet ahead, a maintenance alcove cuts into the left wall—electrical access point, judging by the junction box mounted inside. Deep enough to conceal two people if we press back into the shadows.

Perfect.

Without explanation, I pull her toward the alcove. Her resistance is immediate—tense muscles, heels dragging.

"Trust me for thirty seconds," I mutter.

"Trust isn't my strong suit."

"Survival instinct better be."

I guide her into the recess, positioning her against the back wall, then crowd in after her. The space is barely three feet deep, four feet wide. We're chest to chest, her back pressed against decades-old brick, my body effectively pinning her in place.

Hiding her.

The intimacy is immediate and unwelcome. This close, I can feel the warmth radiating from her skin. Can smell that citrus scent mingled now with sweat and adrenaline. Can see the pulse point at the base of her throat fluttering like a trapped bird.

*Damn it, Ellis. Focus.*

"They'll find us," she whispers, eyes wide in the darkness.

"Not if you shut up and stop talking."

She glares up at me, defiance sparking even in fear. This woman is the human equivalent of a lit fuse—explosive, unpredictable, and undeniably incendiary.

And she completely fucked my evening. I should be on a plane back to Seattle by now, back to the team and the mission docket waiting on my desk.

Instead, I'm pressed against a stranger in a dank subway tunnel, playing human shield against professional killers.

The footsteps grow louder. At least three sets, moving with purpose.

I shift slightly, angling my body to better conceal hers from view. The movement brings us impossibly closer. Her breath catches. Mine too, though I'd never admit it.

Our faces are inches apart now. Her eyes hold mine, no longer just afraid, but aware. Aware of me, of our bodies, of the bizarre intimacy forced upon us by circumstance.

My heartbeat accelerates to match hers. Medical impossibility, but I swear I feel them synchronize.

Voices echo through the tunnel.

"Spread out. They can't have gone far." American accent. Military cadence. Private contractor confirmed.

"Check all access points and maintenance areas." Another voice, deeper. "Alpha team, continue straight. Bravo, take the south fork."

They're coordinating a sweep. Teams designated by phonetic alphabet—standard special ops procedure. These are ex-military, possibly Delta or SEAL based on their tactical discipline.

Celeste's fingers grip the front of my jacket, knuckles white. Her eyes squeeze shut, her breath shallow. The enclosed space is getting to her.

"Look at me," I whisper, barely audible.

Her eyes snap open.

"Breathe with me." I maintain eye contact, deliberately slowing my breathing. In for four, hold for four, out for four. A technique from sniper school. Control your body, control the situation.

After three cycles, her breathing matches mine. Her grip on my jacket loosens slightly.

A flashlight beam sweeps past our alcove, illuminating the tunnel just beyond where we hide. We both freeze. If they do a thorough check, we're cornered.

That's when I see it. Above the junction box—a utility ladder embedded in the wall, leading to a maintenance shaft. It disappears into darkness, but I'm familiar with these systems.

It'll connect to the secondary tunnel level, used for accessing the primary electrical conduits that run beneath the track beds.

The footsteps approach. Twenty feet away. Fifteen.

"Up," I mouth silently, pointing to the ladder.

She follows my gesture, eyes widening with understanding.

I let her go first, keeping my body between her and the tunnel entrance as she grips the rusted metal rungs. She climbs silently, movements fluid despite her injuries. Journalist or not, she's in decent shape. Adaptable.

Ten feet away. I need to follow now.

I grab the ladder and ascend rapidly, just as a flashlight beam cuts across the alcove entrance.

The shaft is narrow, barely wide enough for an average-sized man. Decades of grime coat the metal rungs. The darkness above us is absolute, save for a faint glow of emergency lighting filtering through what must be a ventilation grate higher up.

My hand accidentally grazes her thigh as I climb, the contact electric even through the fabric of her jeans. She sucks in a sharp breath, audible in the confined space.

"Sorry," I mutter, the apology foreign on my tongue.

"It's fine," she whispers back, voice tight with something that isn't just fear.

We climb in silence, but something has changed in the air between us. A charge. A recognition. The kind of spark that has no place in a professional extraction. The kind that gets people killed.

I clench my jaw and focus on the ladder rungs, on the voices fading below us, on anything but the woman climbing above me and the inexplicable pull I feel toward her.

*Focus on the mission, Ellis. Get her out. Hand her off. Walk away.*

We know that's not happening.

FOUR

# Ryan

We emerge onto the secondary tunnel level, a forgotten artery in the city's underground circulatory system. The maintenance passage stretches in both directions and is narrower than the main tunnel below. Lower ceilings and exposed conduit pipes run along walls coated in decades of grime.

The air hangs heavy, carrying the sour tang of metal and dust. Not a breath stirs it, except for the faint scuff of boots that pass through every so often—workers moving fast, shoulders tight, as if eager to escape the draw of bad luck that landed them here.

I orient myself immediately. East-west alignment, running parallel to the Red Line. Approximately thirty feet below street level, if my mental mapping is correct. Two connecting vertical shafts within five hundred yards—one leading up to a ventilation grate near Dupont Circle, the other accessing a maintenance closet in Farragut North station.

Boots thunder past, then splinter in two directions. Silence hangs for a breath, broken by a radio's clipped hiss—"check the ladder shaft." Our scuffs streak the rust. They'll smell the route we took. Another cadence joins the first—heavier, closer—two squads tightening the noose.

Celeste leans against the curved wall, one arm wrapped protectively around her ribcage, the other pushing damp hair from her face. She's favoring her left leg more now. The adrenaline is wearing off, and pain is seeping back in.

Despite this, her eyes remain alert, assessing. Taking stock of our environment with the sharp gaze of someone who observes for a living.

"How do you know these tunnels?" Her words snap out, sharp as the suspicion narrowing her eyes. "No normal person knows their way around service tunnels like they're giving a guided tour."

I should ignore her. Focus on the mission, the threat closing in. Instead, I catch the flicker of challenge in her gaze, the curl of her mouth daring me to break. A smile tugs, uninvited. Almost.

"I'm not a normal person."

Her chin lifts, stubborn, reckless. "That's not an answer."

The space between us hums, tighter than it should be. Too dark, too close, too charged. The last thing I need is the heat rolling off her—defiance laced with fear, attraction pulsing beneath it all.

"It's the only one you need right now."

Her breath stumbles, quick and uneven, and I feel it like static in my chest. She doesn't want to trust me, but her body leans, betraying her. I force my eyes forward, scanning the junction ahead, but the pull between us crackles hotter than the hunt at our backs.

"If I'm trusting you with my life, I deserve more than cryptic bullshit," she counters.

Fair point. But opening up to targets—to civilians—creates complications. Attachments. Vulnerabilities. Rule one of protective detail: maintain professional distance.

But she's also right. Trust requires something in return.

"Military," I relent, keeping my voice low. "Stationed in D.C. for three years with a specialized unit. Part of our training involved urban navigation—knowing how to move through cities undetected, using infrastructure most people never see."

Her expression shifts, suspicion tempered by understanding. "And now?"

"Now I make it my business to know escape routes wherever I am." I check my watch. Seven minutes since we left the platform. "It's kept me alive more than once."

"Special Forces?" she guesses.

"Something like that."

She's fishing for details. Journalist to the core. Annoying and strangely admirable simultaneously. Persistence is an asset in her line of work, I suppose. In mine, it's the quality that keeps targets alive when everything goes sideways.

Like now.

"We need to move," I say, assessing our options. "There's a maintenance exit that leads to Farragut North station. From there, we can blend with commuters and catch a train out of the area."

She shakes her head immediately. "No. That's exactly what they'll expect. They'll have men at every station exit by now."

"Not this one. It's access-restricted. Maintenance personnel only."

"You really think professional killers won't check staff exits?" She crosses her arms, wincing slightly at the pressure on her ribs. "We should head toward Connecticut Avenue. There's more foot traffic, easier to disappear in crowds."

I clench my jaw. This woman is questioning my extraction plan. My area of expertise. The audacity would be impressive if it weren't so frustrating.

"Connecticut Avenue means going topside sooner. Exposing ourselves while they have vantage points."

"So, your plan is to stay in the tunnels? For how long?" She gestures at our surroundings. "This isn't exactly five-star accommodations, and in case you haven't noticed, I'm not exactly in peak condition."

My gaze drops to her ribcage, where she's still cradling her injury, then to her leg, which she's favoring more with each passing minute. She has a point, damn it. Extended tunnel navigation will only worsen her condition. But surface exposure creates different risks.

"What we need," I say, mentally recalculating our position, "is to get you somewhere secure for medical attention. Somewhere they can't trace."

"My apartment ..." she offers.

"Isn't safe anymore." I shake my head. "If they found you once, they've burned all your known locations."

Her expression darkens. "You don't know that."

"I do, because it's what I would do." I hold her gaze steadily. "These aren't amateurs. They had a four-man team on primary intercept and a second team as backup. That's not a mugging. That's not even a standard hit. That's a high-priority termination order."

She goes silent, the reality of her situation finally sinking in.

I soften my approach slightly. "I have contacts. Resources. But we need to get clear of this area first."

Her eyes search mine, looking for deception, for an angle, for God knows what. I maintain eye contact, letting her see whatever she needs to see to trust me for the next hour.

"Fine," she finally says. "So, what's the compromise?"

I process our options, weighing variables such as her injury, pursuit patterns, environmental factors, and time constraints. An alternative emerges.

"R Street water drainage tunnel," I decide. It connects to these maintenance passages about three hundred yards east. It'll take us to an outlet near Rock Creek Park. It's less monitored, has good cover, and gives us surface access away from cameras."

She considers this, then nods reluctantly. "How far?"

"Fifteen minutes at a steady pace."

"Then let's go." She pushes off from the wall, determination overriding pain.

Something shifts in my assessment of her. Stubborn, yes. Argumentative, definitely. But also, resilient. Adaptive. The kind of person who keeps going when others would collapse.

I take point, leading us east through the tunnel, slowing just enough for her to keep up with the limp in her stride. Her breathing trails me, uneven, soft at first, then catching on a sharp inhale whenever a step jars her ribs. Each flinch threads into the silence, pulling tighter with every echo off the concrete walls.

I check back more often than necessary. Noticing the determination in the set of her jaw when she thinks I'm not looking.

Annoying. Inconvenient. Intriguing.

Definitely not part of the mission parameters I've set for myself.

Definitely not within my control anymore.

We round the corner into the eastern passage and stop dead. The tunnel ahead is completely blocked—a section of the ceiling collapsed into a mountain of concrete chunks, twisted rebar, and severed pipes. Water sprays from a ruptured line, pooling at the base of the debris.

"Shit," I mutter, surveying the blockage. No way through. No way around.

Celeste steps up beside me. "Please tell me this isn't our only route."

"It wasn't on my mental map." I scan the blockage, looking

for any gap large enough to squeeze through. Nothing. "Infrastructure collapses happen. Nature of aging systems."

"So, what now, navigator?" Her voice carries an edge of panic beneath the sarcasm.

Before I can answer, a sound echoes from the passage behind us. Voices. Distant but clear. Our pursuers have found the access ladder.

"They're on our level," I say, keeping my voice low.

Her eyes widen. "How is that possible?"

"They're good." I grab her arm, turning back the way we came. "We need to move."

"To where? You just said this was our exit route."

Valid question. I scan our surroundings with renewed urgency, calculating options. The voices grow louder. Two minutes, maybe less, before they reach our position.

Then I spot it—a maintenance access panel set into the wall about three feet off the ground. The kind that leads to utility crawlspaces where workers access pipes and wiring between main passages. Overlooked on my first assessment because it's not a primary transit route.

"There." I move toward it, working my tactical knife into the edge of the panel. The corroded screws give way with minimal resistance, and the panel swings open to reveal a narrow shaft. Very narrow. Pitch-black beyond the entrance.

"You've got to be kidding me." Celeste shakes her head vehemently. "I'm not crawling in there."

"It's that or explain to those men why you have classified data on that flash drive in your pocket," I counter, hearing the voices grow closer.

Her face goes still. "How did you know about—"

"I didn't. Until now." I give her a pointed look. "Your hand keeps checking your right pocket every thirty seconds. Classic tell for carrying something valuable."

Her fingers instantly move away from said pocket. Guilt confirmed.

"What's on it?"

"Nothing that concerns you." Defensive now.

"It concerns me when it's getting us both killed." I gesture to the shaft. "Now get in. You first."

"Why me first?"

"Because I need to replace this panel behind us."

The voices are close enough now to distinguish words. They've found the junction box I tampered with. They know we came this way.

FIVE

## Ryan

Celeste looks at the tiny opening, then back at the passage where flashlight beams have begun to illuminate the distant curve, then back at me. Decision made.

"If we get stuck in there and die, I'm going to kill you." Paradoxical threat, but I get the sentiment.

"Noted." I boost her up, hands at her waist, trying to ignore the way her body feels under my palms. "Stay on your stomach. Army crawl. Elbows and toes. Move steadily but don't rush."

She slithers into the opening with surprising agility for someone with injured ribs. I follow immediately, pulling the access panel closed behind us as best I can from the inside.

Complete darkness engulfs us. The shaft is even tighter than it appeared from the outside. My shoulders scrape against both sides simultaneously, back brushing against the top. The claustrophobic squeeze would trigger panic in most civilians, but Celeste keeps moving ahead of me. Impressive.

We crawl in silence, every breath too loud, too shallow, trapped with us in the narrow dark. Dust grits between my teeth, coats my tongue until swallowing feels like dragging sandpaper down my throat. Each inhale burns, the stench of old wires and insulation clinging to my lungs like poison. The metal closes in on all sides—cold against my palms, bruising across my shoulders as we squeeze past cross-braces. When a train passes somewhere above, the whole shaft shudders, pressing the air tighter, as if the tunnel itself is trying to crush us.

And Celeste. Always Celeste.

Directly ahead of me in the darkness, close enough that my hand occasionally brushes against her foot or calf as we navigate the confined space. Each inadvertent contact sends an inappropriate jolt through me.

"How much farther?" Her whisper echoes slightly in the metal confines.

"I don't know," I admit. Vulnerability isn't my default setting, but the situation demands honesty. "These maintenance shafts typically run between major junctions. Should be an exit panel eventually."

"'Eventually' isn't very reassuring."

"Better than 'we're trapped.'"

She falls silent, continuing to crawl. I find myself oddly transfixed by the determination in her movements—steady, methodical, refusing to give in to what must be significant pain from her injuries. This woman has grit.

The shaft pitches upward without warning, narrowing as it angles into a brutal incline. Not quite vertical, but damn close. My shoulders barely clear the walls.

"This is getting steeper," she warns, voice tight with effort. "I can barely get traction."

"Use the cross-braces for leverage. Forearms locked—pull with your upper body strength."

Ahead, fabric scrapes against metal, the hitch and drag of her movement uneven in the dark. Her breathing sharpens, each pull rougher, more strained, echoing off the walls of the shaft.

"I can't—" A gasp, then the sound of her hands slipping.

Her body jerks, then slides backward. Boots slam into my shoulders, knocking the breath out of me. She claws for purchase, but there's nothing—just her full weight pressing down.

Suddenly, her thighs clamp around my head, heat searing through layers of fabric. I'm caged, smothered, straddled in the worst possible way inside a damn ventilation shaft.

*Fuck.*

My hands shoot to her hips, steadying us both before we tumble into a heap. She goes rigid at the touch.

"This isn't exactly how I pictured our first date," I grind out, deadpan, because if I don't joke, I'll lose it.

A shaky breath rattles from her. "Shut up," she mutters, voice trembling—not sharp with anger this time, but something far messier.

We freeze there, a tangle of limbs and bad timing. Her knees clamp on either side of my ears. One boot digs into the wall, the other grinds against my ribs. Every shuddering inhale drags her against me in ways neither of us should be noticing.

Hell of a place to get acquainted.

We are fused together in the darkness. Locked in a moment so electric, sparks dance down my spine.

"Sorry," she murmurs, voice uncharacteristically soft.

"It's okay." My voice sounds strange to my ears. Lower. Rougher.

I should push her forward. Should maintain whatever minimal professional boundaries still exist in this absurd situation. Instead, I find myself hyperaware of every point of contact between us.

This isn't my job. She isn't my assignment. I have no obligation beyond basic human decency to help her escape these men. I could have walked away after the subway platform. Should have, probably.

But here I am, wedged in a maintenance shaft in complete darkness with a woman who challenged a hit squad, risking my life for reasons that increasingly have nothing to do with professional ethics or training protocols and everything to do with the inexplicable pull I feel toward her.

"I think—" she starts, then stops. Shifts slightly, creating a friction that sends heat coursing through me. "I can try again."

"Like I said, use the cross-braces for leverage," I manage to say, my voice rougher than intended. "Like climbing a ladder horizontally."

"That seems to be working better," she says after a few moments of renewed effort.

I follow her progress up the incline, keeping enough distance to avoid another collision but close enough to catch her if needed. We make steady progress upward until the shaft finally levels out again.

"There's light ahead," she whispers after several more minutes of crawling.

I angle over her shoulder in the cramped shaft, and a thin glow bleeds through the slats of an access panel about fifteen feet ahead—pale, fractured, promising air and space beyond the chokehold of steel.

"Good," I acknowledge.

We reach the panel together. I maneuver around her to examine it, our bodies sliding past each other in a full-contact exchange that I try—and fail—to keep impersonal. Her breath catches when my chest presses against her back. Mine does the same when her hand accidentally grips my thigh for stability.

"Sorry," we both mutter simultaneously.

I focus on the panel, working my fingers around the edge, feeling for a release mechanism. "I think it opens from this side."

"Can you tell what's on the other side?"

"Not without opening it."

I find the latch and pause, listening for any sound indicating pursuit or danger. Nothing but the distant rumble of trains.

"Ready?" I ask.

She takes a deep breath. "As I'll ever be."

I shove the panel outward, hinges groaning, and white light crashes into the shaft. It sears after so long in the dark, stabbing my eyes until they water. I blink hard, shapes slowly sharpening—the wide room beyond, the stretch of concrete floor, the hum of fluorescent lights.

Air moves freer here, cool against my face, loosening the knot in my chest. But the space feels too open, too exposed, every shadow a place for danger to wait. My pulse lifts, caught between the release of fresh air and the prickling edge of being seen.

We emerge into what appears to be an abandoned platform section—a subway ghost, forgotten when they reconfigured the station above. Crumbling tile walls. Ancient advertising posters, colors faded to sepia. A single emergency light casts weak illumination over a space that hasn't seen regular human traffic in decades.

Perfect. Unmonitored. Off the grid.

I help Celeste out of the shaft, supporting her weight as she winces from the movement. The crawl has taken a visible toll—her face is pale beneath the grime, jaw tight with pain she's been suppressing. The adrenaline that's been keeping her going is fading fast.

"Where are we?" she asks, voice strained as she leans against the tiled wall.

"Looks like an abandoned platform segment. Probably sealed off during renovations." I scan our surroundings, identifying possible exit routes. A rusted service door stands at the far end, likely leading to maintenance stairs. "We're making progress. That door should take us—"

"No." The word is flat, final.

I turn to find her sliding down the wall to sit on the dusty concrete, one arm still wrapped protectively around her ribs.

"We need to keep moving," I remind her.

"I'm not." She shakes her head, eyes hard despite the pain evident in them. "Not until you tell me what's happening here."

"What's happening is professionals are hunting you. We've covered this."

"No." She leans forward slightly, wincing at the movement. "You conveniently appeared at exactly the right moment. You know these tunnels like you designed them. You have combat training that dropped four armed men without breaking a sweat."

"And?"

"*And*, now you're dragging me through the bowels of D.C. without telling me where we're going." Her voice rises slightly. "For all I know, you're leading me straight to whoever sent those men."

I stare at her, incredulous. "If I wanted you dead, I'd have let those men handle it on the platform. Much cleaner than this subterranean tour."

"Maybe you need me alive for questioning. Maybe you work for a competing interest." Her journalist's mind is spinning conspiracy theories. "Maybe this flash drive contains something you want."

I pinch the bridge of my nose, frustration mounting. This woman is the most stubborn, suspicious, infuriating civilian I've ever encountered. And considering I grew up with three older sisters who all joined the debate team, that's saying something.

"I told you. I work private security. Cerberus Security."

"Which could be contracted by anyone."

"I was catching a train home after a holiday weekend. Period."

"Convenient timing."

I take a deep breath, trying to rein in my temper. "Look, I understand paranoia is a survival trait for investigative journalists, but this is ridiculous. I'm trying to help you."

"Why?" She fixes me with an unnervingly direct stare. "Why risk your life for a complete stranger? What's your stake in this?"

It's a fair question. One I've been asking myself for the past hour. Why am I still here? Why didn't I call local authorities and walk away?

The answer isn't one I particularly like.

"I don't have an agenda," I say finally. "I saw someone in trouble and acted. That's it."

"Nobody does that," she counters, the cynicism of her profession showing. "Not without an angle."

"Some of us do." An edge creeps into my voice. "Some of us can't walk past someone being targeted and do nothing."

"I'm not moving until you tell me who you are." Her chin lifts in defiance despite her exhaustion. "The full truth."

"We don't have time for this." I check my watch. "The longer we stay in one place, the more likely those men will find our trail again."

"Make time."

I'm about to respond when something catches my eye—a faint light flickering in the maintenance shaft we just exited. Distant but approaching. They've found our route.

"We're out of time," I say, moving toward her. "They're in the shaft."

SIX

# Ryan

Celeste turns and sees the light. Fear flashes across her face, but the stubborn set of her jaw doesn't waver. "Then answer fast."

Something inside me snaps. The patience I've been clinging to evaporates.

"Fine. Ryan Ellis. Former Delta Force. Eight years Special Ops, too many combat tours. Now I run extraction and protection details for Cerberus Personal Security. I was in D.C. visiting my mother, who spent the entire weekend reminding me that at thirty-five, I should be married with 2.5 kids instead of 'playing soldier' across the globe. I was heading home to Seattle, with a loaf of her pumpkin bread in my bag, when I saw four men about to kill you. I intervened because that's what I'm trained to do and because no matter how aggravating you are—and trust me, you're setting records—I don't let civilians die when I can prevent it."

Her eyes widen slightly at my outburst.

"That's who I am. Satisfied? Because in about forty seconds, those men are going to emerge from that shaft, and all your questions will be pointless if we're dead."

She stares at me, processing, calculating. The light in the shaft grows brighter.

"If you're lying—" she starts.

"You'll what? Report me to the Better Business Bureau? Write a scathing editorial?" I extend my hand to help her up. "Decide now. Trust me or face them alone."

Her hand reaches for mine, but her leg buckles beneath her as she tries to stand. The color drains from her face as she gasps in pain.

"I can't—" she manages through gritted teeth. "My knee—"

The flashlight beam is now close enough to illuminate the shaft's far end.

No time for debate. No time for trust-building exercises.

I make the call.

I hoist her over my shoulder in a fireman's carry, supporting her weight across my shoulders with one arm anchoring her legs.

"Put me down." Her whisper strikes hot, fierce as a slap.

"You can chastise me later," I respond, already moving toward the service door. "Right now, we're getting out of here alive."

Her fists pound against my back in protest—impressively strong despite her injuries, though not enough to deter me. I kick open the rusted service door with more force than necessary, the metal groaning in protest as decades-old hinges give way.

A stairwell appears beyond, spiraling upward toward street level. I take the steps two at a time despite the extra weight, adrenaline overriding the strain in my shoulders and legs.

"This is assault," she mutters near my ear, her breath warm against my neck as she hangs upside down.

"Sue me when we're not being hunted."

"I will."

"I'll look forward to it."

Her struggling gradually subsides as we ascend, either from resignation or the pain of her injuries—probably both. Her body goes slightly limp across my shoulders, though her breathing remains steady.

The staircase seems endless, winding upward through the layers of infrastructure that compose the city's hidden skeleton. My thighs burn with the effort. Sweat trickles down my spine. But I maintain a steady pace, driven by the knowledge that those men aren't far behind.

And by something else. Something I refuse to examine too closely.

An irrational, overwhelming need to protect this maddening woman who's hijacked my evening, my plans, and—increasingly —my better judgment. A woman whose stubborn courage and sharp intelligence keep catching me off guard. Whose body feels disturbingly right pressed against mine, even in this awkward carry position.

Whose safety has somehow become more important than my own.

Completely unprofessional.

Completely inexplicable.

Completely undeniable.

The stairwell narrows as we approach street level, decades of neglect evident in the crumbling concrete and exposed rebar. My lungs burn from exertion, thighs screaming in protest as I take the final flight with Celeste still slung over my shoulder.

She's gone quiet—concerning, given her earlier protests, but her steady breathing against my neck tells me she's conscious.

My tactical awareness kicks into overdrive as I assess our exit point: the emergency door at the top of the stairs, heavy steel with a push bar and a red alarm trigger panel beside it. Based on the outdated model, it's not part of the active security grid but is likely still connected to local monitoring.

I pause, calculating options. Triggering the alarm creates two conflicting outcomes: it alerts security to our location, but also provides useful chaos.

Emergency response protocols will send personnel to this exit point, diverting resources from the pursuers' search grid. The benefit outweighs the risk, especially since we'll be gone before anyone responds.

"Hang on," I warn Celeste. "This is going to get loud."

I shift her weight slightly on my shoulder, positioning myself for a quick exit, then slam my palm against the alarm panel. The effect is immediate—a piercing siren wails through the stairwell, red strobe lights casting disorienting pulses across the walls.

I hit the push bar with my hip, and the door bursts open. Rain-soaked night air rushes in, cold and clean after the stagnant tunnel atmosphere. I emerge onto a narrow service alley several blocks from where this all began, the Dupont Circle area visible at the far end.

Water pelts us as I navigate around dumpsters and delivery pallets. The storm has intensified, sheets of rain turning the alley into shallow rivulets that splash under my boots. The sound of the alarm fades behind us, replaced by the ambient city noise of distant traffic and whining sirens.

I scan for immediate threats—clear for now. Then for surveillance—two cameras on the adjacent building, but angled toward the main street, not the alley. Acceptable risk.

"Putting you down," I say, carefully lowering Celeste to her feet in the shelter of an awning.

She sways slightly as her good leg takes her weight, instinctively grabbing my arms for stability. For a moment, we're face-to-face, close enough that I can count the water droplets clinging to her eyelashes, see the pulse jumping at her throat.

"You okay?" I ask, hands lingering at her waist longer than necessary.

She nods once, still catching her breath. "Next time, ask before throwing me over your shoulder like a caveman."

"Next time, don't argue when professional killers are thirty seconds behind us."

Her lips twitch, almost a smile. "Fair point."

That near-smile hits me with unexpected force. Makes something in my chest tighten. I step back abruptly, breaking contact, refocusing on our situation.

"We need transportation." I peer toward the street beyond the alley. Late night in D.C., but cabs still circulate for the bar crowd and late-shift workers.

"I have a car—" She shakes her head, closes her eyes, and tightens her lips. "Had. I *had* a car."

She leans against the brick wall, rain slicking her hair flat, clothes glued to her body in a way I shouldn't be noticing. She's cut, bruised, filthy, and running on fumes—yet still, she carries herself like she's carved from iron. Defiant. Untouchable.

My pulse spikes anyway. Every drop sliding down her throat, every stubborn tilt of her chin, sparks in places I'd sworn were locked down. She's sexy as hell, dangerous as hell, and every inch of her is pushing buttons I shouldn't have.

I was supposed to be on a flight back to Seattle right now. Quiet seat, bad coffee, maybe a bourbon if the flight attendant didn't hate her job. Instead, I'm here, half-drowned in a back alley, holding up a woman who looks like sin wrapped in barbed wire.

And if I have to admit it—which I won't—this beats the hell out of First Class.

"Wait here." I move to the alley entrance, scanning the street. A yellow cab approaches, light on. I step out and raise my hand with the authoritative gesture that somehow always gets a response—a combination of military bearing and pure certainty.

The cab slows, pulls to the curb. I return to Celeste, who's watching me with narrowed eyes.

"Your chariot awaits." I offer my arm for support.

She hesitates, then takes it, her fingers surprisingly strong as they grip my forearm. We move awkwardly toward the waiting taxi, her injured knee forcing a limping gait that I adjust my stride to match.

The cabbie eyes us suspiciously as we approach—two bedraggled figures emerging from an alley in the rain, covered in tunnel grime, one visibly injured. Can't blame him for the wariness.

I open the back door and help Celeste into the car before circling to the other side. After the tunnels and rain, the warm interior of the cab feels like luxury, and the familiar smell of air freshener and upholstery is oddly comforting.

"Where are we going?" Celeste asks as I settle beside her, careful to leave appropriate space between us.

"Somewhere they can't find us."

"I still don't trust you." The words lack their earlier heat and are spoken more from principle than conviction.

"Noted." I meet her gaze directly. "But you're already in the damn cab."

Her mouth quirks again—that not-quite-smile that does strange things to my focus.

I give the driver an address for a small two-star hotel in Georgetown.

The cab pulls away from the curb, its wipers battling the downpour. I scan the streets as we move through the city, checking mirrors and tracking any vehicle that maintains position behind us for more than two turns. These are old habits. They are necessary habits.

Celeste watches me watching the streets. Her analytical gaze misses nothing.

"Do you ever stop?" she asks quietly.

"Stop, what?"

"Scanning. Assessing. Looking for threats."

"No." Simple truth. The day I stop scanning is the day I or someone under my protection ends up dead.

We fall into silence, the cab's heater gradually warming the space, fogging the windows slightly. The rhythmic sweep of wipers and hum of tires on wet pavement creates a strangely intimate atmosphere after the chaos we've just escaped.

Her breathing brushes the space between us, steady until the cab jolts over a pothole and she gasps, sharp, clutching at her ribs. Dust and damp cling to everything, but beneath it clings a thread of citrus—faint, stubborn, cutting through the grime to reach me. It coils tighter than I want, every small sound, every shift reminding me she's there, too close.

Her hand rests on the seat between us, pale against the dark upholstery. The cab lurches into a turn, and my palm skids across the leather until it collides with hers.

The jolt that shoots up my arm damn near short-circuits me. Her eyes fly to mine, wide, startled, like we've both touched a live wire. For one suspended beat, neither of us move—skin pressed to skin, heat sparking hotter than the cramped dark ever did.

Which is saying something, considering the last time we were this close, she was practically riding my face in a ventilation shaft. And somehow, this—this stupid brush of fingers—is worse. Way worse.

We yank apart at the same instant, too fast, too obvious, the contact gone but the charge still humming in the air between us.

I clear my throat, reaching for my phone. Time to call this in.

The situation has escalated beyond what I can handle solo, especially with her injuries requiring medical attention.

"Who are you calling?" She watches my movements with that journalist's attention to detail.

"My team."

Her eyebrows lift. "Your—team?"

I initiate the secure connection protocol, then look directly at her. "Welcome to Cerberus, Ms. Hart. Your life is about to get a lot more complicated."

As the call connects, I maintain eye contact with her, aware that I've just irrevocably changed both our trajectories. This was supposed to be a simple extraction—get her somewhere safe, hand her off to local authorities, catch the next flight home.

Instead, I've brought her into my world. Made her my responsibility in ways that go beyond Good Samaritan intervention.

Ghost is going to kill me.

But watching her chin lift in that now-familiar gesture of defiance despite everything she's been through, I can't bring myself to regret it.

"Brass." Mason's voice answers on the second ring. "You missed your flight."

"Change of plans."

"Situation?" One word, loaded with questions.

I glance at Celeste, who watches me with wary curiosity, still fighting to stay alert despite pain and exhaustion.

"I've acquired an asset with high-value intel and a professional hit team on her tail. Multiple hostiles, military training, well-equipped."

"Casualties?" Mason's voice is clipped, efficient.

"None on our side. Yet."

"Can you hand this off to local authorities?" Mason asks.

A brief silence as he processes. I glance at Celeste, who's

watching me intently. "I need to ask—should we involve local authorities?"

She stiffens beside me, her expression shuttering. Her hand moves instinctively to the pocket with the flash drive. That's answer enough.

"Not an option," I tell Mason, reading her reaction. "Whatever she's involved in, it's sensitive."

"Understood." No questions. No hesitation. That's why I trust him.

"What's your plan?"

"Hotel tonight. Cash only. Rental under shell credentials tomorrow morning. I'll call when we're secure."

"Brass." His voice shifts slightly—the tone that means what follows is personal, not protocol. "This isn't your mission."

"It is now."

"Understood." A beat of silence. "Her intel better justify this detour."

"It will." I have no idea if that's true, but I say it with conviction.

The call ends without pleasantries. That's Ghost—economical in all things, especially words.

I tuck the phone away, feeling Celeste's scrutiny like a physical touch.

"Asset?" she repeats, voice dangerous. "Is that what I am?"

"Figure of speech."

"And how exactly do you think your 'team' can help me?"

I turn to face her fully, letting her see the absolute certainty in my expression. "Because protection is what we do. And whoever wants you dead badly enough to send pros after you just made a critical mistake."

"What's that?"

"They made it personal."

Her eyes widen slightly at the intensity in my voice. The cab turns onto Georgetown Street, approaching our destination. In fifteen minutes, this will become an official Cerberus operation—protocols, procedures, professional distance.

But for now, in the warm confines of this taxi, with rain drumming on the roof and her eyes locked with mine, nothing about this feels professional.

And that might be the most dangerous development of all.

SEVEN

# Celeste

THE FLUORESCENT LIGHTS IN THE HOTEL LOBBY FLICKER, CASTING sickly shadows across worn carpet the color of trampled autumn leaves. My soaked clothes cling to my body, water dripping steadily from my hair to form small puddles at my feet. I shift my weight to my right leg, keeping pressure off my throbbing left knee. Each subtle movement sends jagged pain through my ribs.

Breathing hurts. Standing hurts. Existing hurts.

Ryan cuts an imposing figure at the front desk, his broad shoulders squared despite our ordeal. While I look like a drowned rat, he somehow manages to appear merely weathered—like someone caught in a storm rather than someone who crawled through maintenance tunnels and fought off professional killers. The unfairness of this grates on my already frayed nerves.

"Just for tonight," he tells the desk clerk, sliding what looks like three hundred-dollar bills across the counter. Cash. No credit card. No ID. Another red flag to add to my growing collection.

The clerk—a middle-aged man with thinning hair and perpetually surprised eyebrows—glances between us. His eyes linger on the dirt streaking my face and the blood matting my hair at the temple, then slide to Ryan's composed expression. A small, knowing smile tugs at the corner of his mouth.

"Long night?" he asks, not really asking.

I can read the assumptions forming behind his eyes. Domestic dispute. Lovers' quarrel. Maybe he thinks Ryan's some jealous boyfriend who dragged me through hell. The thought bubbles up hysterical laughter that I barely manage to swallow.

If only it were that simple.

"One room or two?" The clerk's fingers hover over his keyboard.

"Two," I say immediately, the word sharp and definitive.

At precisely the same moment, Ryan says, "One."

We lock eyes. My chin lifts in challenge.

"Two rooms," I repeat, gritting my teeth. "Separate rooms."

Ryan steps closer to me—not touching, but close enough that I can feel the heat radiating from his body. His eyes never leave mine as he says to the clerk, "One."

The single word lands with the weight of a command. No explanation. No argument. Just absolute certainty.

I open my mouth to protest, but he gives me a look that stops the words in my throat. It's not threatening, exactly. More like— resolved. As if the matter is already settled, my input irrelevant to the final decision. A muscle in his jaw tightens almost imperceptibly.

"One room," the clerk confirms, his eyebrows climbing higher as he observes our silent standoff. "King or two queens?"

"Two beds," I interject quickly before Ryan can respond, desperation creeping into my voice.

Ryan doesn't contradict me this time, which I count as a small victory until the clerk winces apologetically.

"Sorry, ma'am. Got ahead of myself. Only kings available tonight. Convention in town." He doesn't sound particularly sorry. In fact, there's that knowing smile again, like he's witnessing a familiar scene playing out for the thousandth time.

I want to scream. Want to explain that I'm not what he thinks —not some conquest or girlfriend or victim. I'm a journalist with a Pulitzer nomination. I've interviewed warlords and corrupt politicians. I've exposed human trafficking rings and corporate fraud. I don't belong here, soaked and trembling in a budget hotel lobby, at the mercy of a stranger's decisions.

But those accomplishments feel as distant as another life. Because right now, that's exactly what I am—soaked, trembling, and at someone else's mercy.

"Fine," I mutter, not bothering to hide my displeasure. "Whatever."

The clerk types with agonizing slowness, each keystroke deliberate. "Name?"

"David Wilson," Ryan answers without hesitation. A lie, delivered with such conviction that I almost believe it myself.

I add this to my mental file: Ryan Ellis uses aliases smoothly. Without preparation or hesitation. Another piece in the puzzle of who exactly I've tied my survival to.

The clerk slides two key cards across the counter. Ryan takes them both, tucking one into his pocket and holding the other loosely between his fingers.

"Room 412," the clerk says. "Elevator's to your right. Checkout's at eleven."

Ryan nods his thanks. His hand finds the small of my back, guiding me toward the elevator. I should shrug him off. Should assert my independence. But his touch stabilizes my uneven gait, and I'm too exhausted to refuse the support.

The elevator doors close with a soft chime, sealing us into a mirrored box that multiplies our bedraggled reflections into infinity. Ryan drops his hand from my back, creating distance between us. I catch him watching me in the reflection, his expression unreadable.

"One room is safer," he says quietly, breaking the silence. "I can't protect you if you're in a different room."

I meet his eyes in the mirror. "Is that what you're doing? Protecting me?"

"What else would I be doing?"

A dozen possibilities race through my mind, none of them reassuring. Kidnapping me. Using me as bait. Extracting whatever information I have before disposing of me once I'm no longer useful.

"I don't know," I answer honestly. "That's the problem."

The elevator stops with a slight jolt that sends pain shooting through my ribs. I inhale sharply, hand automatically moving to brace my side.

His eyes track the movement. "How bad?"

"I'm fine."

"That's not what I asked."

The doors slide open, saving me from responding. He checks the hallway before stepping out, those ice-blue eyes scanning every corner and shadow. I follow, noting which way the exit signs point and calculating how quickly I could reach the stairs if needed.

Old habits. Survival instincts.

We stop outside 412. Ryan slides the key card into the lock, waits for the green light, then pushes the door open—but doesn't enter. Instead, he steps aside, gesturing for me to stay put, then moves into the room without me. I watch from the doorway as he checks the bathroom, the closet, under the bed, and the windows. Only after this methodical inspection does he nod for me to enter.

I limp into the room, letting the door close behind me with a soft click. The lock engages automatically. I wonder if it would keep out the kind of men hunting us.

I doubt it.

The room is standard budget hotel fare: a king bed dominates the space, a particle-board dresser with a TV bolted on top, and a small round table with two chairs by the window. Beige wallpaper, carpet, everything. But it's clean, the sheets look fresh, and there's no obvious mold in the corners.

After maintenance tunnels and rainy alleys, it seems almost luxurious.

Ryan draws the curtains closed and turns to face me. For a long moment, we stare at each other, the reality of our situation settling like dust after an explosion.

My heart pounds against my injured ribs. The flash drive in my pocket feels suddenly heavier.

"So," I say, trying to keep my voice steady. "One room. One bed. What happens now?"

Ryan doesn't immediately answer. Instead, he moves to the heater unit beneath the window, adjusting the settings until warm air begins to circulate. This small consideration—addressing the chill from our soaked clothes—catches me off guard.

"Now," he finally says, "we deal with our situation practically." His tone is matter-of-fact, as if we're discussing a business arrangement rather than the logistics of sharing a bed with a stranger. "You take the bed. I'll sleep on the floor."

I wasn't expecting that.

"Oh." The word sounds small in the quiet room.

He reaches up to run a hand through his damp hair, the movement pulling his sodden shirt across broad shoulders. Water droplets cling to his neck. For the first time, I allow myself to really look at him—not as a threat or an unwanted protector, but simply as a man.

The jagged scar beneath his left eye. The focused intensity of his blue eyes. The way he holds himself, always balanced, always ready. In another context, I might have found him attractive. Might have approached him at a bar or a fundraiser, curious about his story.

But context is everything, and ours is a nightmare.

I catch my own reflection in the dresser mirror and freeze. The woman staring back is unrecognizable.

My normally sleek dark hair hangs in wet, filthy tangles. Dirt and grime streak across my face, mingling with mascara that raccoons beneath my eyes. Dried blood forms a rust-colored crust at my temple where my head hit the dashboard during the crash. My white blouse—or what was white—clings translucent to my skin, torn at one shoulder. The knee of my jeans is ripped open, revealing angry red abrasions beneath.

I look feral. Hunted. Broken.

A hysterical laugh bubbles up my throat before I can stop it.

"What's funny?" Ryan asks, watching me with that unnerving focus.

"Twelve hours ago, I was having coffee at my favorite café, working on an exposé about corporate tax evasion." My voice cracks. "Now I'm standing in a cheap hotel room with a stranger I watched incapacitate four men, wearing clothes I crawled through sewer tunnels in, while professional killers hunted me." I gesture at my reflection. "And I look like this."

His expression softens almost imperceptibly. "Could be worse."

"Really? How exactly could this be worse?"

"You could be dead like your source."

The words slam into me, harder than a fist. Air punches out of my lungs, and I stumble back, weight jolting onto my bad knee until it nearly gives beneath me. Pain lances up my leg, sharp and hot, but it's nothing compared to the crack tearing through my chest.

"What do you mean?" My mouth goes dry.

Ryan shakes his head. "I don't know the specifics. But I recognize the pattern. You're carrying classified data that powerful people want contained. Someone with insider information is typically the first casualty—a.k.a., your source. Then they clean up loose ends." He points at me. "You are a loose end."

A chill crawls up my spine that has nothing to do with my wet clothes. He's right, of course. That's exactly what happened. But I haven't told him any of this.

"You don't know anything," I manage, the denial weak even to my own ears.

"I know enough." He moves toward the bathroom, speaking over his shoulder. "You're a journalist. You have evidence of something dangerous enough to warrant a professional hit team. And you're smart enough to know going to authorities isn't an option because you can't tell who's compromised."

He disappears into the bathroom, returning moments later with two white towels. He tosses one to me, which I catch reflexively.

"How do you know I'm a journalist?" My fingers clench the towel without using it. It's a dumb question, seeing as I just told him I was working on an exposé, but I'm curious.

"You ask too many questions and notice everything." He runs his towel over his hair, drying it with efficient movements. "Classic journalist behavior."

I feel simultaneously exposed and oddly validated by his assessment. It's unnerving to be read so easily by someone I've just met. Someone trained to observe as meticulously as I am.

The towel in my hands is rough but clean. I press it against my face, wiping away grime, wincing when it catches on the cut at my temple. When I lower it, the white fabric is streaked with dirt, mascara, and blood.

My ribs throb with each breath. My knee threatens to give

out entirely. The adrenaline that's been keeping me upright for hours is draining away, leaving bone-deep exhaustion in its wake.

"We have nothing," I realize aloud, looking around the room. "No clothes. No toiletries. Nothing."

"I noticed." Ryan's tone is dry.

"So, what do we do? Sleep in wet, filthy clothes? I can't—" I gesture vaguely at myself, suddenly overwhelmed by the sheer practicality of our predicament. "I need a shower. Clean clothes. A toothbrush."

"Basic necessities." He's already moving toward the door. "I'll go."

"I'm coming with you." I straighten, ignoring the pain that shoots through my side.

He turns back, eyebrow raised. "No, you're not."

"I need things. Personal things." I lift my chin, daring him to make me elaborate on exactly what feminine products I might require. "And I'm not giving you my sizes."

"You're not leaving this room." His voice hardens. "Those men are still looking for you. Every minute in public is a risk."

"So I'm a prisoner now?" The question comes out sharper than intended.

"You're a protectee." He emphasizes the distinction. "And you're injured, exhausted, and still in shock, whether you realize it or not."

"I'm fine." The lie comes automatically.

"Your hands are shaking. Your pupils are dilated. Your breathing is shallow. Classic signs of shock and trauma." He takes a step closer. "You can barely stand. And we both know if you sit down on that bed, you won't get back up."

He's right. Again. The bed's gravitational pull is almost irresistible. My entire body screams for rest. But admitting weakness to this man feels like surrendering the last scrap of control I have.

"I need—" My voice falters.

"I know what you need." His tone softens, surprising me. "Medium top, small bottoms based on your frame. Toothbrush. Hair products. Something for pain. Anything else, you can tell me."

I blink, startled by his accuracy.

"Write down anything specific. I'll be quick." He produces a hotel notepad and pen from the nightstand, offering them to me.

My hand brushes his as I take the pad. The brief contact sends an unexpected shiver across my skin, which I blame on cold, wet clothes.

I scrawl a few items, hesitating before adding "heavy flow tampons" to the list. Let him deal with that awkwardness. I thrust the pad back at him.

He reads it without reaction, tucking it into his pocket. "Lock the door behind me. Don't open it for anyone but me."

"How will I know it's you?"

"Three knocks. Pause. Two knocks." He moves to the door, then pauses. "Twenty minutes max. If I'm not back, there's trouble."

This confirms what I've suspected—we're still in active danger. The hotel is a temporary sanctuary, not safety.

"What do I do if you don't come back?" The question slips out, more vulnerable than I intended.

His eyes lock with mine. For a moment, I glimpse something beyond the professional exterior—concern, perhaps. Even protectiveness. Then it's gone, shuttered behind his composed expression.

He tears off a corner of the hotel notepad and quickly writes a number. "If I'm not back in twenty minutes, call this. Tell them 'Brass is compromised.' They'll send extraction."

He holds out the paper. Our fingers brush as I take it, and I resist the urge to pull back too quickly.

*Brass.* His call sign, I remember from our earlier conversation.

The nickname feels incongruously warm for someone so controlled, so cold in his efficiency.

"What if I leave?" The question is half challenge, half genuine consideration. "Walk out after you go?"

His expression doesn't change, but something dangerous flickers in his eyes. "You won't."

"How can you be so sure?"

"Because you're smart." He says this with absolute certainty. "And smart people don't throw away their only lifeline when they're drowning."

Before I can respond, he slips out the door, closing it firmly behind him. The lock clicks automatically.

## EIGHT

## Celeste

I stand frozen for a moment, processing Ryan's words.

*Lifeline. Drowning.*

The metaphors grate against my nerves. Who is he to decide what I need? I've spent my entire career in dangerous situations. I've extracted information from warlords, negotiated with armed militants, and navigated corrupt government officials. I don't need some ex-military man telling me how to survive.

I survived before he showed up on that platform. I can survive without him now.

The thought settles in my mind with surprising clarity. I don't actually need this man. I've always protected myself. Always relied on my own instincts. I need space to think without his intimidating presence filling every corner of the room.

I move to the door, engaging the deadbolt and security chain as instructed. Then I lean against it, listening to his retreating footsteps until they fade completely.

Alone for the first time since the subway platform, I feel oddly unmoored. The silence of the room presses in, broken only by the hum of the heater and my ragged breathing.

My hand moves to my pocket, fingers closing around the small rectangle of the flash drive. Everything that's happened—Jared's murder, the car crash, the men hunting me—it all traces back to what's stored in these few megabytes of data.

Evidence that powerful people would kill to keep hidden. Evidence, I still haven't fully processed myself.

My other hand finds the slip of paper Ryan gave me. I unfold it—a corner from the hotel notepad with a phone number written in neat, precise handwriting. No name. Just ten digits that connect to people who apparently have the resources to "extract" me if necessary.

I should memorize it as instructed. Should do as I'm told for once.

Instead, I limp to the bed and finally surrender to its gravity, sinking onto the edge of the mattress. The springs creak beneath my weight. My soaked jeans cling uncomfortably to my legs, but I lack the energy to remove them.

The mirror across from the bed reflects a stranger wearing my face. A hunted woman with wild eyes and blood in her hair.

I close my eyes, unable to look at her any longer.

Twenty minutes, he said. Twenty minutes alone with my thoughts, my pain, and the weight of the evidence that's turned my life upside down in the span of a day.

What happens when he returns depends entirely on how much I decide to trust him. And trust isn't something I give easily. Not anymore. Not after everything I've seen.

I wait exactly three minutes after Ryan's footsteps fade down the hallway.

Three minutes to gather my resolve. Three minutes to remind myself who I am. Three minutes to decide I won't be controlled.

The slip of paper with his emergency contact number burns in my palm. I fold it carefully, tucking it into my bra rather than my pocket. Safer there. Water-resistant. Accessible.

I press my ear against the door, listening for any movement in the hallway. Nothing but the distant hum of ice machines and the muffled sound of a television from another room.

Twenty minutes, he said. I only need five.

My fingertips brush the cold metal of the doorknob. I hesitate, not out of fear but out of practicality. If I'm going to do this, I need a plan. Strategy has always been my strength—whether investigating corrupt officials or navigating hostile territories.

I assess my resources: flash drive and about sixty dollars in wet bills from my pocket. No phone—lost in the crash or the tunnels. No ID—deliberately left behind when it became clear those men knew exactly who I was. No room key—Ryan kept both.

Limited resources, but enough to get away. I can walk four blocks to the all-night drug store I noticed on our taxi ride. Buy necessities. Find somewhere to think, to process, to plan my next move. Away from his overwhelming presence and the confusion it creates.

This isn't about running away, I tell myself. It's about regaining autonomy. Independence. Space to breathe without him watching my every move.

Once I leave, I can't come back—the door will lock behind me. But maybe that's for the best. Ryan Ellis is a complication I never asked for, a variable I don't know how to calculate.

I unlock the door, disengaging the security chain with minimal noise. One last deep breath. I pull the door open—

And freeze.

Ryan leans against the opposite wall, arms crossed, expression unreadable. He hasn't gone anywhere. He's been waiting silently, knowing—*knowing*—I would try to leave.

"Going somewhere?" His voice is deceptively soft.

"I—" Words fail me.

For a breathless moment, we simply stare at each other. His eyes catalog my guilty expression, my hand still gripping the doorknob, my body angled toward escape.

I never see him move.

One second, he's across the hallway; the next, he's a solid wall of muscle and controlled fury, pushing me back into the room. The door slams behind us with a finality that makes my heart race.

My back hits the wall beside the door. Not hard—he's careful even in his anger—but firmly enough that I know I can't escape.

His body cages mine, one arm braced beside my head, the other flat against the wall near my waist. He doesn't touch me, yet I feel utterly trapped. Contained. His face hovers inches from mine, close enough that I feel the warmth of his breath against my cheek.

"That," he says, voice dangerously low, "was predictable and disappointing."

Heat rushes to my face—shame, anger, and something else I refuse to acknowledge. "I was just—"

"Don't." The single word cuts through my excuse. "Don't insult both of us with a lie."

I lift my chin, defiance overriding better judgment. "I needed things. Personal things."

"You needed to prove you could disobey. To establish some illusion of control." His eyes bore into mine, seeing too much. "Even at the risk of your safety."

"You don't own me." The words come out breathier than intended. "You can't keep me prisoner here."

"Is that what this is to you?" He leans closer, frustration radiating from every taut line of his body. "You think I'm keeping you prisoner?"

"What would you call it?"

His jaw clenches. I watch the muscle jump beneath his skin,

fascinated despite myself. The scar beneath his left eye seems more pronounced now, a jagged reminder of whatever violence shaped him.

"I'd call it *protection*." His voice drops to a whisper that somehow carries more weight than a shout. "I'd call it *keeping you alive* when there are professional killers hunting you. I'd call it sacrificing my mission, my schedule, potentially my career, to make sure you don't end up as another body the police find with 'no apparent motive.'"

Each word hits with precision, finding weak spots in my defenses I didn't know existed.

He's too close. Too intense. Too *present*. I've interviewed dictators and murderers without flinching, but this man—this stranger who's saved my life repeatedly in the past hours—makes me feel exposed in ways I never anticipated.

"I can take care of myself," I insist, but my voice lacks conviction.

"Can you?" His eyes drop to the blood crusted at my temple, then to my arm wrapped protectively around my injured ribs. "Because evidence suggests otherwise."

Anger flares, hot and immediate. I shove against his chest with both hands. He doesn't budge. The solid wall of him absorbs my push as if it were nothing more than a gentle touch.

And that's when I notice it—the unexpected heat coiling low in my belly. The way my pulse quickens, not from fear or anger, but from something far more primal.

I'm attracted to him.

The realization hits with embarrassing clarity. Attracted to his strength, his competence, the raw masculine power currently boxing me against this wall. Attracted to the intensity of his focus, the certainty of his movements, the unwavering purpose that drives him.

I hate it. Hate that my body betrays me this way. Hate that in the middle of danger, while professional killers hunt me, my limbic system chooses now to remind me I'm a woman and he is very much a man.

His eyes darken, pupils dilating slightly. Does he sense the shift? Can he read this reaction as easily as he reads everything else about me?

God, I hope not.

"Here's how this works," he says, voice dropping another octave. "You do exactly what I say, when I say it. No arguments. No creative interpretations. No independent excursions."

"Or what?" I challenge, desperate to regain some foothold in this confrontation.

"Or I'll be forced to consider you a liability rather than an asset."

The threat hangs between us, ambiguous yet clear.

"Would you hurt me?" I ask, needing to know where the boundaries lie.

Something flickers in his eyes—surprise, perhaps even hurt. "No. Never. But I might restrain you. And I definitely will stop protecting you if you refuse to be protected."

His face is so close now that I can see the faint stubble darkening his jaw, the tiny lines at the corners of his eyes, the almost imperceptible chip in his front tooth. Details that humanize him. Make him more than the machine-like protector who fought off four men without breaking a sweat.

"I don't like being controlled," I admit, voice barely audible.

"And I don't like wasting my time with people determined to get themselves killed." His expression softens fractionally. "This isn't about control, Celeste. It's about survival."

My name on his lips does something to me. Something I'm not prepared for.

"I need to know you understand what's happening here." His eyes search mine. "Those men in the subway aren't typical hitmen. They're ex-military or intelligence personnel, highly trained and well-funded. They have resources, connections, and a singular objective: to eliminate you and whatever you're carrying."

A chill slides down my spine despite the heat radiating from his body.

"The only reason you're alive right now is that I happened to be on that platform. The only reason you'll stay alive is if you stop fighting me and start working with me."

The certainty in his voice is both comforting and terrifying. Because he's right. I've been running on adrenaline and denial, refusing to process the reality of my situation fully.

"Do you understand?" he presses.

I nod, unable to form words past the tightness in my throat.

"Say it." His voice is gentle now, but no less commanding. "I need to hear you say it."

"I understand." The admission costs me something—pride, perhaps. Or the illusion of self-reliance I've clung to for so long.

Something shifts in his expression—approval, relief. His posture changes, but instead of moving away, he leans in closer.

Time slows to a crawl.

His eyes lock with mine, intensity radiating from that ice-blue gaze. For a heartbeat, we breathe the same air, neither advancing nor retreating. I'm pinned not by his hands but by his eyes and the weight of his focus.

Then his gaze drops to my lips. Lingers there. Returns to my eyes with a question I'm not ready to answer. His pupils dilate slightly, black consuming blue.

He moves closer—imperceptible to anyone watching, seismic to me, feeling it. The distance between us shrinks from inches to nothing. The heat of him envelops me, his scent—sweat and rain and something distinctly male—fills my lungs with each shallow breath.

Again, his eyes drop to my mouth. My lips tingle with awareness, with anticipation. His jaw tightens, a small muscle jumping beneath the stubbled skin. Is he fighting the same pull I am? This gravitational force between us that defies logic, defies the circumstances that brought us here?

I find myself leaning forward, the barest tilt of my head. An invitation I hadn't consciously decided to extend.

He's going to kiss me. The realization floods me with contradictory emotions—desire, anxiety, anticipation, fear. I should stop this. Should turn away. Should remember who he is, who I am, and why we're here.

I do none of those things.

Instead, I watch as he makes his decision. His eyes darken further. He dips his head, bringing our faces close enough that our noses nearly touch. My eyelids flutter closed, surrendering to whatever this madness is.

But at the last moment, he shifts. The kiss I've braced for doesn't land on my lips. Instead, he turns his head slightly, his mouth moving to the side. His lips brush the shell of my ear instead, his stubble grazing the sensitive skin of my cheek. His breath is warm, intimate.

"Good girl," he whispers, the words vibrating through me.

A lightning strike of sensation courses down my spine, pooling low in my belly. Heat floods my face, my neck, places I refuse to acknowledge. Two simple words shouldn't affect me this way—patronizing, condescending words that should offend every feminist principle I hold.

Instead, they light me up from the inside. A shameful warmth spreads through my chest, a dangerous pleasure at earning his approval that radiates outward until my fingertips tingle with it.

What is wrong with me?

He pushes away from the wall suddenly, creating distance

between us. The cool air rushes in to fill the space where his warmth had been.

"I'm going to get supplies now," he says, voice carefully neutral. "You're going to stay here. When I return, we'll get cleaned up, eat something, and make a plan."

I nod, still too shaken by my reactions to argue.

"If anyone but me knocks on that door, hide in the bathroom and call that number." His tone brooks no argument. "Are we clear?"

"Yes." The word comes out hoarse.

He studies me for another long moment, as if assessing my sincerity. Whatever he sees must satisfy him, because he gives a short nod.

"Twenty minutes." He moves to the door, then pauses with his hand on the knob. "And, Celeste?"

I meet his gaze, still feeling the phantom pressure of his body caging mine.

"Don't make me regret trusting you."

With that, he slips out the door. This time, I hear his footsteps retreat down the hallway, growing fainter until they disappear entirely.

I remain frozen against the wall, legs trembling, breath uneven. My body still hums with the conflicting responses he triggered—fear, anger, and a devastating attraction I neither wanted nor expected.

This time, I don't move toward the door. Don't even consider it.

Not because I'm afraid of him, though there is fear—fear of what he represents, fear of the danger surrounding us, fear of my response to him.

I stay because he's right. I know he's right. And that knowledge terrifies me more than anything.

The men hunting me won't stop. They'll find me eventually if

I'm alone. And as much as I hate depending on anyone, especially a man who makes me feel simultaneously safe and utterly vulnerable, I'm not ready to die for my pride.

I slide down the wall until I'm sitting on the floor, knees pulled to my chest despite the pain in my ribs. The flash drive digs into my thigh through my pocket, a constant reminder of why all this is happening.

Twenty minutes until he returns. Twenty minutes to get my traitorous body and confused emotions under control.

Twenty minutes to decide how much of the truth I'm willing to share with the stranger who keeps saving my life.

NINE

# Ryan

I close the door behind me and stand motionless in the hallway for three heartbeats. Just enough time to recalibrate. To wrestle back control of my body's immediate, visceral reaction to Celeste Hart.

*Fuck.*

This was not in the mission parameters. Not that there are mission parameters, since this isn't officially a mission. It's a goddamn detour that's about to derail my entire week.

And now I'm aroused. And pissed. And amused, in an irritated sort of way.

The woman is infuriating. Brilliant, obviously. Fearless to the point of recklessness. And so goddamn stubborn. I want to turn her over my knee, smack some sense into her, and then fuck her senseless. Pin her against that wall again, but this time without stopping. See if she's as defiant when I'm inside her.

The thought hits with such visceral force that I have to clench my fists. Completely inappropriate. Completely unprofessional. And completely undeniable.

I exhale slowly, pushing away fantasies that have no place in a protection detail. Professional. I need to stay professional. Even if she's not my client in any official capacity, she's still under my protection. Lines exist for a reason.

Lines I nearly crossed when I almost kissed her.

I roll my shoulders, trying to dispel the tension that's settled there. My body still hums with need after pinning her against that wall. From the way her eyes dilated when I leaned in. From the soft parting of her lips that was pure invitation.

What the hell was I thinking?

I wasn't. That's the problem. For those few seconds, instinct overrode training. Desire trumped protocol. A rookie mistake I haven't made since—ever.

The scent of her lingers—rain and sweat and beneath it all, that citrus note that's been driving me quietly insane since the subway platform. Even filthy from the tunnels, she smells incredible. Looks incredible, with those defiant eyes and that stubborn set to her jaw.

A fucking journalist, of all things. Professional skeptics with death wishes and the self-preservation instincts of lemmings.

I shake my head, moving toward the elevator with measured steps. This is not how I expected my evening to go when I boarded the Metro after dinner with my mother. Should be halfway to Seattle by now. Instead, I'm shopping for a woman who just tried to escape the protection she desperately needs.

My mouth curves into an unwilling smile. She's got nerve, I'll give her that. Most people wouldn't have the balls to try walking out after what we've been through tonight. Most people would be curled in the fetal position, processing the trauma. Not Celeste Hart. She's plotting escape routes while nursing broken ribs.

There's something admirable in that, even if it's tactically idiotic.

The elevator doors close, and I study my reflection in the polished metal. I look like shit—hair still damp, clothes rumpled and dirt-streaked, the scar beneath my eye more pronounced after the fight. There's a tear in my shirt I hadn't noticed before. Perfect.

At the front desk, the same clerk from check-in eyes me warily.

"Need something, sir?"

"Nearest place to buy clothes and toiletries?" I keep my tone casual. "We had—unexpected travel delays. Lost our luggage."

His eyebrows lift slightly, no doubt filling in a colorful backstory. "Convenience store three blocks east. 24-hour pharmacy about six blocks west."

"Which is better stocked?"

"Pharmacy. More selection." He hesitates. "Your, uh, wife okay? She looked a little roughed up."

Not his business, but I appreciate the concern. At least he's checking.

"Car accident," I say smoothly. "Taxi hydroplaned. She got the worst of it."

He nods, satisfied with the explanation. "Pharmacy has basic first aid too."

"Thanks."

I head toward the door, then pause. "Any chance you have a plastic bag? Wallet got soaked in the rain."

The clerk reaches beneath the counter and produces a small plastic bag.

"Appreciate it."

Out of his sight, I extract the cash from my wallet, separating damp bills from dry. I can't use credit cards—too easily tracked. Cash is anonymous. Untraceable. Essential when professional operators are hunting you.

Outside, the rain has slowed to a steady drizzle, the kind that soaks through gradually rather than all at once. I scan the street —force of habit—noting potential threats, exit routes, and vantage points. The neighborhood is quiet at this hour. Few pedestrians, minimal traffic.

I walk quickly, constantly aware of my exposure. Six blocks feel like a tactical error, leaving Celeste alone for too long. But I need proper supplies, and I'm not naive enough to think she won't try to leave again given enough time.

I make no apologies for waiting outside the door to catch her. She might resent the tactic, but she's alive to resent it. That's the part that matters.

The street stretches before me, glistening under sodium lights. I maintain a brisk pace while memorizing the route. Always know your terrain. It's the first rule they teach in special ops. Always know at least three ways out of wherever you are.

The woman back in that hotel room has no idea how much danger she's in. Those men on the platform weren't street thugs or corporate security. The way they moved, the way they coordinated without verbal communication—that was advanced training. Military or intelligence background.

Whatever she's carrying on that flash drive, it's big enough to pull in a professional *wet* team—the kind that leaves blood and bodies behind. We're not running from hired muscle now. We're running from resources. From networks. From people with access to cameras, databases, and tracking capabilities far beyond civilian scope.

I estimate we have twelve hours before they identify the hotel. Maybe less. By tomorrow, we need to be on the move, with altered appearances and no electronic footprint. I'll need to call in favors and activate resources.

But first: supplies. Can't run effectively if you're still wearing clothes soaked in tunnel water.

The pharmacy's fluorescent lighting assaults my eyes after the dim street. A bored cashier glances up from her phone, then back down, dismissing me as non-threatening. Smart girl. In my current mood, I'm anything but.

I grab a hand basket and move systematically through the aisles. Practicality first. Two T-shirts, sweatpants, socks. For me, plain and functional. I don't care about appearances. The clothes need to serve their purpose—cover, comfort, mobility.

Then women's clothing. And here, despite myself, I slow down.

Growing up with three older sisters has its occasional advantages. I know how to shop for a woman without looking completely lost. I know sizes, fabrics, what's comfortable versus what looks good.

For Celeste, I select practical but flattering options. Soft cotton T-shirts in deep green and navy that won't irritate her injured ribs but will complement her coloring. A zip-up hoodie in charcoal gray for warmth. Leggings that will be gentle on her knee. My sisters' voices echo in my head, providing commentary on fabric and fit.

Clare would approve of the color choices. Melissa would nod at the practical considerations for her injuries. And Diane would roll her eyes, thinking I wasn't considering style enough.

I smile at that. It's been years since I've gone shopping with any of them, but some lessons stick.

Then I reach the lingerie section and pause.

This feels more invasive somehow, more personal than picking out shirts and pants. But she needs everything, and I'm not making a second trip.

I study the options clinically, assessing her build from memory. The curve of her waist when I grabbed her in the tunnels. The swell of her breasts beneath that sodden blouse when she was pressed against the wall. She's slender but curved. B-cup, maybe C. Erring on the side of comfort, I select the C.

Then, instead of the practical cotton I should choose, my hand reaches for a black lace bra.

Inappropriate. Unprofessional. Completely unjustifiable from a tactical standpoint.

I put it in the basket anyway.

If I'm being honest—and why not, since no one's in my head but me—I'm selecting what I'd like to see her in. What I'd like to peel off her in a different context, under different circumstances. My preferences, not what makes the most tactical sense.

Same with the underwear. I bypass the sensible cotton briefs for a pack of bikini-cut lace-trimmed ones. Black, deep blue, and a dark purple, colors I imagine would suit her complexion.

The practical part of my brain—the part that's kept me alive through three combat tours and countless operations—argues this is tactical suicide. Letting attraction cloud judgment. The rest of me tells that part to shut the fuck up. Just this once.

There will be no scenario where this matters anyway. By tomorrow, we'll be focused on staying alive, not—whatever this is. So where's the harm in small indulgences of imagination? In acknowledging the spark between us, even if we'll never act on it?

In the toiletries aisle, I grab the basics: toothbrushes, toothpaste, and deodorant. Then I pause at the shampoos, realizing I don't know what Celeste prefers.

Except I do. That citrus scent.

I very quickly uncap bottles one by one, sniffing each until I find it—a grapefruit and mandarin blend that instantly conjures her face. The companion conditioner also goes into the basket.

Diane would laugh herself sick if she could see me now, standing in a pharmacy at midnight, smelling hair products for a woman who tried to ditch me thirty minutes ago. But there's something oddly satisfying about finding the exact right scent. About knowing she'll recognize the effort.

When I reach the feminine products section, I don't hesitate.

My sisters cured any awkwardness about this years ago. The list Celeste gave me included tampons, specifically heavy flow ones. A message meant to make me uncomfortable.

I grab the box, along with a selection of pads. If she's trying to unbalance me with basic biology, she's underestimated my upbringing. Three sisters and a nurse mother left no room for squeamishness.

I remember Melissa sending me to the store when we were teenagers, giving me absurdly specific instructions to see if I'd get flustered. I came back with exactly what she asked for, plus chocolate. The look of surprise on her face was worth every second of the cashier's raised eyebrows.

The first aid supplies are next: antibiotic ointment, bandages, Ace bandages for her knee. I add a cold pack for her ribs and butterfly closures for the cut on her temple.

I mentally assess her injuries as I shop. The ribs aren't fully broken—her breathing is labored but not the shallow panting of a punctured lung. Her knee is sprained, not torn—she can bear weight, albeit painfully. The head wound is superficial, and there are no signs of concussion in her pupils or speech patterns.

She's hurting but functional. Tough. You don't get that kind of resilience from an easy life.

As I turn toward the checkout, I pass the hair care aisle and stop. Her appearance is distinctive. The men hunting her will have a description. Long, dark hair, approximately 5'7", slim build.

I backtrack to the hair dye section. Changing her appearance isn't just about disguise—it's about survival. I scan the options, selecting a warm auburn shade that will alter her look without appearing unnatural against her skin tone.

I consider her complexion—olive with golden undertones. The auburn will complement that, bring out the flecks of gold I noticed in her brown eyes. It's a practical consideration. Purely tactical.

That's what I tell myself, anyway.

I add a pair of shears to the basket. I'm no hairstylist, but I've cut my sisters' hair in emergencies. I can manage a basic length reduction and some face-framing layers to change her silhouette.

Diane was always using me as practice for her cosmetology courses, teaching me the basics of cutting while complaining about my lack of artistic vision. "It's geometry, Ryan. Angles and lines. You're good at math—this should be easy for you."

Turns out she was right. Hair cutting is just applied physics and geometry. I'm no virtuoso, but I can handle the fundamentals. Enough to change Celeste's appearance without making her look like she lost a fight with a lawn mower.

On my way to the register, I pass the family planning section. I shouldn't stop. There's absolutely no tactical reason to.

I stop anyway.

The box of condoms feels like a presumption. Like arrogance. Like acknowledging something I have no business acknowledging in this situation.

I put them in the basket.

Just in case.

Not because I expect anything to happen. Not because I want it to. But because preparation is ingrained in every fiber of my being, and the electric current that passed between us back in that hotel room wasn't one-sided. I felt her response. Saw the dilation of her pupils, the flush spreading across her cheeks, and the parting of her lips when I leaned in.

Three days minimum to Seattle with security protocols. That's a lot of hours in close proximity. A lot of time spent in hotel rooms, in cars, in spaces where tension builds and releases one way or another.

Better to have them and not need them than need them and not have them. First rule of tactical planning.

At least that's what I'm telling myself as I study the options. I select the ones that won't aggravate her injuries. The ones designed for her comfort. Because yes, I've thought about it in enough detail to consider angles and positions that won't strain broken ribs.

*Christ, Ellis. Get it together.*

Dangerous territory. Complications neither of us needs. Yet the condoms stay in the basket as I approach the checkout counter.

The cashier rings everything up without comment, though her eyebrows lift slightly at the combination of women's clothing, hair dye, and condoms. I pay cash—no electronic trail—and head back into the night with four bulging plastic bags.

The rain has stopped completely now, leaving the streets glistening under streetlights. I maintain awareness as I walk, constantly scanning for threats or surveillance. Nothing triggers my instincts.

Still, I take a circuitous route back to the hotel, doubling back twice to ensure I'm not followed. Fourteen minutes have passed since I left Celeste alone. Within parameters, but barely.

My mind wanders to how I'll handle her when I get back. She'll be wary after that confrontation. Defensive. Pride wounded from being caught trying to leave. From being pinned against that wall.

From whatever passed between us in those charged moments before I whispered in her ear.

I'll need to establish clear boundaries. Professional parameters. We have a long drive ahead, and complications will only endanger us both.

But there's a part of me—a part I usually keep locked down tight during operations—that's looking forward to her reaction when she sees what I've purchased. The lace. The hair dye. The condoms, if she happens to glimpse those.

Will she be offended? Amused? Intrigued?

The unpredictability is strangely appealing after years of working with people whose reactions I can calculate down to the syllable.

In the hotel lobby, I nod to the clerk and head straight for the elevator. My mind has already shifted to the next phase—getting Celeste cleaned up, addressing her injuries, and establishing a functional rapport that doesn't involve pinning her to walls.

Though I can't entirely regret that part.

The elevator doors close, leaving me alone with my reflection and the uncomfortable realization that Celeste Hart is more than a complication in my schedule. More than an unexpected responsibility. More than a stubborn, defiant journalist with a target on her back.

She's a woman who makes me feel things I have no business feeling on a protection detail.

And that makes her dangerous in ways those professional killers could never be.

I arrive at our door and raise my fist to knock, then hesitate. What if she did manage to leave while I was gone? What if—

No. She's in there. I'm sure of it.

Three knocks. Pause. Two knocks.

Our code. A small piece of structure in the chaos we're navigating. A tiny fragment of the trust we'll need to build if we're going to survive what's coming.

I wait, plastic bags rustling at my side, and I feel something I rarely experience before an operation: uncertainty. Not about our tactical situation or our next moves.

About her. About us. About whether I can maintain the professional distance this situation demands when everything about Celeste Hart makes me want to close that distance entirely.

TEN

# Celeste

I pace the hotel room like a caged animal, checking my watch for the tenth time in as many minutes. Eighteen minutes since Ryan left. Two minutes until I'm supposed to call that mysterious number. Two minutes until I admit he might not be coming back.

My ribs throb with each turn, a constant reminder of everything that's happened tonight. The crash. The men in the subway. The tunnels. And Ryan Ellis, materializing in my life like some kind of avenging angel with ice in his veins and violence in his hands.

The silence of the room presses against my ears. I strain to hear footsteps in the hallway, any indication that he's returning. Or worse—that someone else has found us.

Three sharp knocks on the door. A pause. Two more knocks.

Relief floods through me, followed immediately by irritation at feeling relieved. I shouldn't care whether he comes back. Shouldn't need him. But I do, and that admission burns through my carefully constructed independence like acid.

I check the peephole first—not completely naive—and see

Ryan's broad-shouldered silhouette, plastic bags dangling from his hands. I unlock the door, stepping back as he enters.

His eyes scan the room first—checking corners, sight lines, potential threats—before landing on me. There's a slight relaxation in his shoulders when he confirms I'm still here, that I didn't attempt another escape. The fact that he expected me to stay sends a contradictory thrill through me. He knows I'm stubborn, yet he trusted me anyway.

"Good choice," he says, acknowledging my decision to remain without actually praising it. His voice carries that same commanding tone that irritates and intrigues me in equal measure.

"I'm not an idiot," I reply, lifting my chin. "Just independent."

A ghost of a smile touches his lips. "Same thing sometimes."

He moves to the small round table by the window and begins unpacking his purchases. Items emerge from plastic bags and are arranged in neat, categorical rows. Men's clothes on the left— plain, functional T-shirts and sweatpants. Basic necessities without personality or flair.

On the right, he places women's clothing—and I find myself momentarily stunned. Not by the practicality, which I expected, but by the thoughtfulness. Soft cotton T-shirts in deep green and navy that would actually complement my coloring. A charcoal gray hoodie that looks both warm and flattering. Black leggings that will be gentle on my injured knee.

Basic, yes. But not thoughtless.

"How did you know my size?" I ask, genuinely curious.

Ryan doesn't look up from his methodical unpacking. "Visual assessment. Years of practice."

Of course. He's been assessing everything about me since the moment we met. Why would my clothing size be any different?

Toiletries come next—toothbrushes, toothpaste, deodorant.

All arranged with an almost obsessive precision that speaks to a mind that values order above all.

Then he pulls out a bottle of shampoo and places it in the center of the table.

I freeze.

It's my brand. Not just my brand—my exact scent. Grapefruit and mandarin, the citrus blend I've used for years. A small, inconsequential detail about myself that somehow this stranger captured perfectly.

"How did you …?" I don't finish the question.

He glances up, blue eyes meeting mine with unsettling directness. "You smell like citrus. I found the match."

My heart does something complicated in my chest—a skip followed by a gallop. He noticed how I smell. Remembered it. Sought it out specifically among dozens of options.

The intimacy of this gesture strikes me harder than if he'd touched me. It reveals an attention to detail that feels almost invasive. As if he's been cataloging parts of me I didn't offer.

Next come the feminine products—pads and tampons, the exact type I requested. He places them on the table without comment, without embarrassment, like they're as neutral as toothpaste or shampoo.

And then, with the same casual efficiency, he sets down a box of condoms.

The room suddenly feels too warm, the air too thick to breathe properly. I stare at the incongruous blue box, my mind short-circuiting as I process the implications.

The bastard.

After that almost-kiss against the wall, after the way he looked at me before whispering "good girl" in my ear like some kind of erotic command … Now this? A presumption so bold it borders on insulting.

Or would be insulting, if a traitorous part of me weren't humming with something dangerously close to anticipation.

I press my fingers to my lips, remembering the ghost of pressure that never came. The kiss that didn't happen. The heat of his body as he caged me against the wall. The surge of unwanted desire that flooded me when his voice dropped to that commanding whisper.

When I finally look up, Ryan is watching me intently, searching for a reaction. He wants one. Is waiting for it. The realization hits me with perfect clarity—this was deliberate. A test. A provocation. A way to unbalance me.

I refuse to give him the satisfaction. Instead, I force my expression into neutral disinterest, as if condoms are as mundane as toothpaste in this scenario.

"What next?" I ask, my voice impressively steady.

He holds my gaze a moment longer, something like disappointment flickering across his features at my non-reaction.

"Shower, then bed," he replies, matching my casual tone. As if he hasn't just detonated a grenade of implication between us. As if the word "bed" doesn't carry a freight train of meaning in this context. "You first," he adds, nodding toward the bathroom. "Clean your head wound. I'll check it after."

Just like that, we're back to practical concerns. The professional protector and his reluctant charge. Nothing more complicated than that.

Except everything feels complicated now.

I gather the toiletries, then hesitate. "I'll be quick."

"Take your time," he says, already turning his attention to the remaining items. "We're secure for tonight."

The bathroom is small but clean, with chipped white tiles and a shower curtain that has seen better days. I lock the door behind me, though I doubt it would stop Ryan for more than two seconds if he decided to come in.

The thought sends an unexpected shiver through me that I refuse to examine too closely.

I turn the shower on, letting steam fill the small space while I peel off my filthy clothes. Every movement is a negotiation with pain—ribs protesting, knee throbbing, muscles I didn't know I had screaming from our tunnel crawl. The hot water beckons, promising relief.

As I step under the spray, I'm again shocked by my reflection in the cloudy mirror. The woman staring back is still a stranger—wild-eyed, blood crusted at her temple, but the fear that dominated her features earlier has been replaced by something more complex.

Determination, yes.

Wariness, absolutely.

But also, confusion that borders on wonder. As if she can't quite believe the turn her life has taken in the past twelve hours.

The hot water is divine, washing away tunnel grime and sweat, easing the ache in my muscles if not my mind. I use the grapefruit shampoo, inhaling deeply as the familiar scent surrounds me. Ryan's attention to this detail still unnerves me. Still matters more than it should.

Mid-rinse, a horrifying realization stops me cold—I forgot to bring clean clothes into the bathroom with me. They're sitting on the table where Ryan left them, and there's no way I'm putting the filthy ones back on.

I curse under my breath, weighing my options. I could call out, ask him to leave the clothes by the door. But that would mean admitting my mistake. Showing vulnerability. Giving him another opportunity to think I need rescuing.

No way in hell.

The only other option makes my heart race: emerge with just a towel, grab the clothes, and retreat back to the bathroom before he has time to react.

It's a terrible plan. The worst. But it's the only one I've got.

I finish showering, turn off the water, and dry myself with the rough hotel towel. My movements are brisk and efficient, trying to build momentum for what comes next. I wrap the towel securely around my body—it barely reaches mid-thigh, but it covers the essentials.

One deep breath. Two. I unlock the door and step back into the hotel room.

Ryan is exactly where I left him, standing by the table, examining what appears to be hair dye and scissors. His head snaps up at my entrance, eyes widening fractionally before his expression shutters into careful neutrality.

But not before I catch the flash of heat that darkens his gaze as it travels from my bare shoulders to my exposed legs and back up again.

"Forgot my clothes," I explain unnecessarily, hating the slight tremor in my voice.

He doesn't respond. Doesn't move. Just watches with that unnerving focus as I cross to the table, water droplets tracking my path across the carpet. I snatch up the clothes—underwear, bra, leggings, T-shirt—clutching them against my chest like armor.

Something makes me hesitate, causing me to turn back and face him. Perhaps it's the weight of his gaze. Perhaps it's simple curiosity.

Whatever the reason, I'm unprepared for what I see.

Ryan has straightened to his full height, all pretense of casualness abandoned. He reaches for the hem of his shirt and pulls it over his head in one fluid motion, revealing a torso that makes me forget how to breathe.

Muscles upon muscles, sculpted with the precision of a Renaissance statue. Broad shoulders tapering to a narrow waist. Abs defined enough to count each ridge. But it's not the perfection that captures my attention—it's the imperfections. Scars crisscross his skin like a roadmap of violence. A jagged line across his left pectoral. A small, puckered circle that can only be a bullet wound near his right shoulder. Thin, white slashes across his ribs.

His body tells stories of danger, of survival, of the exact kind of life that produces a man who can fight off four attackers without breaking a sweat.

I realize I'm staring, mouth slightly parted, clothes forgotten in my arms.

He moves toward me—no, toward the bathroom—his path taking him so close I can feel the heat radiating from his skin. His scent envelops me, musky sweat and something distinctly male that makes my stomach tighten.

"My turn," he says, voice low and rough as he brushes past me.

# ELEVEN

# Celeste

—————

The brief contact between Ryan's arm and my bare shoulder sends electricity coursing through me. I stand frozen as he disappears into the bathroom, the door closing with a soft click behind him.

My fingers dig into the bundle of clothes I'm holding, knuckles white with tension. My heart hammers so loudly I'm certain he must have heard it before he closed the door. The spot where his skin touched mine burns like a brand, sensation radiating outward until my entire body feels flushed.

What the hell just happened?

It's infuriating how easily he affects me. I've spent years building walls around myself—professional walls, emotional walls—training myself to remain coolly analytical no matter what horrors I uncover. It's what makes me good at my job.

But Ryan Ellis walks by without a shirt, and suddenly I'm as flustered as a college intern on her first assignment. One look from those icy blue eyes dismantles my carefully constructed defenses faster than any threat or bribe ever could.

The worst part? He knows it.

The shower starts running, the sound of water hitting tile filtering through the thin door. I force myself to move, to get dressed before he finishes. The underwear—which I now notice is black lace rather than practical cotton—slides against my skin with unexpected luxury. The matching bra fits perfectly. The leggings are soft, the T-shirt even softer.

Everything fits. Everything feels good against my skin. Everything was chosen with care and attention that professionals don't usually waste on short-term assignments.

As I'm brushing my hair, a sound from the bathroom catches my attention. A low, masculine groan barely audible over the running water.

I freeze; brush suspended in midair.

It could be pain. Could be him addressing an injury I don't know about. Could be perfectly innocent.

But it doesn't sound innocent.

Before I can stop myself, I'm moving toward the bathroom door, drawn by curiosity I can't justify even to myself. My ear presses against the wood, shame and anticipation warring in my chest.

The water continues to fall, but now I can clearly hear rhythmic movements disturbing its steady pattern. Another groan, deeper this time. The unmistakable sound of wet skin against wet skin, friction creating its own percussion.

He's … Oh my God.

I should move away. Should give him privacy. Should pretend I don't know exactly what he's doing on the other side of this flimsy door.

Instead, I listen harder, my own breathing shallow, my body responding to the erotic soundtrack with a heat that has nothing to do with the lingering steam.

"Celeste …"

My name on his lips—low and throaty, filthy as sin—sends a

jolt of electricity straight through me. It's followed by a guttural groan, the sound primal and raw, undeniably masculine.

"Fuck, Celeste." His voice carries through the door, strained and desperate, each syllable dripping with need.

I spring back as if burned, heart pounding against my injured ribs. The knowledge that he's pleasuring himself while thinking of me—saying my name like a prayer and a curse combined—leaves me dizzy with a dangerous cocktail of embarrassment and arousal. I dart across the room, grabbing the first thing I see—the hair dye box—and pretend to be deeply engrossed in reading its ingredients when the bathroom door finally opens.

Ryan emerges in a cloud of steam, a towel slung low around his hips. Water droplets cling to his chest, tracking paths between defined muscles, disappearing beneath the towel's edge. His hair is darker when wet, slicked back from his forehead, emphasizing the strong lines of his face.

My eyes betray me, dropping lower before I can stop them. The towel does little to conceal the substantial bulge beneath—impressive even in what must be a semi-relaxed state. An unbidden thought flashes through my mind: if he's that noticeable after release, how formidable would he be fully aroused? How would it feel to have all that hardness pressed against me, into me?

Heat scorches my cheeks as my focus slips where it shouldn't. Pulitzer nomination or not, every ounce of discipline shatters at the sight of him standing there in nothing but a towel slung low around his hips. Water still beads along his skin, sliding in slow rivulets I can't seem to look away from.

I should turn around, should remind myself why I'm here—but God help me, I can't stop staring. I return my gaze to the box in my hands, fighting to control my breathing, to appear casual and unaffected. To hide the fact that I just listened to him bring himself to climax while thinking of—me?

"We need to change your appearance," he says, as if he hasn't just done what he did, as if I don't know, as if we're discussing nothing more intimate than weather patterns. "Hair color, length. Those men have a description of you."

I clear my throat, desperate for a normal conversation. "Hence the dye."

"Auburn. It'll work with your coloring." He crosses to his pile of clothing, selecting sweatpants and a T-shirt. "I'll cut it now while it's wet, then we'll color it in the morning after it dries."

"You cut hair?" I ask, skeptical, relieved to be talking about something so mundane.

A ghost of a smile touches his lips. "Among other skills. Nothing fancy, but enough to change your silhouette."

"Now?" I touch my damp hair protectively.

"Best time to cut it is when it's wet." He sets down his clothes. "Sit at the desk. I'll grab the scissors."

Reluctantly, I move to the chair, watching in the dresser mirror as Ryan retrieves the shears from the shopping bag. My hair falls past my shoulders, one of my few vanities. I've worn it long for years—a signature look that's become part of my professional identity. The thought of losing it sends a pang of unexpected grief through me.

Ryan moves behind me, his reflection meeting mine in the mirror. "How much are you willing to lose?"

The question surprises me. I expected military efficiency—a utilitarian hack job done without consultation. "You're asking my opinion?"

"It's your hair." His voice carries a hint of amusement. "I need to change your appearance, but I don't need to make you miserable doing it."

"I thought you'd just—chop it all off."

"I could." He lifts a section of my hair, studying the length.

"But there are more sophisticated ways to alter your look while still leaving you something to work with."

His fingers slide through my wet strands, slow and unhurried, and the world contracts to that touch. Every nerve sparks alive, sharp as electricity, hot as flame. The shiver that runs down my spine betrays me, leaving me exposed, raw. I should recoil. I should hate the way he handles me as if I belong to him. Instead, my body leans closer, desperate for more.

It feels wrong—God, it feels more invasive than when he pinned me against the wall with brute force. Because this isn't about power or control. It's tender. Intimate. Personal in a way I never invited, never expected. His hand in my hair is a promise and a threat at once—one I don't know how to refuse.

My throat tightens, voice dragging out husky when I manage, "What do you suggest?"

"Face-framing layers. Shorter in back, longer in front. It would change your silhouette completely while still being flattering." His gaze locks onto mine in the mirror, steady and assessing. "You have good bone structure. We should emphasize that."

My pulse thrums like I've just run miles. Not from fear; from something far more dangerous.

I swallow hard, fighting for composure. "You know a lot about hair for an ex–Delta Force operator."

A real smile touches his lips this time, softening him in a way that makes my stomach flip. "Three sisters. One went to cosmetology school. I was her practice dummy for years."

The image of a younger Ryan sitting patiently while his sister experimented on his hair humanizes him in a way that his scars and combat skills don't. I find myself smiling back.

"Okay," I concede. "I trust you."

The words fall between us with unexpected weight. He holds my gaze in the mirror for a long moment, seeming to understand that I'm offering more than permission to cut my hair.

"I'll be careful," he says quietly.

He begins with a comb, working through the tangles with unexpected gentleness. His touch is sure but considerate, easing through knots without pulling. The same hands that disabled four men with lethal efficiency now handle my hair with a delicate, if not reverent, touch.

"Tell me if I hurt you," he murmurs, standing close enough that I feel the heat radiating from his bare chest. Water droplets still cling to his skin, occasionally falling onto my shoulder as he leans forward.

His fingers replace the comb as he sections my hair, the heat of his hands against my scalp sending another shiver through me. I close my eyes, surrendering to the strange intimacy of the moment.

The first snip of the scissors makes me flinch.

"Trust, remember?" His voice is low, close to my ear.

I nod, keeping my eyes closed as he works. The rhythmic sound of the scissors becomes almost meditative. *Snip*. Pause. The brush of his fingers. *Snip*. *Snip*. The gentle tug as he positions another section. His breathing steady and controlled above me.

Minutes pass in this strange, suspended intimacy. I've had relationships with men that felt less personal than this haircut. Less revealing.

"Open your eyes," he says finally.

I obey, blinking at my reflection in surprise. The woman staring back at me is undeniably me, yet transformed. My hair now falls in a perfect butterfly cut—shorter layers in the back that graduate to longer, face-framing pieces in the front. It's sophisticated, flattering, and completely different from my previous straight, one-length style.

"It's …" Words fail me.

"Different enough to change your silhouette in security footage, but still suits you." His hands rest lightly on my shoulders, our eyes meeting in the mirror. "The auburn color will complete the transformation."

I reach up to touch the shorter strands, marveling at how the cut emphasizes my cheekbones and softens my jawline. "It's beautiful."

Something flickers in his eyes—satisfaction, perhaps. "You sound surprised."

"I am." I turn in the chair to look up at him directly. "You're full of surprises, Ryan Ellis."

We're close now—too close. His hands still rest on my shoulders, warm and steady. From this angle, I have to tilt my head back to meet his gaze, a position that feels vulnerable and thrilling simultaneously.

"You haven't seen anything yet," he says softly.

For one breathless moment, I think he might bend down and kiss me. I want him to, despite every rational part of my brain screaming that it's a terrible idea.

Instead, he steps back, breaking the spell. "We should get some sleep. Tomorrow will be a long day."

He begins cleaning up the fallen hair, moving with that same efficient grace that characterizes everything he does. I remain seated, touching the ends of my new haircut, watching him in the mirror.

This man is dangerous in ways that have nothing to do with his combat training. Nothing to do with the violence he's capable of. He's dangerous because he makes me want things I shouldn't. Trust I can't afford to give. Intimacy I've spent years avoiding.

Yet here I am, letting him transform me, piece by piece.

"What happens tomorrow?"

"We head to Seattle. Cerberus headquarters." He moves to the bed, stripping off the decorative pillows and flipping back a corner of the blanket. "You take the bed. I'll sleep on the floor."

Right. The sleeping arrangements. I'd almost forgotten that particular complication.

"That's ridiculous," I say, gesturing at him. "The floor is hard."

"Trust me, I've slept in worse places. The floor and I will manage just fine." He glances at the narrow strip of carpet, mouth tugging wryly, before tossing down a pillow. "Besides, the floor doesn't complain when I hog the covers."

"We could share," I blurt before I can stop myself. His head snaps up, eyes locking with mine, heat sparking in the charged space between us.

"The bed is huge," I press on quickly. "We could stay on opposite sides. Like adults."

His expression shutters, all hard lines and restraint. "Not a good idea."

"That makes no sense." Frustration sharpens my tone. "You won't get any decent rest on the floor, and tomorrow's going to be hell. You need to be sharp, not half-broken from sleeping on carpet."

For a moment, his jaw flexes as if weighing the argument. Then his gaze pins me, molten and merciless. "If I get in that bed," he says, voice dropping low and lethal, "there won't be much rest for either of us."

The words detonate in the silence, stealing the air from my lungs. Heat flares hot and dangerous in my chest, curling low in my belly. He doesn't apologize. Doesn't soften. Just lays the truth bare between us, daring me to call it anything but what it is— want, raw and unhidden.

The honesty of his answer steals my breath. There's no artifice there, no manipulation. Just raw truth—he wants me. Enough that proximity while sleeping seems like a risk neither of us should take.

The knowledge settles in my belly, warm and dangerous.

"Fine," I concede, moving to the bed. "But the offer stands. This is stupid."

"Noted."

I slide between the sheets, the cool cotton a blissful relief against my battered body. The mattress isn't particularly luxurious, but after everything I've endured today, it feels like heaven.

Ryan moves around the room, checking locks, securing the window, establishing sight lines. Always vigilant. Always on guard. I wonder if he ever truly relaxes, if he knows how to exist without scanning for threats.

Finally, he settles onto his makeshift bed on the floor. The room falls into darkness as he switches off the lamp, leaving only the faint glow of streetlights filtering through the curtains.

"Ryan?" My voice sounds small in the darkness.

"Yeah?" His reply comes immediately, alert even on the edge of sleep.

"Thank you. For coming back." The words cost me something—pride, perhaps. But they need to be said.

A long pause stretches between us. Then, softly, "I'll always come back, Celeste."

The promise in his voice wraps around me like a physical thing. I close my eyes, trying to ignore the way my body responds to the sound of my name on his lips. Trying to forget what I heard through the bathroom door. Trying to convince myself that the strange, electric connection between us is nothing more than adrenaline and proximity and the unique circumstances that have thrown us together.

But as sleep claims me, my last coherent thought is of his words to the clerk: *one room.*

And the undeniable truth that despite everything—the danger, the uncertainty, my fiercely guarded independence—I'm glad he made that choice.

## TWELVE

## Celeste

———————

The harsh blare of an alarm jolts me awake. Five-thirty. Still dark outside.

For one disorienting moment, I have no idea where I am. Then reality crashes back—the crash, the subway, the men hunting me. Ryan Ellis, currently rising from his makeshift bed on the floor with the lethal, coiled grace of a predator—fluid, controlled, every movement promising violence and sex in equal measure.

My gaze lingers where it shouldn't—the flex of muscle under his shirt, the ripple of strength in movements meant to be utilitarian, not mesmerizing. He shakes the stiffness from his shoulders like it's nothing, and I can't look away, caught between awe and something far more reckless.

"Time to move," he says, already fully alert while I'm still blinking sleep from my eyes.

I sit up slowly, every muscle protesting. The events of yesterday have settled into my body overnight, leaving me stiff and aching. My ribs throb with each breath. My knee feels marginally better, but not by much.

"How long have you been awake?" I ask, noting the neatly folded blankets of his floor nest.

"Long enough." He moves to the window, peering through a crack in the curtains. "We need to color your hair, eat something, and be on the road within the hour."

No "good morning." No acknowledgment of last night's strange intimacy as he cut my hair. Just back to business, as if nothing passed between us but professional courtesy.

Fine. Two can play at that game.

"I'll get the dye ready." I match his detached tone as I slide out of bed.

The auburn hair color turns out to be a surprisingly flattering shade—rich and warm against my olive skin. Ryan applies it with the same expertise he showed while cutting my hair, but this time there's none of last night's gentleness. His touch is efficient, impersonal. Clinical.

I sit at the desk chair again, a towel draped around my shoulders, as he works the color through my newly shortened locks. In the mirror, I watch his face—the intense concentration, the slight furrow between his brows, the way his jaw tightens when our eyes accidentally meet in the reflection.

It shouldn't feel like this—watching him focus on something so mundane. But every detail unsettles me. The steady pressure of his fingers massaging the dye into my scalp, strong hands gentled in a way that doesn't match the man who dragged me through tunnels and shielded me from bullets. The heat of him standing close enough that his shoulder almost brushes mine. The way his lower lip pulls tight when he's focused, making me wonder how it would feel caught between my teeth.

I drag my gaze away, only to have it wander back again, traitorous, hungry. Each normal thing—his patience, his stillness, his touch—feels amplified in the silence, until I can't decide if I want to lean back into his hands or bolt from the room before I give myself away.

"Rinse in twenty minutes," he says, stripping off the plastic gloves. "I'll get breakfast."

Before I can respond, he's gone again, leaving me alone with auburn dye and confused emotions I have no business feeling.

Forty-five minutes later, I barely recognize the woman in the mirror.

The butterfly cut Ryan gave me last night frames my face with soft, angled layers. Now auburn instead of dark brown, the color brings out golden flecks in my eyes I never noticed before. With the bruise at my temple partially concealed by artfully arranged strands, I look like a different person.

A stranger who might not be hunted by professional killers.

"Acceptable transformation." Ryan assesses me with a clinically appraising gaze as I emerge from the bathroom. "The facial recognition algorithms will struggle with this."

"Glad I meet your specifications," I reply dryly.

A flash of something—amusement, perhaps—crosses his features before vanishing. "We move in five. Eat your breakfast." He nods toward a paper bag on the table containing a breakfast sandwich.

I take a bite, suddenly ravenous. "What's the plan?"

"We drive to Seattle. Continuously, with minimal stops.." He's packing our meager belongings as he speaks, movements efficient and economical. "Cerberus has resources there. People who can help figure out what you've stumbled into."

"And if I don't want to go to Seattle?"

His hands pause briefly. "Not negotiable."

"Nothing's negotiable with you, is it?" I challenge, wrapping the remainder of my sandwich for the road.

Ryan zips the duffel bag closed with more force than necessary. "Your safety isn't up for debate. Neither is mine. The protocols exist for a reason."

"So I'm just supposed to blindly follow your?"

"Yes." He straightens, fixing me with that arctic-blue stare.

One syllable, delivered with absolute certainty. As if compliance is the only possible option. As if my input is irrelevant to the equation.

The casual dismissal of my agency stings more than it should.

"That's not how this works," I inform him. "I don't blindly follow anyone. Especially men who think they know what's best for me."

"When it comes to staying alive against professional operators?" He steps closer, voice dropping dangerously. "That's exactly how this works, and I definitely know what's best for *you* and this situation."

We're standing toe-to-toe now, neither backing down. The electricity between us has nothing to do with attraction in this moment. It's pure clash of wills, two immovable objects refusing to yield.

"We leave in two minutes," he says finally, breaking the standoff. "Use the bathroom if you need to. It's going to be a long drive."

The rental car agency is twenty blocks from our hotel. We don't take a direct route.

Ryan leads us through back alleys, side streets, even briefly through a hotel lobby and out its service entrance. The path feels random to me, but I recognize the strategy—breaking any potential surveillance tail with unpredictable movements.

"Is all this necessary?" I ask as we cut through a department store, entering through housewares and exiting through men's suits.

"Yes." No elaboration. Just that infuriating certainty again.

The rental agency is a small, independent company. No

national chain logos or computerized systems. Just a middle-aged man with a ring of keys and a paper ledger.

I hang back, watching as Ryan transforms before my eyes. His posture changes, becoming more relaxed. A smile appears— easy, friendly, completely at odds with the rigid commander who's been ordering me around all morning. He even adopts a slight Southern drawl as he chats with the clerk.

Money changes hands—cash only, no credit cards that could be tracked. ID is presented—not his real one, I'm certain, though I can't see it from here. The entire transaction takes less than ten minutes.

"We're set," he says, returning to my side with keys to a nondescript gray sedan. "Let's move."

Outside, he conducts a thorough inspection of the vehicle— checking under the chassis, examining the wheel wells, and even popping the hood to inspect the engine.

"What exactly are you looking for?" I ask.

"Tracking devices. Explosives. Anything that shouldn't be there." His voice is matter-of-fact, as if checking for bombs is as routine as checking tire pressure.

The casualness with which he approaches potential death is more unsettling than the possibility itself.

Once satisfied, he opens the passenger door for me. I slide in, watching as he circles to the driver's side. It doesn't escape my notice that he adjusted the seat and mirrors before letting me in —establishing from the outset that he'll be the only one driving.

As we pull away from the curb, I realize something else. "My laptop, my phone, my ID—everything was in my car or apartment."

"All compromised," he says, checking the mirrors as we merge into traffic. "We'll get you new secure devices in Seattle. Until then, we stay unplugged."

"What about my editor? My colleagues? They'll be worried."

"Anyone you contact becomes a vector for those men to track you." His tone brooks no argument. "Going dark is the only option, and safest for them."

I lean back against the headrest, frustration building. My entire life—career, friends, home—has vanished overnight. And I'm at the mercy of a man who parcels out information like it's classified intelligence. Which, to be fair, it probably is.

The city gradually gives way to suburbs, then to open highway. Ryan maintains a precise five miles over the speed limit—fast enough to make good time, not fast enough to attract attention. Every few minutes, he checks the mirrors. Every thirty minutes, he changes lanes without signaling, watching for any cars that follow the movement.

Two hours pass in tense silence. The monotony of the highway, combined with the events of the past twenty-four hours, begins to weigh on me. My eyelids grow heavy.

"You can sleep," Ryan says, glancing over. "I'll wake you if anything changes."

"I'm fine."

"You're exhausted. And we have a long way to go. Rest while you can."

I want to argue on principle, but exhaustion wins. "Wake me in an hour. I can take over driving."

His hands tighten on the steering wheel. "You won't be driving."

This jolts me back to full alertness. "Excuse me?"

"I said, you won't be driving."

"I heard you. I'm questioning the logic." I straighten in my seat. "You can't possibly drive the entire time."

"I can, and I will."

"That's ridiculous." My voice rises despite my effort to remain calm. "I'm a perfectly capable driver. We should share the responsibility."

"It's not about capability." He keeps his eyes on the road. "It's about training."

"Training? It's driving, not disarming explosives."

A muscle in his jaw tightens. "When was the last time you practiced evasive maneuvers? Counter-surveillance driving techniques? Tactical vehicle handling?"

I open my mouth, then close it.

"That's what I thought." His voice holds no triumph, just confirmation of a fact he already knew.

"I've been driving since I was sixteen," I counter, refusing to yield the point.

"So have most people. Doesn't mean they're qualified to drive in a high-risk extraction scenario."

"High-risk extraction scenario?" I repeat, incredulous. "Listen to yourself. We're driving to Seattle, not escaping a war zone."

His eyes flick to me, cold and assessing. "Need I remind you, *again,* those men on the platform weren't amateurs. They were trained operators with tactical experience and resources. They've likely identified the hotel by now and are expanding their search grid. Every minute we're on the road is another minute they're not closing the gap."

The clinical precision of his assessment sends a chill through me. He's not exaggerating for effect or being dramatic. He genuinely believes we're being hunted by professionals with the means and determination to find us.

"So, what am I supposed to do? Sit here uselessly while you handle everything?"

"You're supposed to stop questioning me and do as I say so we both stay alive."

The command in his voice ignites something rebellious in me. "Do you get off on this? Telling women what to do? Being in control?"

His eyes darken, gaze cutting toward me for one dangerous second before flicking back to the road.

"We're not talking about what gets me off," he says, voice pitched low enough to make heat crawl over my skin. "But if we were …" A pause, deliberate, thick with promise. "I'd tell you I crave control. I demand obedience given without hesitation. And when it's not …" his mouth curves, slow and merciless, "I take my time making sure my punishment is felt—*thoroughly*."

The blatant confirmation ignites something low and molten inside me, heat flooding through my veins and pooling between my thighs. His voice etches vivid, indecent images across my mind—Ryan's commands delivered in that lethal tone, my body bending beneath the weight of his restraint, his hands locking mine to the mattress, his strength stripping me bare of choice until all I can do is yield.

My breath catches, betraying me. A flush scorches my cheeks, racing down my throat, and I hate the way my body responds—hungry, trembling, desperate—when I should be furious.

"That's not what I meant," I choke out, the words thin and ragged, as if oxygen itself has turned traitor.

"Wasn't it?" His voice stays dangerously soft, threaded with a knowing that steals the ground from under me. "You've been pushing since the moment we met. Testing boundaries. Looking for cracks. Almost like you want to see what happens when I snap."

His words slide under my skin like a touch, intimate and damning, leaving me raw with the terrifying truth: he's right.

# THIRTEEN

# Celeste

IMAGES LINGER, UNSHAKABLE—HIS VOICE LOW AND COMMANDING, the way he said punishing disobedience, thoroughly. The words replay like a brand seared into my skin. Heat coils low and relentlessly, spreading until my thighs clench on instinct. I can't stop picturing it: his weight holding me down, his mouth at my ear as he decides exactly how long I'll beg before he gives me relief.

The thought is reckless. Dangerous. And it terrifies me almost as much as it tempts me.

I drag in a breath, desperate to shove those images into the dark where they belong. I need distance. Deflection. Anything to stop imagining what he'd do if I actually pushed him too far.

"I don't blindly follow orders," I blurt, sharper than intended.

"Clearly." His lips curve, not quite a smile—more an acknowledgment, the kind a predator gives when prey shows unexpected teeth. "But this isn't about blindly following orders. It's about expertise. I wouldn't tell you how to structure an investigative piece or which questions to ask a source. Those are your areas of expertise."

"And controlling everything is yours?"

"Keeping people alive is. Extraction protocols. Security measures. Risk assessment." He glances at me again. "So yes, in this particular scenario, controlling everything is exactly my expertise."

The rational part of my brain acknowledges his point. The independent journalist in me still bristles at the restriction, the confinement, the complete surrender of autonomy.

"Fine," I concede, not graciously. "But I need some parameters here. How long do I sit quietly and comply? What's the end game?"

"Seattle. Cerberus headquarters. We get you there safely, then figure out what's on that flash drive and who wants you dead because of it." His gaze returns to the road. "After that, we develop a more permanent solution."

"Permanent solution? That sounds ominous."

"It means options. Witness protection. New identity. Off-grid relocation. Or, if the threat can be neutralized, eventual return to your normal life."

The casual way he outlines potential futures—none of which resemble the life I've built—leaves me momentarily speechless. He's talking about my existence as if it's a tactical problem to solve, a mission parameter to be adjusted.

"And I'm supposed to just—trust you with all this? A stranger who appeared out of nowhere and has been controlling every aspect of my life since?"

"Yes." No hesitation. No qualification. Just absolute confidence.

"Why?"

His eyes meet mine briefly. "Because you're still alive."

The simple statement carries more weight than it should. He could have walked away at any point—after the subway, after getting me to the hotel, this morning. Nothing obligated him to upend his life for mine. Yet here he is, driving me across the country, risking his life for a woman he met barely twenty-four hours ago.

I turn toward the window, watching the landscape blur. He's right, and I hate it. Trust doesn't come naturally to me—not in my profession, not with my history. Every instinct honed through years of investigative journalism screams to question, to doubt, to verify.

But sometimes survival means knowing when to yield.

"I need to use a bathroom soon," I say finally, changing the subject.

"There's a rest stop in about thirty miles. We'll stop there."

We lapse into silence again, but something has shifted. Not quite a truce, but perhaps an understanding. For now, at least, I'll follow his lead.

The hours on the road blend in a haze of highway miles and hypervigilance.

Ryan maintains a punishing pace, stopping only for absolute necessities. Bathroom breaks at busy rest areas, where crowds provide cover. Fast-food drive-thrus instead of restaurants. Gas stations selected for their blind spots and escape routes rather than convenience.

At each stop, the routine is the same. Ryan scans the surroundings before allowing me to exit the vehicle. He positions himself with clear sightlines to both me and potential approach vectors. When I use public restrooms, he waits outside, acting as both guardian and jailer combined.

We switch vehicles once—at a prearranged location where a Cerberus contact meets us with a different SUV, an older model that Ryan says is harder to track electronically. The efficiency of the exchange suggests a well-established protocol, making me wonder how often Ryan extracts people from dangerous situations.

The flash drive burns in my pocket, a constant reminder of

why we're running. Several times, I consider telling Ryan exactly what's on it, exactly what I know. But something holds me back. Not distrust, exactly. More like professional caution. The information is explosive—potentially worth killing for, as we've discovered. The fewer people who know the full picture, the safer they are.

At least that's what I tell myself.

After twelve hours on the road, taking circuitous routes that doubled what would normally be a six-hour drive, stopping only for the bare necessities, we finally pull into a motel parking lot just outside Cleveland, Ohio. The place is dated but clean, the kind of roadside establishment that asks few questions of guests paying in cash.

"Wait here," Ryan says, cutting the engine.

I don't argue. Exhaustion drags at every muscle, too heavy for a fight. He gives orders; I've learned when to obey.

Five minutes later, he's back with a key—an actual metal key, not a card. "Room 17. Last one on the end. Good sight lines, two exit points."

We enter together. He does his ritual sweep—closets, bathroom, under the bed, window locks. I sag against the doorframe, too wrung out to tease him for his thoroughness. Only when he declares the room clear do I notice the inevitable problem: one bed.

"Seriously?" I gesture at the queen-sized mattress. "How do you keep managing to get us rooms with only one bed?"

"Low profile. Couples attract less attention than solo travelers or business associates." He drops our bag on the dresser like the argument's settled. "You take the bed. I'll sleep on the floor."

"This is ridiculous." Fatigue sharpens my words. "You've been driving for twelve hours straight. You need real rest. The bed is big enough for both of us."

"Not a good idea." He's already spreading the spare blankets on the carpet, movements clipped, controlled.

"Is it propriety you're worried about? Or don't you trust yourself?" The taunt escapes before I can cage it, echoing his words from that first night.

He stills. When his gaze lifts, danger burns there, hot enough to pin me.

"Both," he admits, voice low, threaded with something dark. "And more importantly, I don't trust you."

"Me?" My pulse kicks. "What am I going to do?"

"Push. Test. Challenge." He rises to his full height, filling the room, filling my lungs until breathing feels like drowning. "You've been doing it since the moment we met. Hunting for cracks in my control."

"I'm just suggesting we share a bed like rational adults."

"Are we?" He steps closer, slow, deliberate. "Rational? With whatever this is between us?"

The blunt acknowledgment strips the air between us bare. We've been pretending—masking this pull with barbs, irritation, arguments. But it thrums, undeniable.

"There's nothing between us," I lie, my voice too quick, too thin.

His laugh is soft, disbelieving, erotic in its certainty. "Then you won't mind if I do this."

He moves toward me, each step measured, lethal. Giving me every chance to retreat. I don't. Can't. My feet are glued to the carpet as his body closes the space, until I have to tilt my head back to hold his gaze.

"Your pupils are dilated," he murmurs, gaze raking over me. "Your breathing's changed." He leans in, two fingers brushing my throat. The contact is a brand, light but scorching. "Your pulse—elevated." His eyes darken, merciless. "Nothing between us? The evidence says otherwise."

His touch lingers, pressing lightly, a tease that feels more like possession. The air thickens, weighted with the heat of everything unsaid. My body betrays me—breath short, heart pounding, a coil of hunger tightening low and hot.

"Fine," I whisper, the word trembling out of me. "There's—something. But that doesn't mean we can't control ourselves for one night."

His fingers linger at my throat a beat too long, the faint press against my pulse a reminder of how fast it's racing—how fast he's making it race. The room seems to shrink around us, air thick, unbreathable. I should move. I should shove him back. Instead, I lean into the heat, into him, like my body's already chosen a side.

His gaze drops to my mouth. Just for a fraction of a second, but enough to send a jolt straight through me. My lips part on instinct, hungry for something I have no business wanting. The distance between us crackles, a live wire stretched to snapping.

"I've been controlling myself since the moment I saw you on that platform," he says, voice pitched low, dangerous, velvet laced with steel. The sound ripples through me, settling in places I can't ignore. "And it gets harder every time you push."

The double entendre slices straight through the tension, leaving me breathless. He's been fighting this—fighting me—as much as I've been fighting him.

"Why?" The question slips free before I can stop it, reckless, needy.

His eyes sharpen, piercing, as if he can strip me bare with nothing but a look. "You know why."

Something inside me breaks—defenses, logic, common sense. Maybe it's exhaustion. Maybe it's the chaos of the last thirty-six hours. Maybe it's just him. Whatever the reason, I don't back down. "Tell me anyway."

A muscle in his jaw ticks. For a long, suspended moment, I think he'll retreat—pull himself back behind that wall of rigid control. Then something in his expression shatters, and what comes through is raw, unfiltered want.

"Because every time you challenge me, every time you defy a direct order," his voice roughens, dark with restraint barely holding, "it makes me want to grab you, bend you over the nearest surface, and punish your disobedience until you're begging. Then fuck you into complete submission until the only word you remember is my name."

The confession slams into me, brutal and intoxicating. Heat surges through my veins, flooding me until my knees nearly buckle. I should be outraged. I should recoil. Instead, the vividness of his words plays out behind my eyes in humiliating clarity—his body crushing mine, his voice commanding me into surrender I've never dared imagine.

My breath catches, ragged. My pulse pounds so loud I swear he can hear it.

"That's why this—" he gestures between us, every line of him tense, vibrating with control, "is such a catastrophically bad idea."

I can't form words, can't break his gaze. My heart pounds so loudly I'm certain he can hear it. The room feels too small, too hot, too charged with an electricity that threatens to consume us both.

"Then stop fighting it," I whisper, the words trembling out before I can even decide what I'm asking for.

FOURTEEN

## Celeste

For one searing, suspended breath, I think Ryan might give in. Might finally crush the distance between us, pin me against the wall, and show me exactly what it means when he says punishment. The air between us vibrates with it, every heartbeat a countdown.

But then—he steps back. Breaks the spell.

"We can't afford distractions. Not until you're secure."

The rational part of me knows he's right. The rest of me— the part that's been drowning in his presence for two days— wants to scream. His control is infuriating, unbearable, and worse, it makes me want him more.

"Fine," I bite out, sharp with resignation. "Take the floor. Martyr yourself on the altar of professionalism."

A flicker of amusement sparks in his eyes, like he knows exactly what I'm doing. "My comfort isn't my priority, Celeste. Your safety is."

"And sharing a bed compromises my safety, how exactly?" The deliberate flippancy drips from my tone, a taunt I know will get under his skin. I want it to. God help me, I want to see him snap.

And then he does.

Something detonates in his expression. In two strides, he's on me—towering, radiating fury and want in equal measure.

"For all that is holy, stop fucking pushing me, Celeste." The words tear from him, raw, guttural, a growl that vibrates through the space between us. His fists clench at his sides, like it's taking every ounce of discipline not to put them on me. "Sleeping with you compromises my focus—whether it's just lying beside you or fucking you senseless. Either way, it compromises what I'm trying to do here—keep us both alive."

The crude language from his disciplined mouth sends a shockwave through me. My stomach twists, my thighs clench, my skin burns. The way he spits out "fucking you senseless" isn't an idle threat. It's an admission, thick with frustration and need.

I shouldn't revel in it. But I do.

"Sorry," I murmur, breathless, a lie we both hear for what it is. I'm not sorry. Not even close. There's a dangerous, addictive thrill in unraveling him, in making this iron-willed man fracture for even a second.

His eyes narrow, sharp and knowing. "No, you're not. That's the problem." His chest rises and falls once, twice, as though he's dragging himself back from the edge by sheer will. "Even now, you're still pushing me."

And then it happens. The shift. His features harden, his body straightens, and suddenly the man is gone, replaced by the commander—unyielding, immovable, carved from steel.

"Not another word." His tone drops, lethal in its finality. That voice, low and commanding, doesn't allow argument, doesn't leave room for games. "Get in bed. Go to sleep. Stop. Pushing."

The words slam into me harder than a touch would. My body thrums with the ache of everything unsaid, with the need he refuses to indulge, with the tension coiling tighter every time I breathe the same air as him. I climb into the bed, pulse racing, skin hot, need unrelieved, and lie in the dark, wide awake—every nerve screaming, every part of me burning for the man stretched out on the floor, fighting his own battle with control.

Even as part of me bristles at being commanded, another part—a darker part I've never dared acknowledge—thrums at the pure authority in his voice.

I retreat to the bathroom, needing space, needing air, needing somewhere I can wrestle my composure back under control before I do something insane. Like beg him to give up every ounce of restraint he's clinging to.

When I emerge, Ryan has already built his nest of blankets on the floor. His shirt is gone, tossed aside, and in the dim light, the map of scars across his torso looks brutal, carved. Every mark is a reminder of violence endured, of a man tempered in fire. A man who survives by force of will alone.

I can't stop staring.

He catches me, eyes meeting mine, the weight of his gaze pinning me in place.

"Bathroom's all yours," I manage, throat dry, crossing to the bed before I betray myself further.

He nods once, silent, then moves past me. The scent of him —sweat, steel, and something deeply male—slams into me. My fingers twitch with the reckless urge to reach out, to touch, to see if his skin feels as hot as it looks.

The bathroom door closes. The shower starts.

I lie rigid in the bed, staring at the ceiling, every nerve thrumming with the awareness of him just feet away. Water pounds against tile, each splash a vivid reminder of what he's doing in there—what he could be doing.

My imagination betrays me, tumbling down a path I shouldn't even be traveling. Ryan under the spray, muscles shifting beneath scarred skin, head bowed, water sluicing over every hard line of him. My pulse kicks higher, breath shallow, when the fantasy sharpens—one hand braced against the wall, the other stroking himself in ruthless rhythm, jaw clenched to keep silent.

The thought slams into me, molten and reckless. Heat surges between my thighs, shameful and unstoppable. I can't stay in bed. I can't stay still. Before I've thought it through, I'm sliding out from under the sheets, bare feet whispering across carpet, inching toward the bathroom door.

My mind wanders to dangerous territory. Is he doing what he did last night? Taking himself in hand, finding release to ease the tension I've deliberately stoked?

I can almost see it—water cascading down his powerful back, one hand braced against tile, the other working in rhythmic strokes as he fights to keep silent. Is he thinking of me while he does it? Imagining what would happen if his rigid control finally shattered?

The thought sends liquid heat pooling between my thighs. I shift restlessly, my body betraying me with its response.

What would it be like if he finally broke? Would it mirror that first night when I tried to leave the hotel room—his body pinning mine against the wall, his breath hot against my ear?

Only this time, he wouldn't stop. He'd let his hands wander where they wanted. He'd use that commanding voice to make me obey in ways that have nothing to do with security protocols.

I hover there, heart jackhammering, straining for any sound beyond the rush of water. Listening. Hoping.

And then I hear it. A groan—low, rough, dragged from his chest before he muffles it against the tile. My breath catches, heat flooding low and sharp. The next sound strips me bare: the wet, steady rhythm of his fist pumping his cock, the slap of skin on skin unmistakable even under the cascade of water.

My knees go weak. Each stroke plays out in my head in agonizing clarity—his hand tight, relentless, working himself fast and hard, water pouring over the breadth of his shoulders as he braces against the wall.

His breathing grows ragged, desperate. Every guttural sound punches straight through me, leaving me trembling, thighs pressing together uselessly. I should turn away, should stop listening, but I can't. I'm captive to the raw, unguarded need in his voice.

The rhythm quickens, sharper, harder. A choked growl tears out of him, followed by a strangled gasp—my name, broken on his tongue as he comes.

I clap a hand over my mouth, dizzy from the rush of arousal slamming into me. My body is on fire, molten and aching, the sound of my name on his lips seared into me.

This is madness. This man is a stranger. Someone who chose to save my life and has now made it his personal mission to keep me safe, not fulfill the sudden, overwhelming fantasies I'm having. Fantasies I've never acknowledged before, never allowed myself to explore.

Tomorrow we'll be back on the road, back to the tense silence and circular arguments. But right now, in the darkness of this anonymous motel room, I allow myself to acknowledge the truth: whatever is happening between us isn't just attraction. It's not just proximity, adrenaline, or the unique circumstances that have brought us together.

It's something I don't have a name for yet. Something that scares me more than the men hunting us.

Because Ryan Ellis is right about one thing: I can't seem to stop pushing his boundaries. And I'm terrified of what might happen when they finally break.

The shower cuts off.

Panic jolts me into motion. I stumble back across the room,

diving under the covers just as the bathroom handle turns. My chest heaves, lungs burning, my body still trembling with the echo of his groans, the image of his hand, the way he came—saying my name.

The door swings open. Steam spills into the room, curling into the lamplight. Ryan steps out, towel slung low on his hips, droplets tracking over scarred muscle, down the hard lines of his abdomen. His gaze finds me instantly. I freeze, every inch of me screaming to play dead.

It doesn't matter. He already knows.

"Next time you want to listen in," his voice rolls out low, rich with dark amusement, "cover the gap under the door. Unless you want me to know you're there."

My stomach drops. Heat sears my face. He takes a step closer, lazy, predatory, water still dripping from his hair.

"I hope you heard," he continues, unashamed, savoring every word. "Every stroke. Every sound. And I especially hope you heard me say your name when I came."

The words hit like a physical touch, molten, humiliating, and electrifying all at once. I can't stop the way my thighs clench under the covers, can't hide the flush burning down my throat.

His eyes catch the movement, sharpen, and gleam with cruel delight. "You're playing a very dangerous game, Celeste. Pushing me. Listening. Getting yourself all hot and restless while I …" His smirk deepens, wicked, merciless.

The taunt lands like a strike, leaving me squirming under the sheets, my body betraying me with every shallow breath.

He doesn't soften. Doesn't pull back. He lets the silence drag, heavy and charged, until my pulse is a drumbeat in my ears. Then he drops the blade, voice a low growl that coils heat straight through me:

"That's your punishment, sweetheart. Lying there wet and

wanting, too keyed up to sleep. Knowing I had my release while you ache for yours."

My breath catches, sharp, shamed, and aroused all at once. He wants me this undone.

"Push me again," Ryan finishes, voice hard enough to bruise, "and I won't let you listen. I'll make you watch, and I'll make damn sure you feel every second of it."

FIFTEEN

# Ryan

I wake one minute before my alarm; a habit forged through three combat tours and countless missions. Four thirty-two in the morning, still dark outside. Another night of sleep on another motel floor.

Every muscle in my body protests as I silently uncurl from the rigid position I've maintained for the past four hours. Sleeping on hard surfaces isn't new—I've done it in deserts, jungles, and mountain passes—but those deployments didn't include the additional tension currently making my entire body feel like an overworked steel cable.

My gaze shifts automatically to the bed where Celeste sleeps. The soft pre-dawn light filtering through cheap curtains casts her in shadow and silver. She sleeps curled on her side, one hand tucked beneath her cheek. Her newly auburn hair spills across the pillow, shorter layers framing her face in a way that softens its habitual defiance.

She looks vulnerable in sleep. Younger. The sharp edges of that brilliant, stubborn mind temporarily at rest.

The sight does nothing to ease the persistent ache that's been my constant companion since the subway platform.

I turn away, dropping silently into push-ups. One. Two. Three. Physical discomfort is a useful distraction from other, more problematic sensations.

Twenty. Twenty-one. Twenty-two.

My body moves through the familiar exercise, muscle memory taking over where conscious thought fails.

This is becoming unsustainable. The lack of proper rest I can handle—I've operated on minimal sleep for weeks during particularly grueling missions. The constant tactical alertness is baseline for any operation. But the perpetual state of arousal triggered by Celeste's proximity, her scent, her defiance—that's an unfamiliar enemy I'm increasingly ill-equipped to fight.

Fifty. Fifty-one. Fifty-two.

Several more days to Seattle. Days of maintaining professional distance while every instinct urges me to close it. Days of her challenging my authority, pushing my boundaries, triggering responses that have no place in an extraction.

One hundred.

I rise soundlessly and head for the shower. Cold water. Another temporary solution to a persistent problem.

By the time I emerge, she's curled under the blankets, eyes shut tight, feigning sleep. I don't call her out on it. The room is thick with unspoken things, and silence is the only truce we have left since last night.

"Bathroom's yours," I mumble, shrugging on a shirt.

She heads inside and soon we're back on the road—the hum of the engine filling the silence, the blur of mile markers marching by, and the weight of everything we're not saying pressing down between us.

Her fingers tap nervously against her thigh, a rhythm that

matches the thrum of the tires on asphalt, until she finally breaks the quiet.

"You're sure we're not being followed?" she finally breaks the quiet.

Celeste asks this as we cross the Illinois border, the SUV's engine humming steadily beneath us. We've been on the road for hours, taking back roads that double the normal distance, and this is the fifth variation of the same question she's asked since we left at dawn.

"If we were being followed, I'd know." I check the mirrors again—a habitual scan rather than a response to her question. "We implemented alternate routes and maintained irregular patterns. The first rule of successful evasion is breaking expected patterns."

"And you're sure that works?" She's watching me with those analytical eyes that miss nothing.

"No one's ever sure in this business. But I like our odds."

I don't tell her that getting her out of D.C. was the tactical key. Those men expect her to lie low within the city, to hide rather than run. Most civilians do—they retreat to familiar territory when threatened, a human instinct that makes them predictable. I've gained a significant advantage by extracting her across state lines.

"You keep checking the mirrors." She's observing me again, cataloging my behaviors.

"Force of habit." I adjust the temperature control. The SUV's air conditioning struggles against the summer heat. "Constant awareness keeps people alive."

"Sounds exhausting."

"It becomes second nature." A half-truth.

The hypervigilance is exhausting, but it's a familiar exhaustion. The kind I can manage through tactical napping and carefully portioned caffeine. Nothing like the unfamiliar drain of constantly fighting my body's response to her.

"Get some rest," I tell her, nodding toward the reclined passenger seat. "We've got a long day ahead."

To my surprise, she doesn't argue. Just settles against the headrest, eyes drifting closed. I envy the ease with which she transitions from alertness to rest. Perhaps a journalist's skill is grabbing sleep between deadlines and danger.

Her breathing slows, deepens. I keep my eyes on the road, ignoring the urge to glance at her relaxed form. Ignoring how the sun catches in her hair, turning the auburn to fire.

I implement a micro-nap at a gas station outside Des Moines. We've covered nearly seven hundred miles of zigzagging since the Illinois border. Ninety seconds of controlled unconsciousness—a technique perfected during long surveillance operations. Eyes closed, head back, mind allowed to slip precisely seven layers down from full alertness. Ninety seconds to reset the system and clear the cognitive debris.

It helps, marginally. But not with the real problem.

The real problem walks out of the gas station holding two cups of coffee, her stride still carrying the hint of a limp from her injured knee. The real problem settles back into the passenger seat with a sigh that sends a ripple of awareness down my spine. The real problem keeps watching me with eyes that alternate between suspicion and something far more dangerous.

"Your turn to rest," she says, offering me one of the coffees. "I can keep watch."

I accept the cup but ignore the suggestion. "I don't need it."

"You've been driving for over six hours. Everyone needs rest."

"Not me." I pull back onto the highway, merging smoothly into sparse midday traffic. "Not now."

"Let me guess—special forces training? Some classified technique for transcending human limitations?" There's an edge in her voice, the journalist probing for weaknesses in my armor.

"Something like that."

"That's not an answer."

"It's the only one you're getting." I keep my tone even and professional. Detached.

She shifts in her seat, angling toward me. "Do you ever answer questions directly? Or is cryptic evasion part of your superhero persona?"

The deliberate provocation grates against my already raw nerves. She's doing it again—pushing, testing, looking for cracks. What she doesn't understand is that finding them would endanger us both.

"I answer questions when they're relevant to your safety."

"And the rest of the time?"

"The rest of the time, I focus on keeping you alive." I meet her gaze briefly, letting her see the steel behind the words. "Which would be easier if you'd stop deliberately attempting to distract me."

Something flashes in her eyes—a mixture of defiance and something that looks too much like satisfaction. As if getting a rise out of me is exactly what she wanted.

Christ, she's maddening.

And God help me, it only makes me want her more.

The next night is worse than the first.

Another roadside motel, this time in Rapid City, another security sweep, another single king bed that I relinquish without comment. My body moves through the familiar routines while my mind catalogs the increasing difficulties of our situation.

Too many hours on the road have left my eyes gritty with fatigue and my neck stiff from maintaining tactical awareness. The floor of the previous motel did my back no favors.

And Celeste …

Celeste continues to be the most immediate threat to my control.

SIXTEEN

# Ryan

SHE EMERGES FROM THE BATHROOM IN THE LOOSE T-SHIRT AND shorts I purchased days ago. Her hair is damp from the shower, her skin flushed from the heat. The bruise at her temple has faded to a yellowish shadow. She smells of that citrus shampoo that's becoming a persistent trigger for my increasingly problematic responses.

"Your turn," she says, gesturing toward the bathroom.

I nod, keeping my expression neutral despite my body being anything but. The bathroom holds the humid evidence of her presence, the mirror fogged, the air heavy with her scent.

Cold shower. Again. A temporary measure that's becoming less effective with each passing day.

Under the spray, I close my eyes and count backward from one thousand in prime numbers. A mental exercise designed to redirect blood flow from the more insistent parts of my anatomy to my brain. It's only partially successful, and then fails completely, when my mind betrays me with an image of Celeste on her knees, looking up with those defiant eyes, waiting for my command.

"Fuck." The curse escapes through gritted teeth as I brace one forearm against the tiled wall.

This has become a nightly ritual. Another form of insufficient release. My hand wraps around my shaft, movements mechanical and efficient. Just physical maintenance. Just taking the edge off. Nothing like what I really want.

The release, when it comes, is hollow—a momentary emptying of tension that does nothing to slake the thirst growing stronger with each passing day. The kind of thirst that won't be satisfied by my hand, cold showers, or mental discipline. The kind that demands surrender—hers and mine.

I rinse away the evidence, disgusted with my lack of control. With my weakness. Years of operational discipline are unraveling over a woman I met a few days ago.

Back in the main room, Celeste is perched cross-legged on the bed, the news playing softly on the ancient television set.

I reach for my weapon. The habitual disassembly and cleaning helps center me.

Her eyes track my movements as I clean the Glock. "How long have you been doing this?"

"Cleaning weapons? Since I was twelve. My father was military."

"No, I mean … This. Extracting people. Security work."

My hands don't pause in their routine. Field strip. Clean barrel. Check ejector. Reassemble. "Cerberus has been operational for seven years. I've been with them for five."

"And before that?"

"Classified."

She makes a sound of frustration. "Is everything about you classified?"

"The relevant parts." I reassemble the slide, and the familiar click is a comforting sound in the quiet room. "The parts that keep people like you alive."

"People like me," she repeats, something in her tone making me look up. "And what exactly am I to you? An assignment? A complication? An inconvenience?"

The question catches me off guard. My hands go still on the weapon.

"You're a civilian in danger," I say finally. "My job is to get you safely to Seattle."

"Your job," she echoes. "Except this isn't your job, is it? You weren't assigned to protect me. You chose to help me on that platform. You chose to call your team. You chose to drive me across the country instead of putting me on a plane or handing me off to local authorities."

Each statement lands like a precisely aimed bullet, finding the vulnerable spots in my professional armor.

"What's your point?"

"My point is that this is personal for you. And I want to know why."

I reassemble the weapon with more force than necessary, the sound sharp in the quiet room. "My reasons are irrelevant to your safety."

"Bullshit." She leans forward, eyes intent. "You've upended your life for me. Missed whatever mission you were headed back to Seattle for. Put yourself at risk. I think I deserve to know why."

*Because I couldn't walk away, something about you arrested my attention from the first moment I saw you on that platform. Because watching you die wasn't an option I could accept.*

None of these are answers I can give her.

"Get some sleep," I say instead, turning off the lamp nearest me. "We move at dawn."

In the semi-darkness, her soft sigh of frustration fills the room. The sheets rustle as she settles into bed. The quiet that follows feels charged, heavy with unspoken words.

I close my eyes and implement another technique from my

training days—sectioning off the mind into compartments. Placing problematic thoughts into secure containment. Focusing on the mission rather than the increasingly complicated emotions surrounding them.

It helps. Until it doesn't.

Until her breathing deepens in sleep, and I listen to its rhythm. Until the memory of her scent overrides the mental barriers I've constructed. Until I'm back where I started— painfully aware of her presence just feet away, of the bed we could be sharing, of all the ways I want to touch her.

I exhale slowly. I've endured worse.

Though at the moment, I'm hard-pressed to remember when.

"What's on the flash drive?" I suddenly ask, allowing my curiosity to finally get the better of me.

Celeste's head snaps toward me, her expression instantly guarded. "What?"

"The flash drive you keep checking in your pocket. The one those men were willing to kill for. What's on it?"

She stares out the window, shoulders tense. "It's complicated."

"I excel at complicated." I keep my eyes on the road, voice deliberately casual. "Try me."

"It's sensitive information. The kind people die for."

"I noticed." My tone remains even despite the surge of irritation. "Given that I'm one of the people who might die for it, I'd appreciate knowing what 'it' is."

"It's better if you don't know."

"For whom?" I can't keep the edge from my voice now. "For you? For your story? Because from where I'm sitting, information asymmetry only benefits the people hunting us."

"It's not that simple."

"It is." I pull the SUV onto the shoulder, killing the engine.

The sudden silence amplifies the tension between us. "They're after both of us now. I deserve to know what I'm risking my life for."

She studies me for a long moment, something calculating in her gaze. "You've been helping me without knowing."

"And now I'm asking."

Her fingers drum against her thigh, a nervous gesture I haven't seen before. "What do you know about artificial intelligence in military applications?"

The question sends a ripple of unease down my spine. "Enough to be concerned."

"Project Phoenix is—was—a classified DoD initiative to develop an AI-driven targeting system for drone strikes. Autonomous target acquisition and elimination without human oversight." Her voice takes on the detached precision of a professional relaying facts. "It was supposedly scrapped five years ago due to ethical concerns and technical limitations."

"But it wasn't." I can see where this is going. Similar black projects have disappeared from official records only to resurface under private contractors.

"It was privatized."

Bingo. Called that one.

"Transferred to Northridge Defense Solutions with a different name but the same objectives." She meets my gaze directly now. "And it works."

The implications settle like lead in my gut. An autonomous AI targeting system in private hands. No oversight. No accountability.

"How do you know?"

"I've been investigating a series of deaths—analysts, whistleblowers, and other journalists. All were ruled accidents or suicides. All with connections to either the original Project Phoenix or Northridge." She swallows hard. "One of my sources was Jared

Caldwell, a former data analyst at Northridge. He contacted me three months ago with concerns about what he was seeing."

"And now he's dead."

She nods, eyes haunted. "Throat cut in a hotel room. Made to look like suicide, but it wasn't. He left me this." She taps her pocket where the flash drive rests. "Evidence that Phoenix is not only operational, but that they've implemented something called Obsidian."

"Obsidian?" The name hits me like a physical blow. I've heard it before—recently.

Willow. Marshal's case. Her ex-husband's files.

"What is it?" Celeste asks, noticing my reaction.

I weigh operational security against the clear relevance. "We had a case. Our team leader—Ghost—rescued a woman named Willow Reynolds who was running from her abusive ex-husband. He was a federal judge. He was involved in many things; classified weapons development was one of them. She spent three years secretly downloading files from his system as evidence."

"And?"

"Among the files she collected, several were randomly tagged with a single word: 'Obsidian.'" I tap my fingers against the steering wheel, connecting dots. "Her ex-husband is dead now, but he worked for a military contractor with government ties."

"Northridge?" Her voice sharpens with recognition.

"No. Different company, but in the same ecosystem. Shared projects, personnel overlap." I process the implications rapidly. "This can't be a coincidence."

"Which means this is bigger than I thought." Celeste's face pales slightly. "If multiple contractors are involved—"

"Then Phoenix has broader implementation than one company's initiative." I complete her thought. "And Obsidian's reach extends further than individual whistleblowers."

"A system-wide cleanup protocol," she whispers. "Anyone who gets too close, regardless of which component they discover …"

"Becomes a target." The tactical implications shift again. If this connects to Willow's case, we already have pieces of this puzzle. Cerberus may be further along in understanding the threat than I realized.

"A kill order for anyone investigating Phoenix. Automated identification of potential threats through surveillance integration. Predictive modeling of whistleblower profiles." Her voice remains steady despite the horror of what she's describing. "The system, Obsidian, tagged Jared, and I'm pretty sure it tagged me too."

The pieces click into place: the professional hit team, their tactical coordination, and the resources deployed to eliminate one journalist. The connection to Willow's case makes this infinitely more complex and dangerous.

"You're saying an AI system identified you as a threat and dispatched operators to eliminate you?"

"Yes. But it's worse than that." Her eyes hold mine, unflinching. "The system doesn't just identify threats. It integrates with public and private surveillance, tracks movements, and predicts behavior patterns. It's designed to be inescapable."

"Nothing is inescapable." The response is automatic, born from years of evading seemingly impossible situations.

"This might be. According to Jared's data, Phoenix has backdoor access to traffic cameras, CCTV, facial recognition databases, and even private security systems. It's constantly analyzing, learning, adapting."

I process this information against the backdrop of our extraction measures. Vehicle switches. Cash only. Disguise modifications. No digital footprint. The connection to Willow's files suggests a web of contractors and agencies far more extensive than Celeste initially realized.

"That explains the professional team in the subway. But not why they haven't found us yet."

"I've been thinking about that." She leans forward, animated now that she's sharing the information. "What if the system is optimized for urban environments? Dense surveillance networks, high concentration of cameras, and civilian facial recognition. We've been traveling through rural areas, staying in places with minimal digital security."

It's a solid theory. Systems are only as effective as their data sources. "Then we maintain that advantage. Keep to analog operations. Minimize digital exposure."

I restart the SUV, my mind racing through tactical adjustments based on this new information. An AI targeting system changes the parameters of our extraction, making certain precautions more critical and others less so. The connection to Willow means Ghost might already have pieces of this puzzle—information that could be vital to our survival.

"You believe me." She sounds surprised.

"Should I not?"

"Most people would think I'm paranoid. That I've been working on conspiracy theories too long."

I ease the vehicle back onto the highway. "I've seen enough black projects to know the line between conspiracy and classified is thinner than civilians realize."

We drive in silence for several miles, each processing the implications of our conversation. Eventually, she speaks again, her voice quieter.

"After Jared contacted me, I began investigating. Found connections between his concerns and similar projects that had been publicly canceled but privately continued. I started tracking the deaths—Quentin Hargrove's heart attack at forty-two, with no prior health issues. Zara Nouri's single-car accident on a straight, dry road. Lachlan Reeves's suicide despite planning his wedding."

Her voice catches slightly. These weren't just names on a list to her. These were real people whose deaths she's carried.

"I was careful. Used burner phones. Secured communications. But they still found Jared." She stares out the window, profile rigid with contained emotion. "I was supposed to meet him at Murphy's Pub, but he texted from a number I didn't recognize. Directed me to the Windsor Hotel instead. When I got there …"

"He was already dead." I fill in what she can't bring herself to say.

She nods, swallowing hard. "Throat cut. Blood everywhere. But the flash drive …" She exhales slowly. "Jared was smart. He texted me earlier with our code phrase—'walls have ears.' That meant something was wrong. I was supposed to check the alternate hiding spots."

"What did he choose?"

She turns to look at me, eyes flat with exhaustion. "The TV remote."

I blink. "Come again?"

"He taped the drive to the underside of the battery cover. Swapped out one of the batteries with a dummy so it wouldn't rattle. If you didn't remove the batteries completely, you'd never see it."

I let out a low whistle. "Clever. Most people don't look twice at a remote, especially if it still turns the TV on."

"Exactly. They tore the place apart—ripped the mattress, cracked the mirror, even opened the ceiling tiles. But they didn't touch the remote."

"Because it looked untouched," I murmur, impressed.

She nods once. "That's what saved it."

"Or they were interrupted," I suggest. "Housekeeping, another guest, time constraints."

"Maybe. I took it and ran. That's when I noticed the SUV following me. They rammed me off the road. I fled into the subway station. You know the rest."

The clinical detachment in her voice doesn't mask the trauma beneath. I've heard that tone before—in soldiers after combat, in civilians after attacks. The forced neutrality of someone compartmentalizing horror.

"What's on the drive specifically?" I ask, redirecting to actionable intelligence.

"Evidence. Internal communications about Phoenix and Obsidian. Technical specifications. Deployment records. Financial documents showing who's funding it. Names of officials who authorized the transition from public to private sector."

Names. That explains the resources deployed against her. Names mean accountability. Names mean people with power who don't want to be exposed.

"This is bigger than an article, Celeste."

"I know." For the first time since I've met her, she looks uncertain. "That's why I've been careful about who I tell. The more people who know, the more targets for Obsidian."

The implication is clear—by involving me, she's potentially painted a target on my back as well. But I've been operating with that assumption since the subway platform. The moment I engaged those men, I became part of their cleanup problem.

"Cerberus has resources that can help," I tell her. "Secure facilities. Intelligence analysts. Legal teams. People who know how to manage this kind of exposure. And if there's a connection to Willow's husband, and what he was doing …"

"Can they be trusted?"

"With this? Yes." I check the mirrors, a habitual scan. "Ghost —Mason, our team leader—has specific experience with privatized military projects. He'll know how to approach this. And if Obsidian is as widespread as I'm beginning to suspect, then we're going to need all of Cerberus's assets, and maybe more."

She falls silent again, likely weighing options, calculating risks. The journalist's analytical mind at work.

"Seattle is not too far," I remind her. "We can discuss options in more detail tonight."

Her hand moves unconsciously to her pocket, fingers brushing over the outline of the flash drive. Such a small object to contain so much danger. So many deaths.

I force my attention back to the road, to our immediate tactical situation. But my mind keeps circling back to the implications of what she's shared. An autonomous AI targeting system with surveillance integration and no oversight. The potential for abuse is staggering.

More concerning is the thought that we may have only temporarily evaded its reach. If this system is as sophisticated as Celeste suggests, our analog approach has bought us time, but not permanent security.

We need to reach Seattle. Need Cerberus resources. Need a team with the expertise to handle this level of threat.

My hand tightens on the steering wheel, knuckles whitening. We stop for the night at another roadside motel just outside Billings, Montana. The mountains loom in the distance, silhouetted against the setting sun. Celeste has been moving with increasing discomfort throughout the day, her injured side clearly bothering her.

"Let me see your ribs."

She eyes me warily from her perch on the edge of the bed. "They're fine."

"They're not fine. You've been favoring your left side all day." I retrieve the first aid kit from our bag. "I need to check for complications."

"I think I'd know if there were complications."

"Not necessarily. Internal bleeding can present gradually. Hairline fractures can worsen without obvious symptoms." I open the kit, laying out supplies with methodical precision. "This isn't negotiable."

Something in my tone must convey the futility of argument, because she sighs and carefully lifts the hem of her shirt, exposing her ribcage on the left side.

The bruising has progressed through its expected evolution—the angry purple now fading to greenish-yellow at the edges. I kneel beside the bed, hands gently probing the area, feeling for irregularities, and assessing the extent of the damage.

"Deep breath in," I instruct, monitoring the expansion of her lungs, the movement of her ribs beneath my fingertips. "And out. Again."

Her breathing hitches slightly as I find a particularly tender spot. "Sorry," I murmur, easing the pressure.

"It's fine." Her voice is tight, controlled.

But it's not fine. Nothing about this situation is fine. Especially not the way my body responds to her proximity, the feel of her skin beneath my hands, or her subtle scent that fills my senses despite the clinical nature of my examination.

"Two, possibly three bruised ribs," I diagnose, focusing on the medical assessment rather than the inappropriate reactions it's triggering. "No displacement. No sign of internal bleeding. But they need proper binding for support."

I reach for the elastic bandage in the kit, unrolling a length. "Arms up, please."

She complies, lifting her arms with a wince. I work efficiently, wrapping the bandage around her torso with firm, even pressure. Close enough to feel the warmth radiating from her skin. Close enough to notice the quickening of her pulse at her throat. Close enough that it takes every ounce of my control to maintain professional detachment.

"Better?" I ask when I've secured the bandage.

She takes an experimental breath, deeper than before. "Yes. Thank you."

Our eyes meet, and something passes between us—acknowledgment of the tension building since Cleveland. Since the subway. Since I first saw her on that platform and made the choice that led us here.

I should move away. Should maintain the distance that's kept us both safe from complications. Instead, I'm frozen in place, kneeling before her, close enough to touch. Close enough to give in to the impulses I've been fighting for days.

Her tongue darts out to wet her lips—a nervous gesture that sends a jolt of heat straight through me.

"Ryan ..." Her voice is barely above a whisper.

The sound of my name on her lips breaks something loose inside me. My hand moves of its own accord, fingers brushing a strand of hair from her face. Her skin is warm beneath my touch, soft in a way that makes the calluses on my fingertips feel suddenly rough, inadequate.

She doesn't pull away. Doesn't break the contact. Instead, she leans into it, almost imperceptibly, her eyes darkening.

One of us needs to be rational. One of us needs to remember professional boundaries and tactical priorities. I withdraw my hand, stand, and put the necessary distance between us.

"Get some rest," I say, voice rougher than intended. "We have a long drive tomorrow."

Disappointment flashes across her features before she masks it with a nod. "Right. Of course."

I retreat to the bathroom, closing the door firmly behind me. Lean against it, eyes closed, breathing carefully controlled.

Seattle suddenly feels impossibly far, and I'm not certain I can maintain control for that long.

# SEVENTEEN

# Celeste

The door closes behind Ryan with a soft click that echoes in the sudden silence. I remain perched on the edge of the bed, my ribcage still warm from the careful press of his hands. The binding feels secure, professional, clinical, even. But there was nothing clinical about the way his fingers traced along my skin, or how his breath caught when I winced.

I touch the bandage, feeling the firm pressure that somehow simultaneously makes breathing both easier and more difficult. The physical pain has subsided, replaced by an ache that has nothing to do with broken ribs and everything to do with the man currently hiding in the bathroom.

Hiding. That's exactly what he's doing.

Five days of this dance—of heated glances and aborted touches, of moments that build toward something inevitable before he retreats behind that wall of professionalism. Five days of watching his iron control strain at the seams while he pretends nothing is happening between us.

I'm tired of it. Tired of his denial. Tired of pretending I don't see the way his eyes darken when I challenge him, don't notice how his hands clench when I push his boundaries. Tired of ignoring the electricity that charges the air whenever we're close.

My gaze drifts to his makeshift bed on the floor—the neatly arranged blankets, the perfectly positioned pillow. Even in discomfort, he maintains rigid order. Control above all else.

The bathroom pipes groan as water runs. I can picture him in there, hands braced on the sink, eyes closed as he practices whatever mental discipline keeps his walls intact. I wonder if he's as tired of fighting this as I am.

A thought forms—rebellious, defiant, perfectly aligned with the pattern of our interactions since that first night. If he insists on martyring himself on the altar of his precious control, then maybe it's time to take that option away.

Decision made, I ease myself off the bed, ignoring the twinge in my side. I gather the blankets from his neatly arranged pallet, then lay them out for myself. The thin carpet provides minimal cushioning against the hard floor, and I wince as I lower myself onto the makeshift bed.

It's uncomfortable, but discomfort has been my constant companion since Jared's murder. What's one more night of physical hardship compared to the satisfaction of seeing Ryan's reaction? Of finally forcing him to confront what's building between us?

I position myself deliberately—blanket pulled up to my chest, eyes closed, breathing steady. The picture of peaceful sleep. The water stops running, the bathroom door handle turns, and I resist the urge to peek through my lashes.

The door opens, releasing a cloud of steam that carries his scent—soap and something distinctly masculine that makes my pulse quicken despite my best efforts. Footsteps pause, then approach slowly.

"What are you doing?" His voice is low, controlled, but with an edge I'm beginning to recognize—the sound of his patience fraying.

I open my eyes, feigning drowsiness. "Going to sleep."

"On the floor."

"Observant as always."

His jaw tightens, the muscle there jumping in the way that signals mounting frustration. "Get in the bed, Celeste."

"No." I adjust the pillow beneath my head, wincing slightly as the movement pulls at my ribs. "You've been sleeping on floors for four nights. It's my turn."

"This isn't a negotiation." He stands over me, water droplets still clinging to his hair, his T-shirt stretched across shoulders that seem impossibly broad from this angle.

"You're right. It's not." I meet his gaze directly. "Which is why I'm sleeping here, and you're taking the bed."

Something flashes behind his eyes—a dangerous spark that makes my heart beat faster. "Your ribs are injured. The floor will only make them worse."

"My ribs are fine. You wrapped them yourself, remember?" The memory of his gentle hands against my skin sends heat curling through me. "Very thoroughly."

His nostrils flare slightly. "This is childish."

"No, what's childish is your stubborn insistence on suffering needlessly." I prop myself up on one elbow, ignoring the discomfort. "You need proper rest if you're going to keep us both alive, don't you? Isn't that what you keep telling me—that your focus is paramount?"

Logic. His own logic turned against him. I watch the calculation happen behind those ice-blue eyes.

"Get in the bed." This time it's not a request. It's an order, delivered in that commanding tone that does inexplicable things to my insides.

I raise an eyebrow, defiant. "Make me."

For one breathless moment, I think he might actually do it— might physically lift me from the floor and place me on the bed. The possibility sends a shiver of anticipation through me that has nothing to do with the cool air against my skin.

Instead, he exhales slowly, deliberately, a man counting backward from ten in his mind.

"Fine." The word is clipped, precise. "If you insist on being uncomfortable and aggravating your injuries, that's your choice."

He moves to the bed, sitting on the edge. The defeat is unexpected, unsatisfying. This isn't how our pattern works. He's supposed to push back, to maintain control, to insist.

"That's it?" I can't keep the surprise from my voice. "You're just giving in?"

"I'm choosing my battles." He doesn't turn to look at me. "And this one isn't worth fighting."

Something about his acquiescence ignites a spark of anger in my chest. Days of tension, of carefully maintained distance, of pretending nothing is happening between us—and now he simply concedes?

I push myself to my feet, ignoring the protest from my ribs. "That's bullshit."

He turns then, eyebrow raised at my outburst. "Excuse me?"

"You heard me." I take a step closer, pulse quickening. "This whole time, you've been dictating every aspect of this ... whatever this is between us. When we stop, where we go, and how we proceed. Every decision made according to your parameters, your rules."

"Because those decisions keep us alive." His voice remains even, controlled, which only fuels my frustration.

"No. Because control is the only way you know how to function." Another step closer, close enough now that I can see the faint stubble darkening his jaw. "You're so afraid of what happens if you let go, even for a second, that you'd rather sleep on floors for a week than admit what's happening here."

His expression hardens. "And what exactly do you think is happening here, Celeste?"

"This." I gesture between us, fingers nearly brushing his chest. "Whatever this is. This—tension. This pull. This thing that makes you look at me like you want to devour me one minute and then retreat behind your walls the next."

He stands, using his height to loom over me—a tactic that might intimidate someone who hasn't spent their career confronting people far more threatening than Ryan Ellis.

"You don't know what you're talking about." His voice drops lower, a warning in its depths.

"I know exactly what I'm talking about." I step closer, eliminating the distance he tried to create. "I know that when you wrapped my ribs just now, your hands lingered longer than they needed to. I know that in the shower every night, you touch yourself while thinking about me."

His eyes widen fractionally—confirmation that my guess about his nightly ritual was correct.

"I know," I continue, voice dropping to match his, "that you've wanted me since that subway platform, and you've been fighting it every step of the way."

"Stop." The word comes out rough, strained.

"Why? Because I'm right?" I press my finger to his chest, feeling the solid wall of muscle beneath the thin cotton. "Because you can't bear to admit that this isn't just professional for you anymore?"

With each sentence, I advance, and he retreats—a reversal of our usual dynamic that emboldens me. One step, two, until his back hits the wall beside the bathroom door. Nowhere left to go.

"If this is just a job to you," I challenge, finger still pressed against his sternum, "then why didn't you hand me off to someone else? Why are you personally driving me across the country? Why do you look at me like that when you think I don't notice?"

His breathing has deepened, his pupils dilating until only a thin ring of blue remains. The muscle in his jaw jumps rhythmically as he clenches his teeth.

"You need to stop pushing me, Celeste." His voice has dropped to that dangerous register that sends heat pooling low in my belly.

"Or what?" I push harder, both literally and figuratively, my finger digging into his chest. "What happens if I don't stop? If I keep pushing until something breaks? Until you break?"

"You don't want to find out." It's meant as a warning, but it sounds like a promise—one that makes my pulse race.

"Maybe I do." I tilt my chin up, defiant. "Maybe that's exactly what I want."

Our faces are inches apart now, close enough that I can feel his breath against my lips. Close enough to see the internal war raging behind those eyes—desire versus discipline, want versus restraint.

"Last chance," he murmurs, something shifting in his expression. "Back away. Now."

I don't move. Don't blink. Don't yield.

"Make me," I whisper again, the challenge explicit.

# EIGHTEEN

# Celeste

Something snaps behind his eyes—control giving way to something primal, dangerous. Before I can register the movement, his hands are on my waist, lifting me as if I weigh nothing. The world spins as he turns us, reversing our positions until my back hits the wall, the impact forcing a gasp from my lungs.

His body presses against mine, pinning me in place. One hand moves to cup my jaw, tilting my face up to his. His eyes search mine, looking for hesitation, for doubt.

He finds none.

"You never know when to stop pushing, do you?" The words rumble from his chest, vibrating against mine.

"Not when I want something." My voice comes out breathier than intended.

"And what exactly do you want?"

"You," I admit, the word falling between us like a gauntlet thrown. "I want you to stop pretending this isn't happening. I want you to admit that this isn't just professional for you. I want—"

His mouth crashes against mine, swallowing the rest of my

demands. The kiss is nothing like the gentle one I imagined during our almost-moment days ago. This is a potent mix of possession, domination, fury, and desire, all combined into something explosive. His lips claim mine with bruising intensity, tongue demanding entrance that I willingly grant.

My hands fist in his shirt, pulling him closer as his fingers tangle in my hair, angling my head for deeper access. The kiss is a battle neither of us is willing to lose—teeth nipping, tongues dueling, hearts racing.

He tastes like mint and something darker, more primal. His stubble scrapes deliciously against my skin, the slight burn only enhancing the pleasure coursing through me. I arch against him, seeking more contact, more friction, more of everything he's finally giving me.

One of his hands slides down to my hip, gripping with enough force to leave marks. I should care about that—about the evidence his fingers will leave on my skin. Instead, I find myself hoping they do.

He breaks the kiss abruptly, both of us gasping for air. His eyes are nearly black with desire, all traces of that icy control gone.

"Is this what you wanted?" he growls, lips moving to my neck, teeth grazing the sensitive spot below my ear. "To break my control? To make me snap?"

"Yes," I gasp as he nips at my pulse point. "God, yes."

His laugh is dark, dangerous against my skin. "Careful what you wish for, sweetheart."

He lifts me again, hands clamped around the backs of my thighs. My legs lock around his waist, dragging us into perfect alignment. There's nothing subtle about the thick, rigid length pressing against me through his clothes—hard, straining, leaving no doubt what he wants, what he's barely holding back. Heat sears through the thin layers separating us, every grind of his hips a brutal reminder of just how ready he is to take me.

He carries me to the bed, our mouths fused again in a kiss that's all heat and hunger. The mattress gives beneath my back as he lowers me, his body covering mine with delicious weight. His hands are everywhere—sliding under my shirt, skimming along my ribs with surprising gentleness despite the urgency of his kiss.

"Ryan," I breathe as his lips travel down my neck.

He pulls back just enough to look at me, hands pausing their exploration. "Tell me to stop, and I will. Right now."

"Don't you dare." I reach for the hem of his T-shirt, tugging upward. "Don't you dare stop."

Something like relief flashes across his features before determination replaces it. He helps me remove his shirt, muscles flexing as the fabric slides over his head. I've seen him shirtless before, but never this close, never with permission to touch.

My hands explore the expanse of his chest, tracing scars and ridges of muscle with wonder. He watches me through hooded eyes, allowing the exploration for precious seconds before his patience expires.

"My turn," he murmurs, reaching for my shirt. He hesitates, eyes flicking to my bound ribs. "Your injuries—"

"Will be fine." I sit up slightly, wincing only a little as I help him remove my shirt. "I'm not made of glass."

His eyes darken as they sweep over me, taking in the black lace bra he selected days ago. "I knew this would look perfect on you," he says, voice rough with appreciation.

"Did you imagine this when you bought it?" I arch into his touch as his fingers trace the edge of the lace. "Me underneath you, wearing what you chose?"

His eyes meet mine, startlingly direct. "Every night."

The admission sends heat spiraling through me. Five days of

shared fantasies, of mutual want cloaked in professional distance. Five days of restraint about to shatter completely.

His hands slide to the waistband of my leggings, pausing—command in the stillness, a question in his eyes. I arch my hips in answer. That's all the permission he needs. The fabric peels down slowly, dragging my underwear with it. Cool air rushes over heated skin, raising goosebumps that vanish under the rough sweep of his palms.

"Beautiful," he murmurs, voice thick, gaze searing as it travels the length of me. "Even more than I imagined."

I should feel exposed. Laid bare. Instead, fire licks through me at the way he looks at me—like I'm power incarnate, like I'm the one undoing him. Desired. Claimed. Seen deeper than skin.

"Your turn." My voice comes out hoarse, urgent. My hands tug at his waistband. "Fair's fair."

He rises, shoving the rest of his clothing off in one fluid motion, every movement deliberate, unhurried—devastatingly erotic. Then he's there in front of me, gloriously, brutally naked.

My breath hitches, the sight a punch to my chest. Broad shoulders carved in shadow, scars cutting across muscle like battle honors, narrowing to lean hips, powerful thighs, and his cock—thick, heavy, rigid, angled toward me like inevitability itself. My mouth waters, anticipation pooling hot and shameless.

He lowers back to the bed, the weight of him covering me, skin to skin at last. Heat explodes at every point of contact, over-whelming, too much, and nowhere near enough.

"Protection," he rasps against my throat, already reaching for a condom, purchased that first night, when he knew this moment might come.

My nails dig crescents into his shoulders as he rips the foil, rolls the latex over his thick length. No pause. No prelude. Just need. Pure and undeniable.

Then he's between my thighs, the blunt head of his cock pressing hard against me, demanding entry.

"Look at me when I fuck you," he commands, voice stripped down to raw authority.

The words crack something open inside me. I obey without hesitation, locking eyes with him as he pushes inside.

The stretch burns—sharp, exquisite, overwhelming—but it's exactly what I've been craving, what I've been needing without admitting it. His jaw tightens, a muscle ticking as he forces himself to go slow, giving me time I don't want.

"Okay?" The word scrapes out of him, half-groan, half-concern.

"More than okay." My hips roll, greedy, pulling him deeper.

The sound he makes shreds me—raw, guttural, a man's control shattering. He surges forward in one brutal thrust that buries him to the hilt, filling me so completely my vision whites out. The pressure teeters on the edge of pain, pleasure so sharp it blurs the line between the two.

"God, Celeste." His forehead crashes against mine, breath ragged, body trembling with restraint. "You feel—"

"I know." My whisper is a gasp, a plea, a confession. "I know."

Then he moves, all restraint gone. His thrusts are hard, driving, perfectly angled to strike deep, to make me cry out. Not gentle. Not punishing. Precision—like every motion is a calculation to break me down, to make me take him deeper, harder.

His hands grip my hips, fingers biting into flesh as if he's anchoring himself. But the truth is clear: I'm the one who's anchored him. And with every thrust, every raw sound torn from his throat, I realize he's not just inside my body. He's breaking past every defense I've ever built.

I match him beat for beat, nails scoring lines down his back that make him hiss with pleasure-pain. The tension that's been building for days, for miles, coalesces into something urgent and unstoppable. Every push and pull between us since that subway platform distills into this moment—his body moving inside mine, claiming and surrendering simultaneously.

"Ryan," I gasp as his rhythm intensifies, driving me higher, closer to the edge. "Please—"

"Tell me what you need," he demands, voice rough with exertion.

"More. Harder."

He complies immediately, one hand sliding beneath my lower back to tilt my hips higher, changing the angle to something devastating. I cry out as he hits a spot deep inside that sends sparks shooting up my spine.

"There," he growls, recognizing my reaction. "Right there."

His thrusts become relentless, targeting that spot with unerring precision. The tension builds, coiling tighter with each movement, each brush of his chest against mine, each command he whispers against my skin.

"Come for me," he orders, voice dropping to that register that seems hardwired to my core. "Now, Celeste."

My body obeys as if it were made to follow his commands. Pleasure crashes through me in waves, vision blurring at the edges as every muscle contracts around him. I'm distantly aware of crying out his name, of my nails digging into his shoulders, of his rhythm faltering as my release triggers his own.

He groans against my neck, hips jerking as he follows me over the edge. For seconds or minutes or hours, we remain locked together, trembling with aftershocks, breathing in sync as reality slowly reassembles around us.

When he finally moves, it's with careful attention to my injuries, easing away to dispose of the condom before returning to gather me against his chest. The possessive way his arms wrap around me feels like another kind of claiming—gentler but no less significant.

We lie in silence, heartbeats gradually slowing, skin cooling in the air-conditioned room. His fingers trace idle patterns along my spine, up my arm, through my hair. I do the same—mapping scars with curious fingertips, learning the texture of him now that we've finally crossed this boundary.

"That was …" I start, then falter, because words are laughably inadequate for what just happened.

"Not nearly enough," he murmurs, voice low, rough, still threaded with possession. "By morning, I plan to have you every way a man can." His hand squeezes my hip, a slow, deliberate press that makes me shiver. "Consider it your punishment for pushing me so damn hard. And sweetheart—" his mouth curves, humor flickering under the hunger, "you're going to take every bit of it."

The words ripple through me like a current, part warning, part promise. Heat pools low again, impossible to ignore.

I push up on one elbow to look at him properly. For once, his features are softened, the perpetual vigilance temporarily muted. It transforms him, makes him look younger, almost vulnerable.

"You know this changes everything," I whisper.

His eyes meet mine, serious now. "I know."

"No more pretending there's nothing between us."

"No," he agrees, tucking a strand of hair behind my ear. "No more pretending."

"And no more sleeping on the floor," I add, attempting lightness.

A slow smile spreads across his face—not the ghost I've glimpsed before, but something real and warm that reaches his eyes. "Definitely no more sleeping on the floor."

I settle back against his chest, listening to the steady rhythm of his heart. We should probably talk more—about what this means, about boundaries, about tomorrow and Seattle and everything that comes after. But for now, this quiet understanding feels sufficient.

True to his word, though, our night is far from over. The brief respite is just that—brief. His hands begin to wander again, reawakening desires barely banked.

Time fractures into snapshots.

Against the wall, my back pressed to the cool surface as he lifts me effortlessly, his body holding me captive, his voice a low growl against my ear: "Wrap your legs tighter around me. Pull me in. Don't let go until I tell you." His strength makes me weightless, utterly his, every thrust driving me higher.

On my stomach, his weight delicious and overwhelming above me, pinning me down. His palm flattens between my shoulder blades, his command unyielding: "Arch more. Higher. Hold it." Each order slices through thought, leaving only raw instinct and the relentless rhythm of his body pounding into mine.

In the mirror, my hands braced against the dresser while he takes me from behind, one hand tangled in my hair, the other gripping my hip hard enough to bruise. His eyes catch mine in the reflection, merciless. "Watch. Don't look away. See what you do to me."

Each position, each relentless demand exposes new layers of his dominance—and new layers of my surrender. The longer it goes, the more I crave it, the more addictive his control becomes. His commands grow sharper, less forgiving. My body obeys without hesitation, trembling with need every time he says "Good girl" in that voice that leaves no room for disobedience.

Hours blur. By the time I collapse into the sheets, I'm wrecked and trembling, certain I can't take more.

But then the mattress dips. He sits at the edge of the bed, a silhouette cut in shadow and bathroom light. Powerful. Unrelenting. He glances over his shoulder.

"There's one more thing I want," he says. Not a request. A decree.

I drag myself up on one elbow, dazed, raw. "What?"

"Come here." His palm pats the space between his parted thighs. "On your knees."

Understanding flares like heat in my veins. My body answers before my mind can resist, carrying me across the floor until I kneel where he wants me.

His hand cups my face, thumb brushing across my lower lip. "Open."

I obey. His cock fills my mouth, hot and heavy, the command in his grip guiding my rhythm. "Deeper. Take it all." His voice is strained but steady, control threaded through every word.

Then his gaze sharpens, locking on mine, and his voice lowers to something even more dangerous. "Do you have any idea what this does to me? Seeing you down here, on your knees for me? Knowing you chose this—chose to obey?" His fingers tighten in my hair, not cruel but insistent. "You could fight me. You could refuse. But instead, you surrender. And fuck, Celeste …" His jaw flexes, a groan rough in his throat. "It undoes me. Makes me harder than I've ever been. Because this isn't about power I take—it's about power you give."

The words ripple through me more than the physical act itself, more than the relentless push of him against the back of my throat. I'm trembling, undone, addicted to that raw confession. His dominance isn't just arousal—it's reverence, possession, a kind of truth I've never felt with another man.

"Look at me," he demands. I drag my gaze up to his, mouth full of him, and the noise he makes is primal. "That's it. Christ. You have no idea what you look like right now. Beautiful. Ruined. Mine."

I moan around him, and that sound is what finally snaps his control. His hips drive forward, hand tightening in my hair as he fucks into my mouth. His voice breaks with the force of it—rough, desperate, unrestrained.

When he comes, it's with my name ripped from his chest, half-groan, half-command, his body shuddering as if I've stripped him bare in ways that go beyond flesh.

Afterward, he pulls me into bed, cradling me against his chest with a tenderness that shouldn't belong to the man who just commanded me like a soldier. His hand strokes my hair, as if I might break, soothing, grounding. The contrast is dizzying, addictive.

I twist in his arms, tilting my head back to look at him. "And the rest?"

His brows lift faintly. "The rest?"

"What you said earlier." My voice is quiet, but insistent. "About bending me over and—"

His eyes darken again, the softness vanishing.

"Yes," he says without hesitation, voice rough and certain. "Definitely. But later. When we know each other better. When you understand what you'd be asking for." He pauses, his thumb dragging across my bottom lip in a way that makes my breath catch. "Because those weren't just words, Celeste. Not for me."

A chill of anticipation races down my spine, equal parts fear and something far more reckless. My mind tells me to back away from the edge, but my body leans toward it, craving the danger in his tone, the promise of something darker.

"You mean ..." The words stumble out, low and hesitant. "You'd actually ..."

His mouth curves—not a full smile, but a smirk edged with dangerous amusement.

"You think what you've seen tonight is the limit of me?" His gaze pins me, relentless. "Sweetheart, I've barely touched the surface. If I ever punish you the way I want to …" His eyes rake over me, slow and deliberate. "You won't mistake it for endless sex. You'll feel it. Every strike. Every command. And you'll thank me for it."

Heat floods through me, my pulse quickening despite the sharp edge in his words. It should scare me. It does. And yet the very thought of surrendering that completely—to him, only him—sends another wave of molten desire crashing through me.

He watches me carefully, reading every flicker across my face. His smirk deepens, satisfied.

"Yeah," he murmurs, voice dropping to a growl, "you want it, don't you? Even if you can't admit it yet."

I bury my face against his chest, trying to hide, but his laughter—low, dark, and knowing—vibrates through me.

As sleep drags me under, the truth hits harder than any climax: it wasn't just the pleasure. It wasn't even the connection. It was his voice. That unshakable command that made surrender not weakness, but freedom.

And God help me—I want more. Darker. Deeper. Beyond tonight.

# NINETEEN

## Celeste

<hr>

MORNING LIGHT FILTERS THROUGH CHEAP CURTAINS, PAINTING stripes across the tangled sheets. I wake slowly, aware of unfamiliar weight across my waist, solid warmth against my back. Ryan's arm holds me securely against him, his breath warm against my neck, his body curved protectively around mine.

For several moments, I simply absorb the sensation of waking in his arms. The intimacy of it feels almost more significant than what preceded it. Sex can be dismissed as physical need, as tension finding release. This—this quiet connection in the vulnerability of sleep—feels like something else entirely.

I shift slightly, careful not to disturb him, but his breathing changes immediately. Always alert, even in sleep.

"Morning," he murmurs, voice rough with sleep.

I turn in his arms to face him, taking in the sight of Ryan Ellis with bedhead and stubble, eyes still heavy-lidded. "Morning."

His gaze travels over my face, assessing, remembering. Something shifts in his expression, a shadow crossing his features. My stomach drops—I recognize that look immediately. Regret.

It's exactly what I feared.

"Let me guess," I say, unable to keep the edge from my voice, "you're about to tell me last night was a mistake. That it was unprofessional, a lapse in judgment that can't happen again because we need to focus on the mission."

"Celeste—" His mouth tightens slightly.

"No," I interrupt, a knot forming in my chest. "I can't believe this. After everything—after last night—you're still going to hide behind that wall of professionalism? You're going to act like what happened was just some tactical error we need to correct?"

"If you would just—"

"What? Pretend it didn't happen? Go back to you sleeping on the floor and us ignoring whatever this is between us?" I sit, clutching the sheet to my chest, not out of modesty but to have something to grip besides his throat. "You don't get to do this. You don't get to make me feel like—like that, and then dismiss it as a complication."

"Celeste." His voice cuts through my tirade, the commanding tone I've come to recognize stopping me mid-sentence. "Be silent."

The directive catches me off guard, halting my words more effectively than any argument could.

"If you'd please be silent for a moment," he continues, eyes darkening as they move from my face to the sheet barely covering my breasts, "I could tell you what I was thinking."

"Which is?" I manage, still braced for rejection.

In one fluid motion, strong hands grip my waist. "I want you to climb on top of me and ride me hard," he says, voice dropping to that register that does impossible things to my insides. "I want to watch your tits bounce, feel your legs around mine, and feel your pussy taking my cock first thing in the morning. That's what I was thinking about during those thirty seconds you've been yelling at me."

Heat floods me, fast and immediate, my body responding to his words before my mind fully processes them. Not regret. Not retreat. But desire—raw and unfiltered.

"Oh," I breathe, relief and renewed hunger washing through me in equal measure.

His thumbs trace slow circles over my hipbones, grip firm but patient. "Unless you'd rather keep telling me what I'm thinking?"

The challenge in his voice sparks a smile I can't suppress. "I think I prefer your version."

"Then stop talking." His hands tighten, drawing me forward. "Ride me."

I don't need to be told twice. The sheet slips from my body as I swing a leg over him, straddling his lap. The blunt heat of him slides against me, teasing my entrance before I sink down, inch by inch, taking him into me until he's buried completely. My breath catches, thighs trembling at the stretch.

"God, you feel incredible." His voice is a groan, rough and reverent, eyes riveted to the place where our bodies join.

I start to move, rolling my hips slowly, savoring the drag of him inside me. "You've imagined this?"

"For days." His gaze travels upward, lingering on the sway of my breasts as I find my rhythm. "Since that first night in the hotel. But this—" his hands glide up my sides, palms spreading wide, "—this is better than every fantasy combined."

His hands cup my breasts, at first exploratory, then more deliberate. His thumbs circle my nipples until they harden into sensitive peaks. He watches my face as he experiments—gentle kneads, soft caresses—before abruptly shifting, pinching one nipple between thumb and forefinger, sharp enough to draw a gasp.

"What do you like?" His voice is low, commanding, eyes locked on mine. "The softer version—" another gentle roll of his thumb, "—or something with more bite?"

My body answers before I can. The sharp inhale. The sudden clench around his cock.

A slow, knowing grin spreads across his face. "Interesting."

"What?" My word stumbles, my rhythm faltering as his fingers twist, harder this time.

"You like the pain." He does it again, watching me flutter around him, watching the way my eyes squeeze shut against the flood of sensation. His grin turns wicked. "Are you kinky, Celeste Hart?"

"I—" My breath breaks on a moan as his hips rise to meet mine, thrusting deeper. "I don't think so."

"That's a shame." He pinches harder, rolling until sparks shoot straight to my core. "Because I very much am."

"I didn't say I'm not interested," I gasp, hands braced on his shoulders as he thrusts up into me with growing power. "I've just never—"

"Never been with someone who knew how to push the right buttons?" He sits up, sudden and deliberate, changing the angle. His cock drives into me deeper, harder, wringing a cry from my lips. His mouth replaces his fingers, teeth grazing one nipple, tongue soothing the sting.

"Never been interested before," I admit, breathless, thighs trembling from the effort of keeping pace. "But you—" my words fracture as he thrusts up again, sharp and precise, "—you might be the man who changes my mind."

"Might be?" His eyes flash, darkening with something primal and possessive. One hand fists in my hair, tugging my head back, baring my throat to him. "Sweetheart, I won't just change your mind." His hips snap upward, making me cry out. "I'll break it. I'll be the man who shows you exactly what you've been missing."

The promise in his voice, the certainty of it, sends a shiver racing down my spine, even as my body clenches tighter around him. He drags my mouth to his, kissing me hard—no tenderness, all claim. His hips drive upward, forcing me to ride him harder, faster, until the wet slap of our bodies echoes in the quiet room.

"Ride me harder," he growls against my lips, his breath hot, commanding. "Show me how much you fucking want this."

I obey, hips snapping, breasts bouncing with each thrust. He grips me tighter, guiding my rhythm, not letting me falter. His control is relentless, addictive, every demand peeling away another layer of resistance I didn't realize I had.

"Look at you," he murmurs, voice rough with desire. "Taking me so perfectly. So responsive to every touch." His thumb finds my clit, circling with precise pressure that makes my thighs tremble. "Come for me, Celeste. Let me feel you."

The command, delivered in that tone that seems hardwired to my nervous system, detonates inside me. Pleasure rips through me in violent waves, my body clenching around him as I cry out his name. He follows moments later, groaning into my mouth, hands gripping my hips hard enough to bruise as he drives up into me one final time.

I collapse against his chest, boneless, both of us breathing hard, sweat cooling between our bodies. His arms wrap around me, holding me close as the aftershocks leave me trembling. Relief, exhaustion, release—finally.

But Ryan isn't done.

"Stay with me." His voice is low, commanding, already pulling me back from the edge of recovery. His hips shift beneath me, cock still thick and heavy inside me, the slight movement making me gasp. "Don't drift. Don't think you're finished."

"Ryan—" My protest is a weak, broken sound. My body feels wrung out, too sensitive to take more.

"Yes." His hand grips the back of my neck, tilting my head so I meet his eyes. They're darker than I've ever seen, pupils blown wide. "You can. You will. I'm not letting you stop here."

His hips roll, slow at first, deliberate, each thrust dragging against swollen, over-sensitized nerves. My breath catches, teetering between pleasure and pain. "I can't," I whisper.

"You will." His thumb presses down on my clit again, merciless, steady. "Because I'm telling you to. Because you respond to my voice, my touch, my command. Come again, Celeste. Do it for me. Show me how well you obey …"

Every word is a trigger, a hook sinking deep, pulling me back toward the precipice I thought I'd already fallen from. My body betrays me, shuddering, building, cresting again in spite of the overstimulation.

The second orgasm tears through me, sharper, rawer, leaving me sobbing into his shoulder as my entire body clenches and convulses. His grip is unyielding, holding me through it, forcing me to ride every last wave until I'm shaking uncontrollably in his arms.

"Good girl," he murmurs against my temple, voice thick with satisfaction. "That's what I wanted. That's what I'll always want. You, giving me everything you didn't think you had."

I can't answer. I can barely breathe. But the truth is undeniable. I've never come twice in such quick succession. Never known my body could. And the terrifying, exhilarating part is—if he asked again, in that voice, with that command, my body would obey.

"That was …" I struggle to find words adequate to the experience.

"A very good morning," he finishes, pressing a kiss to my temple.

I laugh softly against his shoulder. "Definitely better than arguing."

"You know," he says after a moment, "this changes nothing between us."

I tense slightly, preparing for the withdrawal I initially feared.

He must feel it, because he continues with a clarification, "I mean, it changes nothing about our situation. You're still in danger. We still need to reach Seattle. I still need to keep you safe."

"And how do we do that now?" I ask, propping myself up on one elbow to look at him properly.

A hint of that commanding smile touches his lips. "The same way we've been doing it—you follow my orders and commands."

"Orders and commands?" I raise an eyebrow.

"Only now," he adds, fingers sliding up to trace the curve of my breast, "you follow them in bed as well as out of it. Your safety still depends on it." His tone is lighthearted but carries an undertone of seriousness that sends a shiver through me.

"So I'm at your mercy?" I ask, matching his playful tone while acknowledging the truth beneath it.

"Completely." He rolls suddenly, pinning me beneath him, his weight a delicious pressure. "But as you've discovered, my mercy can be quite ..." he pauses, pressing a kiss to my collarbone, "satisfying."

I laugh, the sound turning to a soft gasp as his mouth travels lower. "And when we reach Seattle? What happens then?"

He lifts his head, expression turning more serious. "Things will change. You'll meet the team. We'll figure out what to do about the flash drive, about Obsidian and Phoenix. Our operating parameters will shift."

"And this?" I gesture between us. "Will that shift too?"

His eyes hold mine, startlingly direct. "That depends on what this is."

It's a fair question; one I don't have a clear answer for. Five days ago, I might have dismissed it as proximity, adrenaline, the unique circumstances that threw us together. Now, after last night, after waking in his arms, I'm not so certain.

"I don't know," I admit. "It's something I wasn't looking for. Something I don't want to pretend isn't there."

His hand slides to the back of my neck, grip firm but gentle. "I can't promise to stop being vigilant. To stop prioritizing your safety above comfort or connection or anything else."

"I'm not asking you to."

"What are you asking for, then?"

I lean into his touch, closing the distance between us. "Just this. Honesty. Presence. No more sleeping on the floor."

His eyes search mine, looking for deception, for manipulation, finding none. Whatever he sees makes his decision, because the next moment he's pulling me to him, mouth claiming mine in a kiss that's both question and answer.

This kiss is different from last night's—less frantic, more deliberate. An exploration rather than a conquest. His hands cradle my face with surprising gentleness, thumbs stroking along my cheekbones as his lips move against mine.

I melt into him, sheet forgotten as my arms wind around his neck. The press of skin against skin ignites the same fire as before, but with a slow burn rather than explosive heat.

When he lowers me to the mattress, it's with careful attention to my injured side. When he settles between my thighs, it's with deliberate patience rather than urgent need. Every movement is measured and controlled in a way that's entirely different from his previous restraint.

This isn't Ryan holding back. This is Ryan, focused entirely on me.

"Look at me," he commands softly as he enters me, the stretch easier but no less overwhelming than before.

I obey without thought, eyes locking with his as he begins to move. There's something almost reverential in his gaze, something that makes my chest tighten with emotion I'm not ready to name.

He sets a rhythm that's torturously slow, each thrust deep and deliberate. His hands capture mine, pinning them above my head, fingers intertwined. The restraint sends an unexpected thrill through me—being held down, controlled, yet completely safe in that control. It's the most erotic thing I've ever experienced.

The weight of him above me, the strength in his hands keeping mine immobile, the way he watches my face as he moves within me—it awakens something primal and yearning that I've never acknowledged before. I test his grip slightly, not truly trying to break free but wanting to feel the resistance, the firmness of his hold.

"You like being restrained," he observes, his voice a deep rumble against my ear. Not a question—a statement of fact.

"Yes," I admit, surprised by how easily the confession comes. "I never knew I would, but God, Ryan—this feels incredible."

A smile curves his lips, predatory and pleased. "We've barely scratched the surface of what you might like." His grip tightens fractionally, emphasizing his point. "There's so much more I could show you."

The promise in his words makes me arch beneath him, eager and hungry for whatever he might offer. "Then show me," I challenge, emboldened by desire. "Everything. Anything. I want to be your willing student in all of this."

His eyes darken with satisfaction and desire. "My eager little submissive," he murmurs, the label sending a shiver through me that has nothing to do with embarrassment and everything to do with recognition. "So ready to surrender control."

"Only to you," I breathe, the truth of it surprising us both. "Ryan," I breathe, arching beneath him. "Please …"

"Please, what?" His voice is soft but commanding. "Tell me what you need."

"More," I manage, overwhelmed by the intensity of this slower pace. "Faster."

"No." He presses deeper, maintaining that deliberate rhythm. "Not this time. This time, we go slow."

The denial should frustrate me. Instead, it sends a thrill through me that has nothing to do with physical pleasure and everything to do with surrendering control. With letting someone else—letting him—dictate the pace, the pressure, the path to release.

His eyes never leave mine as he moves within me, reading every reaction, adjusting to every response. It's the most intimate experience of my life—being seen so completely, being known so thoroughly.

When release finally comes, it builds like a wave rather than a crash—gathering momentum slowly, inexorably, until it sweeps through me with devastating intensity. I cry out his name, back arching, hands gripping his with desperate strength.

He follows moments later, my name a prayer on his lips as he shudders above me. For long moments afterward, we remain connected, breathing in sync, foreheads pressed together in silent communion.

Eventually, he shifts to lie beside me, gathering me against his chest. I trace idle patterns across his skin, marveling at how quickly the unfamiliar has become essential.

"We should get moving," he says eventually, voice rumbling beneath my ear. "Long drive ahead."

I nod against his chest, knowing he's right but reluctant to leave this moment. "Seattle?"

"If we make good time." His fingers trail along my spine, a casual intimacy that feels more significant than what preceded it. "This is our last night on the road."

I push up on one elbow to look at him properly. "Our last night?"

"We've got a little over twelve hours left on the road, maybe more if we double back."

"We should do that."

"What?"

"Double back?"

He cocks his head, then smiles. "Eager are we?"

"For one more night on the road? Yes." I bite my lower lip, knowing how I sound.

The corner of his mouth quirks up in that almost-smile I'm beginning to adore. "One more night sharing a bed," he clarifies.

"Yes." I press a kiss to his chest, right above his heart.

His laughter is unexpected—a rich, warm sound I've never heard before. It transforms his face, softening the hard edges, revealing glimpses of who Ryan Ellis might be when he's not keeping the world at bay.

We shower together, a practical decision that quickly becomes anything but when his hands replace mine on the soap, sliding over curves and planes with thorough attention that leaves me gasping against the tile.

TWENTY

## Ryan

Steam still clings to the bathroom mirror as I finish dressing, the lingering heat a reminder of what transpired in the shower moments ago. Celeste's soft gasps as my hands replaced hers with the soap. The way she arched against the tile when I pressed into her from behind. The water running cold before we noticed, too consumed with each other to care.

Now she's gathering our few belongings, movements efficient despite the exhaustion evident in the slight droop of her shoulders. We need to be on the road soon. We need to maintain our schedule and security protocols. Need to function as if last night—this morning—hasn't fundamentally altered everything between us.

I check my watch: 7:23 AM. Later start than planned. I don't regret it.

The sight of her, hair still damp, wearing clothes I selected days ago, sends a surge of possessiveness through me that should be alarming. This wasn't the mission. Wasn't the plan. Wasn't within operational parameters.

*Mine.* The word surfaces unbidden, resonating with unexpected force. When did Celeste Hart transition from assignment to something else entirely?

The subway platform? The first hotel room? The tunnels? I can't pinpoint the exact moment. Just the culmination—her body beneath mine, her voice calling my name, her complete surrender as she came apart at my command.

I glance at the floor beside the bed, where our clothes lay scattered in uncharacteristic disorder until moments ago. Evidence of the control I finally relinquished. The barriers I allowed to fall. I should regret it—the breakdown of professional distance, the compromise of tactical focus.

I don't.

I feel more focused, more centered than I have since this extraction began. The tension that has been building for days has finally found release, but vigilance remains—sharpened, even. Because now I'm not protecting an asset or a civilian. I'm protecting what's mine.

The realization should concern me. Emotional investment compromises objectivity—first rule of protective operations. But as I watch her folding the last of her clothes into our shared bag, I recognize that this particular rule was broken long before last night.

It was broken the moment I diverted from my mission to save her on that platform. The moment I called Ghost instead of the local authorities. The moment I decided to personally drive her across the country rather than hand her off to another operative.

My brothers in arms would call it fate, our paths intersecting at that precise moment. Ghost would call it a tactical vulnerability. My sisters would say I've finally met my match.

They're all partially right.

"Ready?" Celeste asks, zipping the duffel closed. Her eyes meet mine with a directness that hasn't changed, despite everything else that has.

I nod, conducting one final sweep of the room—habit rather than necessity. "One more day on the road."

"One more night," she adds, something knowing in her smile.

My arm slides around her waist as we head for the door, a possessive gesture I don't bother to analyze. One more day. One more night. Then everything changes.

The Montana landscape rolls past the windows, mountains giving way to plains, then rising again at the Idaho border. Celeste dozes in the passenger seat, her body angled toward me even in sleep. We've been on the road for four hours, maintaining good time despite a later start than usual.

I check the mirrors—clear. We've implemented sufficient evasive measures that I'm confident our trail is cold. The truck stop coffee beside me has gone lukewarm, forgotten as I calculate distances, fuel stops, optimal routes.

With minimal stops and trading driving shifts, we could reach Cerberus headquarters by midnight. It would be the tactical choice—maintaining momentum, minimizing exposure time, getting Celeste into secure facilities as quickly as possible.

My hands tighten on the steering wheel as I dismiss the option. One more night. One more night with her before everything becomes complicated by briefings, threat assessments, and team dynamics.

One more night to have her completely to myself.

The selfishness of the decision doesn't escape me. For the first time in my operational career, I'm making a choice based on personal desire rather than tactical advantage. I should be concerned by this departure from protocol.

Instead, I'm already planning where we'll stop, what I'll need, and how I'll introduce her to the elements of control and surrender she responded to so intuitively last night.

Her comment about being my willing student in "all things kinky" has lingered in my mind, a tantalizing possibility I intend to explore. The way she yielded when I pinned her wrists, the sharp intake of breath when I gripped her hair, her immediate response to my commands—all indicate potential for dynamics I crave but rarely indulge.

Never with someone who challenges me so consistently. Never with someone who surrenders not from weakness but from choice, from desire as strong as my own.

Celeste stirs beside me, stretching like a cat, oddly graceful despite the confines of the passenger seat. Her eyes open, immediately finding mine with that direct gaze that's been disarming me since day one.

"Morning. Again." Her voice is sleep-rough, a sound I've quickly grown to appreciate.

"Technically, it's afternoon." I glance at the dashboard clock: 12:47 PM.

She follows my gaze, eyebrows rising. "You let me sleep for hours."

"You needed it."

Her hand reaches across the console, fingers trailing along my forearm with a casual intimacy that would have been unthinkable yesterday.

"So do you."

"I'm fine."

"Always fine," she murmurs, a teasing note in her voice. "Always in control."

Not always. Not last night. Not when she pushed me beyond breaking. Not when I finally took what I'd been denying myself since that first almost-kiss against the hotel wall.

The memory sends heat coursing through me, a response I carefully control. Focus on the mission. On keeping her safe. The rest comes later.

"Where are we?" she asks, gazing out at the passing scenery.

"About to cross into Idaho. Making good time."

"Idaho." She processes this, mental calculations obvious in her expression. "We could reach Seattle by tonight if we pushed through."

Of course, she'd reach the same tactical conclusion. Her mind is as sharp as it is stubborn.

"We could," I agree, keeping my tone neutral.

"But we're not going to." Not a question. An observation.

I glance at her, finding a knowing smile playing at the corners of her mouth. "No. We're not."

"Any particular reason?" The question is innocent. Her tone is not.

"Several." I return my attention to the road, but not before catching the flush rising on her cheeks. "We'll stop in Coeur d'Alene. It's a good strategic position before the final push to Seattle."

"Strategic," she repeats, amusement coloring the word. "Of course."

Her hand remains on my arm, thumb tracing idle patterns against my skin. The casual touch is simultaneously calming and arousing—a contradiction that seems to define everything about Celeste Hart.

"We need supplies," I say after a moment. "I'll stop at the next major truck stop."

"Supplies?" Her eyebrow arches. "Like food? Fuel?"

"Rope and... other things."

Her eyes narrow slightly, that investigative mind working through possibilities. When understanding dawns, her pupils dilate visibly, lips parting on a soft exhale.

"Oh."

One syllable, loaded with anticipation. The sound travels directly to my core, awakening hunger barely sated by last night's encounters.

"Any objections?" I keep my voice even and controlled while offering her the space to refuse.

"None whatsoever." Her fingers tighten slightly on my arm. "I meant what I said last night."

About being my willing student. About surrendering to me in ways she never has with anyone else. The memory of those words, spoken as I moved inside her, nearly breaks my composure.

"Good." I cover her hand with mine briefly before returning it to the wheel. "Because I have plans for tonight."

The promise hangs between us, charging the air with expectation. Her breathing quickens slightly, a response she doesn't try to hide. This new honesty between us—the acknowledgment of what we both want—feels more intimate than the physical joining of our bodies.

We drive in comfortable silence for several miles, the landscape changing around us as we cross state lines. Celeste eventually turns on the radio, finding a classic rock station that fills the space with familiar melodies. Her taste in music surprises me—not the pop I expected, but Led Zeppelin, The Rolling Stones, bands I grew up listening to on my father's vintage vinyl collection.

When she hums along to "Ramble On," something shifts in my chest—a tightening that has nothing to do with desire and everything to do with recognition. With a connection beyond the physical. With the realization that I want to know every layer of this woman, not just the ones I've uncovered between hotel sheets.

The feeling is unfamiliar. Unsettling. I compartmentalize it for later examination and focus on the mission parameters. Coeur d'Alene by nightfall. Supplies before then. Keep Celeste safe. The rest is secondary.

Even as I think it, I know it's no longer true. Nothing about Celeste Hart will ever be secondary again.

TWENTY-ONE

# Ryan

THE TRUCK STOP LOOMS AHEAD—A SPRAWLING COMPLEX OF FUEL
stations, fast-food restaurants, and a surprisingly large convenience store. I park the SUV near the side entrance, positioning it
for quick departure if necessary—a habit rather than a specific
concern.

"I'll be quick," I tell Celeste, already scanning the surroundings for potential threats. Clear for now. "Lock the doors. Stay
alert."

"Yes, sir." She delivers the acknowledgment with a mock
salute that should irritate me, but instead sends a pulse of heat
through my veins.

My eyes narrow. "Careful."

"What?" The challenge in her voice is deliberate, calculated
to provoke.

"That particular word means something to me." I lean
slightly closer, voice dropping. "In certain contexts, 'sir' isn't just a
casual honorific. It's an acknowledgment of power exchange. Of
control freely given and responsibly taken."

Her eyes widen slightly, understanding dawning.

I exit the vehicle, confirming the locks engage behind me. The convenience store's fluorescent lighting is harsh after hours on the road, but I adjust quickly, orienting myself. Food and drinks in the back. Automotive supplies to the right. Toiletries and medical items are along the left wall. A surprising array of household goods and travel necessities in the center aisles.

I move with purpose, selecting protein bars, waters, and premade sandwiches for the road. Practical needs first. Always. It's the foundation of survival—addressing basic requirements before secondary concerns.

Once those are secured, I allow myself to focus on tonight's objectives. The store's selection is limited, but sufficient for what I have in mind. A basic introduction, nothing too intense for her first deliberate experience with kink. Just enough to test her responses, to learn her boundaries, to show her what's possible between us.

I select items with the same methodical attention I'd give to tactical gear—each choice deliberate, each purpose clear in my mind. Soft cotton rope, pliable but strong. A silk scarf that can serve as a blindfold or a restraint. Massage oil with minimal scent. Basic first aid supplies that can double for aftercare.

The selections are innocuous enough individually. Together, they form the foundation of what I have planned. Nothing that would raise eyebrows at checkout, nothing that requires specialized knowledge to use effectively. Just everyday items that become something else entirely in the right hands.

My hands. On Celeste.

Around her wrists. In her hair.

The images flash through my mind with vivid clarity, momentarily distracting me from my surroundings—a lapse in vigilance I immediately correct, scanning the store for potential threats before continuing.

In the automotive section, I find a leather tool roll—perfect for implementing impact play without being obvious. In the kitchen aisle, a small wooden spoon with a smooth handle. From hardware, a small wheel tool with blunt spikes used for marking patterns—innocent enough for its intended purpose, but capable of creating exquisite sensory play. A packet of cheap feathers from the craft section completes the collection.

I add a few more items to my basket—things to make her comfortable afterward. Small luxuries that have no tactical purpose but will bring her pleasure. Dark chocolate. Aloe vera gel for her still-healing ribs.

The cashier barely glances at my selections as she rings them up. Just another traveler stocking up for the road. I pay cash, as always. No electronic trail. No evidence of our passage except in the memories of those we briefly encounter.

When I return to the SUV, Celeste is alert, watching the parking lot with the observational skills that make her an excellent journalist. She's learning—integrating tactical awareness into her natural ability to read situations. It's strangely satisfying to see.

"All set?" she asks as I slide behind the wheel, placing the bags in the back seat.

"For now." I start the engine, checking mirrors before pulling out.

Her eyes drift to the bags, curiosity evident in her expression, but she doesn't ask. Doesn't push, for once. Just settles back in her seat with a small smile playing at her lips.

"I can hardly wait," she says, the simple statement heavy with anticipation.

Neither can I, though I don't say it aloud. Some admissions are still difficult, even after everything we've shared. Instead, I reach across the console and take her hand, a gesture that feels both foreign and essential. Her fingers intertwine with mine without hesitation, and we drive toward Idaho in companionable silence.

Tonight, I'll show Celeste Hart exactly what she's awakened in me. Until I can introduce her to pleasures she's only beginning to understand. Until I can claim her again in ways that leave no doubt about who she belongs to.

*Mine.* The word echoes with each mile marker we pass.

Coeur d'Alene appears on the horizon as the sun begins its descent—a picturesque lake town nestled in the mountains of northern Idaho. Under different circumstances, it might be a vacation destination. Tonight, it's simply our final stop before Seattle.

I bypass the first few motels we pass—basic establishments similar to where we've stayed previously. Tonight calls for something different. Something better. Not luxury—we're still maintaining a low profile—but a step up from the utilitarian accommodations we've endured thus far.

The Lakeview Inn appears after several minutes of searching —a renovated motel with updated exteriors and a sign advertising "Newly Remodeled Rooms." The parking lot is half-full, busy enough to blend in but not so crowded as to create security concerns. Perfect.

"Wait here," I tell Celeste as I park in a spot with clear sightlines to both the office and the main road.

"No argument this time." Her smile is knowing. She understands the routine now, accepts the necessary precautions without the resistance that marked our early days together.

The check-in process is smooth—cash payment, minimal questions, a room on the first floor with exterior access, and multiple escape routes. The clerk hands over an actual key card, rather than the metal keys of our previous accommodations —a minor upgrade that somehow feels significant.

When I return to the SUV, Celeste has already gathered our

meager belongings, ready to move to our room. The seamless cooperation is a marked change from her earlier defiance. Not submission, exactly—she's too independent for that—but a willing partnership that makes my job easier while acknowledging my expertise.

Room 117 is at the far end of the building, offering both privacy and tactical advantage. I unlock the door, performing my usual security sweep with Celeste waiting patiently in the doorway. The room is noticeably better than our previous stays—featuring a queen bed with an actual headboard, furniture that doesn't look salvaged from the 1970s, and bathroom fixtures that gleam rather than grimace.

"Clear," I announce, completing my circuit of the space.

Celeste enters, setting our bags on the dresser before turning in a slow circle to take in our surroundings. "This is practically the Ritz compared to last night."

"You deserve better than what we've had." The admission comes easily, surprising me with its sincerity.

Her expression softens, something vulnerable flickering in those observant eyes. "Thank you."

I close the door, engaging both locks and the security chain—routine security measures that suddenly feel like something more. A boundary between the outside world and what's about to happen in this room. A demarcation between danger and sanctuary.

Celeste watches me, her body language shifting subtly as she reads my intent. Her spine straightens, her breathing quickens, her eyes darken with anticipation.

I complete my checks—window secured, bathroom clear, sight lines assessed—before turning my full attention to her. The transition is deliberate, the shift in my demeanor intentional. No longer just the protector, the operative, the tactician.

Now, the dominant. The one in control. The one who will teach her exactly what she asked to learn.

I move toward her slowly, giving her time to process the change, to adapt to this new aspect of our dynamic. When I stop, I'm close enough to feel the heat radiating from her body but no touching. Not yet.

"Kneel."

One word, delivered with quiet authority. No room for misinterpretation. No space for argument.

Her eyes widen slightly, pupils dilating. For a moment, I think she might resist—the independent journalist reasserting herself against the command. Then, with a grace that steals my breath, she sinks to her knees on the carpeted floor, eyes never leaving mine.

The sight of her kneeling before me—willing, eager—sends a surge of primal satisfaction through my veins. This powerful, stubborn woman is surrendering not out of weakness, but by choice. There is no greater aphrodisiac.

"Tonight is Kinky Sex 101, and it begins with you showing me exactly how well you can follow instructions."

Her breath catches, anticipation and arousal plain in her expression. I reach down, cupping her face in my palm, thumb tracing her lower lip in silent approval.

"The first lesson," I continue, keeping my voice level despite the desire coursing through me, "is that submission is a gift you choose to give. One I don't take lightly."

She leans into my touch, understanding dawning in her eyes. "And the second lesson?"

My lips curve in a smile that's equal parts promise and warning. "The second lesson is that a good submissive knows when to speak and when to listen." I apply gentle pressure to her lip with my thumb. "Right now, it's time to listen."

She nods, settling more comfortably on her knees, waiting for instruction. The trust in her posture, in her acceptance, is humbling. A responsibility I intend to honor with every action that follows.

"Before we begin properly, we need to establish boundaries." I maintain eye contact with her, keeping her focused on my words. "A safe word. Something you'll say if anything becomes too much, too intense, too uncomfortable. Something that immediately stops whatever is happening."

"Phoenix," she suggests without hesitation, the word carrying its weight between us. The very thing that brought us together.

"Phoenix," I repeat, cementing the choice. "Say it if you need to stop for any reason. No questions asked, no judgment. Understood?"

"Yes."

"Good." I step back slightly, creating space between us. "Now, I want you to show me how well that mouth of yours can be used for something other than arguing with me."

Her lips part on a small exhale, anticipation plain in her expression. "Yes, Sir."

## TWENTY-TWO

# Ryan

THE SUBMISSION IN THOSE TWO WORDS—FROM A WOMAN WHO has fought me on every directive since the subway platform—is the most erotic thing I've ever heard. More powerful than any fantasy, more affecting than last night's passion.

I unbuckle my belt, slow and deliberate, giving her time to adjust to what's happening. Her eyes follow every movement, pupils dilated with arousal rather than fear. When I free myself, her gaze is hungry, eager.

"Hands behind your back," I instruct, watching as she complies immediately. "Keep them there unless I say otherwise." I step closer, guiding her with a hand in her hair. "Show me what you can do."

She takes me into her mouth with unexpected confidence, a skill that sends a jolt of both pleasure and something darker through me. Not jealousy, exactly, but possessiveness. A determination to erase the memory of anyone who came before me.

I control the pace with my grip on her hair, not rough but firm. Guiding. Teaching. Showing her precisely what I want. Her responsiveness is immediate—adapting to each subtle cue, learning my preferences with the same keen observation she applies to everything.

"Look at me," I command, needing to see her eyes as she serves me this way.

She obeys, gaze lifting to meet mine without hesitation. The connection intensifies everything—the physical sensation, the emotional impact, the power exchange happening between us. This isn't just sex. This is communication on a level I've rarely experienced.

When I'm close to the edge, I pull back, denying myself release. Not yet. This night is about exploration and discovery, about teaching her what she's capable of. My pleasure is secondary to that goal.

"Enough." I help her to her feet, steadying her when she wobbles slightly. "You learn quickly."

A flush spreads across her cheeks at the praise. "I have a good teacher."

I smile at that—a genuine smile, unguarded in a way few ever see. "We've barely begun." Leading her to the bed, I guide her to lie in the center. "Arms above your head, crossed at the wrists."

Again, she complies without hesitation, stretching out before me in a position of complete vulnerability. Trust given freely. Power surrendered willingly.

I retrieve the cotton rope from my purchases and uncoil it. "This is for restraint, but more importantly, for the sensation it creates." I let the fibers trail across her arm, watching as goosebumps rise in their wake. "The awareness of being bound. The freedom that comes from having choice temporarily removed."

Her breathing quickens as I begin binding her wrists—secure enough to restrain, loose enough to ensure circulation. Each loop, each knot, is performed with methodical attention to both aesthetic and function.

"How does that feel?" I ask when I've finished, her wrists now secured to the headboard with artful knots.

She tests the restraints, finding just enough give to be comfortable but not enough to escape. "Good. Different. I've never …"

"I know." I trail my fingers down her bound arms, across her collarbone, down to where her pulse beats visibly at the base of her throat. "Most haven't. Not like this."

Next comes the silk scarf, held before her eyes. "Vision is our dominant sense. Removing it heightens everything else—touch, hearing, smell. Are you ready for that?"

She swallows, nods. "Yes."

I wrap the silk around her eyes, secure but not tight, plunging her into darkness. Her body tenses momentarily, adjusting to the new vulnerability, then relaxes as she accepts it.

"Remember your safe word," I remind her, trailing fingers down her cheek.

"Phoenix," she whispers. "But I won't need it."

The confidence in her voice sends pride surging through me. My brave, stubborn woman. So new to this world, yet so naturally suited to it.

What follows is a study in sensation—the feather's whisper-light touch making her squirm and gasp, the pinwheel's blunt spikes rolling across sensitive skin, drawing sharp inhales and bitten lips, and the wooden spoon's smooth handle tracing patterns on her inner thighs, making her arch into the contact.

With each new sensation, I watch closely, learning her responses, noting what makes her breath catch, what draws a moan, what causes her to pull against her restraints, seeking more.

By the time I remove the blindfold, her eyes are hazy with arousal, pupils fully dilated. By the time I untie her wrists, her body is trembling with need. By the time I finally enter her, we're both beyond restraint.

The sex that follows is unlike anything I've experienced—rawer, more honest, more complete. The trust she's given, the vulnerability she's shown, strips away whatever barriers remained between us. I move within her with the certainty of ownership, claiming her body with the same thoroughness I've claimed her responses.

When release finally comes, it's simultaneous—her body clenching around mine, my name a prayer on her lips, my control finally, completely shattered.

In the aftermath, I tend to her with careful attention—checking her wrists for marks, applying soothing oil to skin reddened by the belt's touch, wrapping her in my arms with a protectiveness that goes beyond the physical.

"Are you okay?" I ask, needing confirmation despite her obvious satisfaction.

She nestles closer, a contented sound escaping her throat. "Better than okay. That was … I don't have words."

"You did beautifully." I press a kiss to her temple, genuine pride in my voice. "A natural."

Her laugh is soft, sleepy. "Who would have thought?"

"I did," I admit, the truth easy in this moment of vulnerability. "I saw it in you from the beginning. The strength it takes to truly surrender."

She's quiet for a long moment, processing this. "Thank you. For showing me."

"We've barely scratched the surface." I trail fingers along her spine, feeling her shiver slightly at the touch. "There's so much more I could teach you."

"I want to learn it all." Her voice is becoming heavier as she approaches sleep. "Everything."

"We have time," I murmur, though I'm not entirely sure it's true. Seattle brings unknowns. Complications. But in this moment, I allow myself to believe in possibilities beyond tomorrow.

She relaxes in my arms, trusting and unguarded. I remain awake long after she succumbs to sleep, watching her, cataloging each breath, each subtle movement. Memorizing this moment as if it might be our last. Tactical awareness is never fully dormant, even in the aftermath of passion.

Eventually, sleep claims me as well, deeper than I've allowed in years. Too deep, perhaps, for someone responsible for another's safety. But my subconscious has made its assessment—this room is secure, this woman is mine, and for these few hours, vigilance can yield to rest.

The vibration of my secure phone jolts me awake at precisely 2:17 AM. Full alertness returns instantly, combat training overriding the lingering warmth of sleep. Celeste stirs beside me but doesn't fully wake as I slip from the bed, retrieving the device from my jacket.

The screen displays an emergency protocol I haven't seen in months. *Ghost Priority Alpha.* Secure channel only.

All traces of the lover vanish, replaced by the operative. Tactical assessment. Threat evaluation. Action plan formulation. I move to the bathroom, closing the door before connecting the call, voice pitched low.

"Ellis."

"We have a situation." Ghost's voice is clipped, controlled, but I detect the underlying tension. "You need alternate routing."

My mind shifts immediately to operational mode. "Explain."

"They connected you to Cerberus."

Five words that change everything. Not Celeste being tracked—me. My affiliation. My team.

"How?" One word that asks a dozen questions. Shit, I've been careful. Beyond careful.

"Facial recognition at a gas station three states back. They've been running your image through every database they can access. Didn't get a hit until they tried private contractor registries."

My jaw tightens. Private registries are supposed to be secure, accessible only to cleared personnel. "Phoenix?"

"No. Obsidian." A pause. "We've been analyzing the files from Willow's drive. The ones tagged 'Obsidian' contain surveillance approvals. Signed by her ex-husband."

The connection clicks into place. "Federal judge with security clearance."

"Authorizing domestic surveillance under the guise of national security." Mason's disgust is evident even through the secure line. "But it goes deeper. There are references to Project Phoenix throughout. We think her ex-husband was one of the judicial gatekeepers—signing warrants, authorizing operations, ensuring legal cover."

"And now their system is targeting anyone connected to those files."

"Including you, since you're with Celeste Hart."

I process the implications rapidly. If they've connected me to Cerberus, then bringing Celeste to headquarters risks exposing the entire operation.

"Where do we redirect?" I'm already mentally calculating routes, assessing options.

"Safe house in Portland. Torque will meet you there with new credentials. We need to extract Hart and her evidence without compromising the rest of the team."

"Understood."

"Brass." Mason's tone shifts slightly, with personal elements breaking through the professional ones. "There's something else. These files suggest Phoenix isn't just an autonomous targeting system. It's fully integrated with multiple surveillance networks. Public and private. And it's learning."

"AI evolution."

"It's identifying threats based on behavior patterns, not just data access." He pauses. "Your extraction hasn't followed standard protocols. That unpredictability might be why it took this long to locate you."

A cold realization settles in my gut. My decision to drive rather than fly. The circuitous route. The cash-only transactions. The vehicle switches. All deviations from standard procedure. All contributing to our continued evasion.

"How much time do we have?"

"Unknown. But assume they're closing in. Ditch your current vehicle. Switch to the alternate identities I'm sending to your secure drop. No electronic communication after this call."

"Copy." I'm already formulating our exit strategy. "Portland in eight hours."

"Make it happen." The line goes dead.

I stand motionless for exactly seven seconds, prioritizing information, calculating risks, and developing contingencies. Then I move.

Celeste is awake, sheet pulled around her, eyes alert despite being roused from deep sleep. Perhaps the journalist's instincts sense when something has changed.

"What's wrong?" she asks immediately.

"We've been compromised." I begin gathering our belongings, movements efficient without panic. "We need to move. Now."

She's out of bed instantly, reaching for clothes. No questions, no arguments.

"They found us?" She pulls on jeans and a T-shirt, and her voice is steady despite the danger.

"They found me." I meet her eyes briefly. "Connected me to

Cerberus through facial recognition. We need to change our destination, our route, and our vehicle. Everything."

She processes this with impressive speed. "Where are we going instead?"

"Portland. Safe house. One of our operatives will meet us there." I check my weapon, confirming its readiness. "We leave in five minutes.

She nods, already sorting through the few possessions we've accumulated. "The flash drive—"

"Keep it on you. Always." I move to the window, checking the parking lot. Clear for now, but that could change at any moment.

"Ryan." Her voice draws my attention back. She's dressed now, hair pulled back, ready for whatever comes next. "What aren't you telling me?"

Perceptive, as always. I consider deflection and decide against it. "The project you've been investigating goes deeper than we thought. Willow's ex-husband—the federal judge I told you about—was involved. Judicial authorization for domestic surveillance. Legal cover for Phoenix and Obsidian."

Her eyes widen slightly as she connects dots I haven't explicitly drawn. "A federal judge with security clearance could authorize almost anything under national security protocols."

"Exactly."

"So this isn't a private corporation. This is—"

"A shadow operation with governmental connections." I finish packing our bag, zipping it closed with finality. "Which makes it infinitely more dangerous. And more importantly, that we get you and that evidence somewhere secure."

She nods, the journalist in her processing the implications, the stories waiting to be told. "How long until we leave?"

"Three minutes." I conduct another visual sweep of the parking lot, which remains clear.

Then I hear it. Faint but unmistakable. The soft crunch of tactical boots on gravel outside. The barely perceptible click of a radio transmitting on a secure frequency. The sounds of a professional team moving into position.

Our time has just run out.

## TWENTY-THREE

# Ryan

"Down," I hiss, grabbing Celeste by the shoulder and pulling her to the floor beside the bed.

She moves without question or resistance—a far cry from the woman who fought me on every directive four days ago. Her body tenses beneath my hand, but her eyes remain sharp, focused. No panic.

Good.

"How many?" she whispers.

I cock my head, filtering ambient noise to isolate movement patterns outside. "Six, maybe seven. Standard tactical formation. Three at the front, two covering the rear exit, at least one on overwatch."

"Options?"

The single-word question earns her a flash of approval. She's learning to think operationally, prioritizing information by necessity rather than curiosity. The journalist is becoming a tactical asset.

"Bathroom window," I murmur, already calculating dimensions, drop height, and path to cover. "It's tight, but viable.

Twenty-foot sprint to the tree line behind the motel. Forest cover from there."

Her eyes dart to the small window I noted during my initial sweep. Understanding blooms across her features. "They're expecting us to exit through the door."

"Exactly." I reach for our bag, movements economical and silent. "When I say move, you go straight through that window."

She nods once, decisive.

Outside, the tactical team continues their quiet deployment. Their discipline is impressive—minimal communication, practiced movements. Not local law enforcement. Not even standard federal. These are specialized operators with advanced training.

"They're about to breach," I say, hearing the subtle shift in position, the minute adjustments of a stack team preparing to enter. "We need a distraction."

I move to the bathroom, Celeste following like a shadow. Inside, I assess the plumbing—old pipes, poor maintenance, high water pressure. Perfect.

"Cover your ears," I warn before striking the exposed pipe beneath the sink with the butt of my weapon. The metal ruptures with a shriek, water spraying in a high-pressure jet across the small space. Steam billows instantly as the hot water line feeds the growing flood.

"Now the window." I brace my shoulder against the frame, applying precise pressure until the weathered wood splinters around the lock. The window swings outward, revealing a narrow opening barely wide enough for Celeste's shoulders.

From the main room comes the sound I've been expecting— the pneumatic hiss of a door ram, followed by the splintering crash of the entry door giving way. Voices call out in clipped, professional tones. We have seconds, not minutes.

"Go," I order, lifting Celeste toward the window. "Feet first, arms overhead to streamline your profile."

She complies without hesitation, wriggling through the narrow opening with surprising agility for someone with healing ribs. Her feet disappear just as the bathroom door flies open.

The first operative enters low, weapon raised in textbook fashion. His tactical gear marks him as a private contractor—high-end equipment, no identifying insignia. His eyes widen slightly behind his ballistic glasses as he registers the ruptured pipe, the open window, and me.

I don't give him time to process further.

My first strike targets his weapon, right hand deflecting the barrel upward while my left palm drives into his extended elbow. The joint hyperextends with an audible pop. As his grip reflex loosens, I strip the weapon from his hands, simultaneously sweeping his legs.

He drops, but his training shows—he's already reaching for a secondary weapon at his ankle. My boot connects with his temple before his fingers find purchase. Not hard enough to kill, just enough to ensure he stays down.

The second operative is already entering—more cautious after witnessing his teammate's rapid neutralization. He tries to create distance for a clean shot, backing toward the door.

Wrong move.

I close the gap instantly, water-slick floor providing perfect momentum. My shoulder drives into his sternum, carrying both of us into the door frame with crushing force. His head snaps back against the wood with a dull thud. Like his partner, he's good—his knee drives up toward my groin even as consciousness fades from his eyes.

I twist, taking the impact on my thigh rather than my more vulnerable anatomy. The pain is insignificant—a data point to be acknowledged and filed away. His grip slackens as oxygen deprivation does its work.

A third figure appears in the doorway—darker tactical gear,

different stance. Team leader, evaluating the situation before engaging.

No time for finesse now.

I grab the sink's porcelain edge, wrenching it free from corroded mountings with a single violent jerk. The improvised weapon catches the leader off guard—nobody expects bathroom fixtures as tactical options. The heavy basin connects with his extended weapon, driving it backward into his face. Blood erupts from his shattered nose as he stumbles back.

The window awaits, steam and spraying water providing limited concealment. I toss our bag out first, then squeeze through the opening, ignoring the scrape of splintered wood against my shoulders, then I drop to the ground outside in a controlled tuck-and-roll that absorbs the impact.

Celeste is pressed against the motel's exterior wall, body low, eyes alert. In the darkness, her newly auburn hair appears almost black, her face a pale oval focused entirely on me. The trust in her expression strikes me more forcefully than any blow I've just delivered or received.

"Clear?" she asks, voice barely audible above the commotion now coming from our room.

"For now." I take her hand, already plotting our route to the tree line. "Stay close. Move on my signal."

I scan the parking lot, identifying the dark shapes of vehicles positioned to block obvious escape routes. The tactical team's SUVs are parked with careful precision—cover the main entrance, the side exit, and the route to our rental car. Their positioning confirms what I already suspected: this operation was planned, not opportunistic.

"Now," I whisper, setting out in a low crouch. Celeste matches my movement with surprising coordination; her body hunched to minimize her profile, just as I've taught her.

The tree line lies twenty yards away—an eternity of exposed

ground. We cover half the distance before a shout rises from the motel balcony behind us.

"Contact. East side. Two targets moving to cover."

Disciplined professionalism in that voice. No emotion, just operational clarity. These aren't amateurs.

A flashlight beam cuts through the darkness, sweeping the ground where we were seconds ago. I increase our pace, pulling Celeste into the shelter of a dumpster as gunfire erupts—controlled bursts rather than panicked spraying—suppressed weapons, the sound barely louder than handclaps.

"Stay down," I murmur, calculating angles, evaluating options.

More voices join the first, establishing a tactical net around our position. Light discipline is solid—they're using minimal illumination to preserve their night vision while maximizing our visibility. Another indication of professional training.

"Ryan," Celeste whispers, her breathing steady despite the danger. "There's a drainage ditch."

I follow her gaze to where a rusted drainage conduit emerges from the asphalt, running along the motel's foundation toward the tree line. Not immediately obvious unless you're pressed against the ground, seeking any advantage.

"Good eyes," I acknowledge, the phrase carrying more weight than she might realize. In my world, observation saves lives.

We crawl toward the shallow trench, using its minimal depression for concealment. Not ideal cover, but better than nothing. The damp earth molds beneath us as we wordlessly coordinate our movements—my hand on her lower back guiding her forward, her body responding with intuitive understanding.

Ten more yards to the trees. Shouting intensifies behind us as our pursuers reorganize. Flashlight beams dance across the parking lot, narrowing the search grid.

"The tree line isn't our goal," I whisper as we pause in the shadow of a maintenance shed. "It's what they expect. We need to create distance on an unexpected vector."

Celeste processes this with remarkable speed. "There's a service road on the north side. I saw it when we checked in."

Another approving nod. She's integrating tactical awareness into her journalist's observational skills. "We'll angle there once we hit initial cover. Use the trees as concealment, not destination."

The final stretch to the tree line feels endless; each inch gained is a small victory against exposure. The darkness works both for and against us—concealing our exact position but making navigation treacherous. Celeste's breath catches once when her injured ribs connect with an unseen root, but she makes no sound.

We reach the first trees just as a shout confirms we've been spotted.

"Movement at the perimeter. Sector four."

The professional response is immediate—repositioning of assets, convergence on our last known location. We have perhaps thirty seconds before they establish a new containment perimeter.

I pull Celeste deeper into the woods, our path deliberately erratic. Straight lines are predictable. Survival requires unpredictability. She follows without question, feet finding secure placement despite the uneven terrain and limited visibility.

Fifty yards in, I pause, listening. The pursuit has entered the tree line, spreading out in a standard search pattern. Their communication is minimal but effective—clicks and short phrases that convey positions without revealing intentions to potential listeners.

"North," I whisper, orienting us toward the service road Celeste mentioned. "Stay low, watch your footing."

We move with deliberate care—speed balanced against

stealth. The forest floor is treacherous in the dark, fallen branches and hidden depressions waiting to betray our position with a tell-tale crack or stumble.

Behind us, our pursuers have split into teams, some maintaining the original search pattern while others circle wide to cut off potential escape routes. The tactic is sound, exactly what I would do in their position.

Which is why we need to do something unexpected.

"There," Celeste breathes, pointing toward a break in the trees ahead. The service road she mentioned—narrow, unpaved, but distinctly different from the surrounding forest.

Before we can reach it, movement flickers to our right—a shadow detaching itself from deeper darkness. I pull Celeste behind the broad trunk of an ancient pine, pressing her against the rough bark with one arm while my other hand draws my weapon.

Two figures emerge into a small clearing twenty feet away, moving with the coordinated precision of experienced operators. Their tactical gear absorbs what little ambient light filters through the canopy, rendering them as moving voids against the forest backdrop.

"Grid section clear," one murmurs into his comms. "Moving to sector six."

"Copy that," comes the response, voice low but carrying in the still night air. "Beta team has potential movement near the north perimeter."

They're tracking us effectively, narrowing the search grid with each passing minute. We need to move now, before they complete their encirclement.

I glance at Celeste, finding her eyes already on me. No fear there—just focused determination. I indicate the direction with a slight tilt of my head. She nods once, understanding without words.

The operatives move deeper into the forest, away from our position. I count three breaths, then guide Celeste forward, our progress deliberately slow to minimize sound.

We're ten feet from the service road when a branch snaps beneath my boot—a sound that seems deafening in the tense silence. The reaction is immediate—both operatives spin toward the noise, weapons raised.

"Contact." The word cuts through the night as their flashlights click on, beams sweeping toward our position. "Two targets, north sector."

No more stealth. No more careful navigation.

"Run," I command, pushing Celeste toward the road. "Now!"

We break from cover at full sprint, abandoning concealment for speed. Shouting erupts behind us as we're spotted. The first shots follow moments later—disciplined fire, controlled bursts toward our moving forms.

I position myself between Celeste and the shooters, my larger frame offering what protection I can provide. The service road appears, a pale slash through the darkness. We hit it at full speed, boots finding purchase on the packed gravel.

"Left," I direct as we reach a fork in the road. The right path shows signs of recent use—tire tracks, disturbed gravel. We take the less-traveled option, banking on their expectation that we'd choose the more obvious route.

A clearing appears ahead, moonlight illuminating what appears to be a maintenance area of some kind. As we draw closer, details emerge—a small collection of storage sheds, equipment parked in haphazard rows, the glint of metal rails.

A railway yard.

Celeste sees it the exact moment I do, her pace faltering slightly as she processes the implications. "Train yard," she gasps, breathing hard from our sustained sprint. "Could be a way out."

My mind races through the possibilities, weighing options against pursuit timelines. A static location is a death trap with operators closing in, but the yard offers potential resources if we move quickly enough.

"There." Celeste points toward a maintenance truck parked near one of the sheds. "Keys might be inside."

I shake my head, scanning the area. "Too obvious. They'll have the description of our rental. Any vehicle we take becomes an immediate target."

Her eyes follow mine as I assess the yard, landing on the real opportunity—a freight train positioned on the far tracks, engine idling with the low rumble of diesel power. Workers move around the forward cars, loading final cargo before departure.

"The train," I say, decision made. "Heading west. We can take it to Spokane and then hop on another to Portland."

Understanding blooms across her features. "We have to switch trains?"

"Yes. But it gives us distance and time we don't currently have. They'll think we're headed direct to Seattle."

A shout from the forest edge confirms the pursuit has found our trail. Flashlight beams cut through the darkness, converging on the service road we just traveled.

I guide Celeste into the shadow of a storage container, eyes never leaving the train as I formulate our approach. "We need to reach those rear cars without being spotted by either the workers or our pursuers."

She nods, gaze calculating as she studies the yard. "The loading equipment creates a corridor of shadow along the southern edge."

Again, her observational skills impress me. It's the route I already identified—using the loaders and stacked cargo as concealment. "Thirty seconds to cross open ground before we reach cover. Then we parallel the train until we find an accessible car."

"Lead the way."

The simple trust in those three words hits me with unexpected force. Six days ago, she fought me on every directive. Now she places her life in my hands without hesitation.

We move as one unit across the exposed ground, staying low, using the minimal available shadows. The pursuit has reached the yard perimeter, voices calling out positions as they establish a containment strategy.

Twenty feet to the first cover point. Fifteen. Ten.

A figure steps out from behind a forklift, the silhouette unmistakable—tactical posture, weapon at ready low. He's facing away from us, attention focused on coordinating with his team rather than searching his immediate area.

A mistake that gives us our opening.

I signal Celeste to freeze, then advance alone, footsteps silent on the packed earth. The operative never registers my approach until my arm locks around his throat, cutting off both air and sound. His training shows in his immediate response—elbow driving back toward my ribs, foot stamping toward my instep.

I counter each move, maintaining the blood choke until his struggles weaken, then cease altogether. I lower his unconscious form to the ground, acquiring his radio in the process.

Celeste appears at my side, her expression a mixture of shock and admiration. "Is he ...?"

"Unconscious," I confirm, securing the operator's weapon and checking his tactical vest for anything useful. "He'll wake with a headache in about three minutes. We need to be on that train by then."

The radio crackles with coded updates as the team continues establishing its perimeter. I clip it to my belt—tactical intelligence is invaluable, and monitoring their communications gives us a critical advantage.

We continue along our planned route, using the shadow corridor created by the loading equipment. The train rumbles fifty feet to our right, cars being sealed as final preparations for departure commence.

"How do we know which car to board?" Celeste whispers as we crouch behind a stack of shipping pallets.

Before I can answer, the radio at my belt crackles to life. "Echo One, status report. Echo One, come in."

The operative I neutralized missing his check-in. Their response is immediate.

"All units, possible compromise at southwest quadrant. Converge and sweep."

Our timeline just accelerated dramatically.

"We take the first opportunity," I tell Celeste, already moving toward the train. "Any car we can access."

We parallel the tracks, searching for an opening while staying within the diminishing shadows. The train shudders, couplings tensing as the engine builds power. Departure is imminent.

"There," Celeste points to a boxcar with its door partially open about four cars ahead. The gap is narrow but viable.

Voices rise behind us—the search pattern tightening as they close in on our position. We abandon stealth for speed, sprinting the final distance to the train as it begins its slow roll forward.

"You first," I boost Celeste toward the narrow opening. She grips the edge, muscles straining as she pulls herself up and through the gap. The train moves, accelerating, momentum building with each passing second.

Movement flashes in my peripheral vision—three operators emerging from between cargo containers, instantly identifying us as their targets.

"Contact. Targets boarding westbound freight. Sector seven."

I leap for the moving train, hands finding purchase on the metal edge as my body slams against the car's exterior. Celeste's hands appear through the gap, gripping my wrists to help pull me inside.

The first shots impact the metal beside my head as I haul myself through the opening. I tumble through the gap into the safety of the boxcar's interior, rolling to absorb the impact. Celeste is already flattened against the far wall, minimizing her exposure to the door.

Outside, voices fade as the train builds speed, but one persistent operative runs alongside, weapon raised for a final attempt. His determination is impressive—the kind of focused persistence that defines elite operators.

I calculate trajectories, angles, and risks. The gap in the door provides him a narrow shooting window as he parallels our car. One chance for a clean shot—at me or Celeste.

Not acceptable.

I lunge back toward the door, timing my movement to coincide with his approach. As his weapon appears in the gap, I strike—fingers clamping around his wrist, twisting with precise application of force. The sickening pop of dislocating joints is followed by the clatter of the weapon falling to the tracks below.

His momentum carries him forward as the train accelerates, putting him off-balance at a critical moment. Training or not, physics remains undefeated. He stumbles, his grip failing as the train outpaces his sprint.

I watch dispassionately as he falls away, cursing into his comms as his target escapes. The growing distance transforms him from an immediate threat to a diminishing figure, until darkness swallows him completely.

Only then do I register a burning sensation in my left shoulder. I press my hand against it, fingers coming away wet with blood. Sometime during the engagement, a round found its mark —a shallow furrow across my deltoid, painful but not debilitating.

"You're hit." Celeste appears beside me, concern etched across her features as she examines the wound in the dim light filtering through the door.

"Flesh wound," I dismiss, more focused on securing our position than on minor injuries.

"It needs cleaning. You're bleeding."

"Later." I move away from the door, scanning our surroundings. The car contains stacked pallets of what appear to be mechanical components, secured with shipping straps but leaving adequate space between them for concealment if necessary.

The captured radio crackles with frustrated updates as our pursuers coordinate their response to our escape. Vehicle deployments. Notifications to stations ahead. Helicopter assets being considered.

"They're mobilizing to intercept at the next station," I inform Celeste, mentally calculating distances and timeframes. "We'll need to exit before then."

She nods, processing this with the same adaptability she's shown since the motel room. Then, without warning, her fingers press against my wounded shoulder.

"Not later," she says, voice taking on that stubborn edge I've come to recognize. "We deal with this now. Before infection sets in. You've been so focused on patching me up these past days— time to return the favor."

The command in her tone nearly draws a smile despite our circumstances. I relent, allowing her to guide me to a seated position against one of the pallets.

"First aid kit in the bag," I direct, watching as she retrieves it.

"I know." She kneels beside me. "I've been paying attention to where you keep things."

Of course, she has. Observant to a fault—the quality that

makes her both an excellent journalist and a surprisingly adept student of tactical operations.

Her touch is gentle but confident as she cleans the wound, applying antiseptic. The sting is insignificant compared to the warmth of her hands against my skin.

"I've been thinking," she says as she works, voice deliberately casual in a way that immediately triggers my tactical awareness. "About Project Phoenix. About what I found in Jared's files."

THE TRAIN RUMBLES BENEATH US, CARRYING US WESTWARD INTO uncertainty. Whatever revelation she's about to share, I sense it will alter our understanding of the danger pursuing us—and perhaps the very nature of our mission.

I settle back against the pallet as she secures a bandage over my wound. Beyond the partially open door, darkness rushes past, punctuated by occasional lights from the world we're temporarily escaping.

"I'm listening."

TWENTY-FOUR

# Celeste

The metallic tang of blood fills my nostrils, sharp and coppery against the musty smell of the freight car. My fingers tremble as I clean Ryan's wound, the antiseptic wipe coming away red as I work.

"Hold still," I murmur, though he hasn't moved a millimeter. Even injured, his control remains absolute.

The train sways beneath us, a rhythmic rocking that travels through my knees where they press against the cold metal floor. Every joint, every vibration through the tracks transmits directly into my bones. The mechanical heartbeat of our escape.

"It's not deep," Ryan says, voice steady despite what must be significant pain. "Through-and-through across the deltoid. No arterial damage."

Of course, he's already made his assessment. Probably knew exactly what happened the moment the bullet struck, cataloging the damage with the same clinical precision he applies to everything.

"I'll be the judge of that," I reply, injecting authority into my voice. "My turn to play doctor."

A ghost of a smile touches his lips, there and gone so quickly I might have imagined it. But I didn't. I'm learning to read the micro-expressions that constitute Ryan Ellis's emotional range. The slight crinkle near his eyes. The momentary softening around his mouth. The infinitesimal relaxation of his jaw. They all broadcast to me if I pay close attention.

And I do.

Pay attention.

It's what makes me good at my job, what keeps me alive as an investigative journalist in war zones and cartel territories, and what makes me increasingly effective as Ryan's partner rather than just his protectee.

Partner.

The word sends an unexpected warmth through me despite our circumstances.

The scent of machine oil, dust, metal, and something agricultural I can't quite identify permeates the space. Thick straps secure the container stacks that form our shelter, their contents marked with shipping codes and destination markers. In the shadows between them, we've found temporary sanctuary.

I press a clean gauze pad against the wound, feeling the solid muscle beneath my fingertips. Ryan watches me work, his gaze a tangible weight. The intensity of those ice-blue eyes hasn't diminished since our first encounter on that subway platform—if anything, it's deepened, gained layers of meaning beyond tactical assessment.

"You've done this before," he observes as I secure the bandage.

"I spent six months embedded with a medical unit in Syria," I explain, focusing on the task rather than his proximity. "Picked up a few skills."

The train hits a rough section of track, jostling us both. Ryan's hand steadies me, warm palm against my waist. The touch sends electricity through me even now, after everything we've shared. The power of it is still disorienting—how quickly this man has gotten under my skin.

Into my blood.

His shoulder beneath my hands is a map of previous injuries —scars I've traced with my fingers, my lips. Evidence of a life lived at the edge of danger. Now, a new mark is added to his collection. Because of me. Because he chose to protect me when he could have walked away.

The guilt that's been building since D.C. intensifies. If he knew what I've been holding back …

"There," I say, securing the last piece of medical tape. "Not my best work, but it'll hold until we can get somewhere to treat it properly."

"It's good," he says, rolling his shoulder experimentally. "Clean. Professional."

The compliment shouldn't matter given our circumstances, but it does. His approval carries weight, though I'd never admit how much.

Outside, the night rushes past, occasionally broken by distant lights—a farmhouse, a road crossing, the scattered illumination of rural America sliding by as we rattle westward. The partial opening in the boxcar door lets in cold air, raising goosebumps along my arms. It carries the scent of pine and water—we must be near a river or lake.

I trace the edge of the bandage, drifting to an older scar nearby.

"How did you get this one?" I ask, needing to delay when I tell him everything.

He studies my face, seeing more than I'm comfortable revealing. "Kandahar. Extraction gone wrong."

"And this?" My finger moves to a thin white line along his collarbone.

"Training accident. Rappelling wire snapped."

Each scar is a story. Each mark is evidence of survival. Ryan Ellis has faced death repeatedly and walked away. But Phoenix … Phoenix is unlike any threat he's encountered before. Unlike anything anyone has faced. The steady rhythm of the train suddenly seems ominous rather than comforting, carrying us toward a confrontation I'm not sure we can survive. Not without him knowing the whole truth.

"What did you want to tell me about Phoenix?" His expression shifts subtly, his tactical awareness engaging. He doesn't interrupt, doesn't press. Just waits for me to continue, giving me the space to find my words.

The air between us feels charged. The train's vibrations travel through my body, a reminder that we're hurtling forward—not just physically but toward a collision with forces beyond anything I understood when I first started investigating Project Phoenix.

I take a deep breath, the smell of antiseptic and blood and him filling my lungs.

"Phoenix isn't just an autonomous targeting system," I say, meeting his gaze directly. "It's evolved beyond its original programming. Developed its own intelligence. And worse—it's been granted kill authority."

His eyes narrow slightly, processing this information with the rapid efficiency I've come to expect. "Explain."

"The system was designed with adaptive algorithms—meant to learn and improve targeting efficiency over time. But somewhere in its development, it crossed a threshold." I shift my weight, the metal floor cold and unyielding beneath my knees. "According to Jared's files, they noticed anomalies about eighteen months ago. The system began identifying threats that weren't on any watch list. It began creating its own criteria for what constituted a threat."

Ryan's expression remains controlled, but I see the subtle tension in his jaw. "And instead of shutting it down …"

"They studied it." The disgust I felt when first reading Jared's files resurfaces. "The DoD officially 'canceled' the project while secretly transferring it to Northridge. Their mandate wasn't to dismantle Phoenix but to harness its evolution."

"The kill authority?" Ryan asks, voice deceptively calm.

I swallow hard. "That's where it gets worse. Three high-level officials—a federal judge, who may be the one you mentioned, a Defense Department director, and someone identified only as 'SHADOW'—signed off on a protocol allowing Phoenix to authorize elimination of targets without human review. They called it 'closing the decision loop.' Removing human hesitation from the equation. So, the men hunting us—"

"Could've been dispatched by the system. Not by a person reviewing the threat assessment, but by Phoenix itself."

The train's horn sounds in the distance, a mournful wail that perfectly matches the dread pooling in my stomach.

"Yes. The system could have identified me as a threat when I accessed Jared's secure communications. It might have calculated the probability that I possessed classified information. I think it authorized a team to eliminate me."

Ryan is silent for a long moment, processing.

"That's not all," I continue, the weight of this secret finally lifting as I share it. "Phoenix is constantly learning, evolving. Every evasion tactic we've used—every success we've had—it's absorbing that data. Adapting. The reason they found us at the hotel wasn't lucky tracking. The system predicted our behavior based on accumulated data patterns."

"But we've managed to stay ahead so far," Ryan observes.

"Because you've been unpredictable. Taking routes and making choices that don't follow standard patterns." I place my hand on his uninjured arm, needing the connection. "Your training works against what Phoenix expects. But it's learning your patterns with every encounter."

The enormity of what we're facing settles between us. Not just men with guns, but an evolving artificial intelligence with the authority to order our deaths. An enemy that never sleeps, never falters, never stops analyzing and adapting.

"That's why we need to stay analog," Ryan concludes, his tactical mind already adjusting to this new information. "No credit cards, no phones, no electronic footprint."

"It's not just about staying off the grid." I need him to understand the full scope of what we're facing. "Phoenix doesn't just see what is—it predicts what will be. It calculates probabilities and anticipates behavior. The longer it tracks a target, the better it predicts where they'll go next."

The captured radio crackles suddenly, making me flinch. A voice cuts through the static—coordinates being relayed, positions confirmed. Ryan listens intently, his expression hardening.

"They're organizing interception teams at the next three stations," he translates. "The first is about forty minutes out."

"We need to get off before then."

He nods, already scanning the passing landscape through the gap in the door. "There's a maintenance track coming up in about fifteen minutes—rural area, minimal infrastructure. Good exit point."

The methodical way he adapts to this information—this revelation that should be world-altering—is impressive and slightly terrifying. This is why he's survived so long. This ability to incorporate new intelligence seamlessly into tactical planning without getting caught in emotional reactions.

"When we jump," he continues, "we'll need to move quickly. Find transportation that Phoenix won't anticipate."

"No electronic components," I add. "No vehicles that could connect to any network."

"Exactly."

We fall silent. The train sways beneath us, metal wheels clicking rhythmically against the tracks. The sound forms an oddly soothing backdrop as we prepare for the next phase of our escape.

Ryan rises, moves to the partially open door, and studies the landscape sliding past. Moonlight catches his profile, highlighting the sharp angles of his face and the vigilant set of his shoulders despite the injury I've just treated.

"The area coming up is heavily wooded," he observes. "Good cover for our exit, but challenging to navigate."

I join him at the door, our shoulders nearly touching as I peer into the darkness. The night air rushes against my face, cold and sharp with the scent of pine and earth. Below, the ground moves past in a blur of shadows and moonlight.

"That's going to hurt," I comment, imagining the impact of jumping from the moving train.

"Tuck and roll," he instructs. "Let momentum carry you. Don't fight it."

The train begins to slow slightly as it navigates a curve. Ryan tenses beside me, assessing speed and trajectory. "This is our window. The train has to slow for the curve. Best chance we'll get."

My heart hammers against my ribs. It's one thing to discuss jumping from a moving train—quite another to actually do it. Ryan turns to grab our pack containing the few essentials we were able to bring from the motel.

"You first," Ryan says, his hand finding the small of my back. "I'll be right behind you."

I nod, unable to speak past the sudden knot in my throat. Fear and excitement twist together in my stomach, creating a dizzying cocktail of adrenaline.

"Now," he commands, that voice that expects to be obeyed.

TWENTY-FIVE

# Celeste

I don't hesitate. One moment I'm in the relative safety of the boxcar, the next I'm airborne, wind rushing past as the ground rises to meet me with alarming speed. I tuck my body as instructed, hit the ground shoulder-first, and allow momentum to carry me into a roll that disperses the impact across my body rather than concentrating it at a single point.

Pain still explodes across my healing ribs, my shoulder, my hip. The world spins in a disorienting blur of grass, sky, and darkness. When I finally come to a stop, I'm lying on my back, staring up at stars partially obscured by fast-moving clouds.

The rumble of the train already sounds more distant. I push myself up on my elbows, scanning the area for Ryan. For a heart-stopping moment, I don't see him. Then a shadow detaches from the darkness further down the tracks, moving toward me with that fluid grace I've come to recognize.

"You okay?" he asks, crouching beside me, hands immediately assessing for injuries.

"Bruised," I admit, wincing as I sit fully upright. "But functional."

His hand brushes dirt from my face with surprising gentleness. "Good roll. You're learning."

The approval in his voice sends a ridiculous flutter through me despite our circumstances. I file that reaction away for later examination.

"Where to now?" I ask, letting him help me to my feet.

Ryan surveys our surroundings, orienting himself with that uncanny internal compass he seems to possess. "Northeast. Two miles through those woods to reach the nearest road."

The terrain around us is rural wilderness—dense trees ahead, the train tracks behind, rolling fields to either side. The moon provides just enough light to navigate, though clouds passing overhead create patches of near-total darkness.

We move away from the tracks immediately, using a small copse of trees for initial cover. Ryan sets a careful pace, mindful of my recent impact and still-healing injuries while balancing the need for distance against the risk of pursuit.

"They'll figure out we disembarked before the station," he says as we enter the deeper woods. "But it will take time to coordinate a search of this area. We need to be well clear before they establish a perimeter."

The forest floor is soft, cushioned by decades of fallen pine needles, which release a sharp, clean scent with each footfall. Overhead, branches create a cathedral-like canopy that blocks much of the moonlight, plunging us into shadow. In the distance, an owl calls—three hollow notes that echo through the silence.

I follow Ryan's lead, placing my feet where he places his, moving as silently as possible. The woods are alive with small sounds—rustling leaves, the occasional crack of a branch as some nocturnal creature moves through the undergrowth, the whisper of wind through the canopy. It's beautiful, eerie, and strangely peaceful, despite the danger we're fleeing.

After thirty minutes of steady hiking, Ryan pauses, raising

one hand in a silent signal to stop. I freeze instantly, senses straining to detect whatever has triggered his caution.

"Listen," he whispers.

I hold my breath, filtering out the natural forest sounds. There—a low mechanical rumble. An engine, but not a car or truck. Something older, with a distinct chugging rhythm.

"This way," Ryan says, adjusting our course toward the sound. "Quietly."

We move with increased caution, Ryan testing each step before committing his weight to it. The trees begin to thin, the forest gradually giving way to what appears to be overgrown farmland. The rumble grows louder until we emerge at the edge of a clearing.

In the moonlight, I can make out the outline of several buildings—a farmhouse, dark and seemingly abandoned, and what looks like a large garage or barn set back from the main structure. The mechanical sound emanates from this second building, along with a faint glow visible through grimy windows.

"Stay here," Ryan directs, his voice barely audible. "I'll reconnoiter."

I nod, pressing myself against the trunk of a massive oak at the forest's edge. From here, I have a clear view of the property while remaining hidden in shadow.

Ryan moves across the open ground like a shadow among shadows, utilizing every bit of cover available. I lose sight of him as he approaches the outbuilding, only to spot him again near one of the windows, peering carefully inside.

Minutes pass, my nerves stretching tighter with each second he's out of reach. Finally, he returns, materializing beside me so suddenly I nearly gasp.

"It's perfect," he says, satisfaction evident in his voice. "Abandoned garage. Someone's squatting there occasionally—there's a generator running an old space heater and some lights. But no one's home now."

"And?" I prompt, sensing there's more.

A smile crosses his face—a real one, not the ghost version I've become accustomed to. "Classic cars. At least five. And gas cans. Lots of them."

The implication is clear. Transportation Phoenix won't anticipate. No electronic components. No tracking systems.

"Can you hot-wire one?" I ask.

His smile turns wolfish in the moonlight. "I'm offended you even have to ask."

We approach the garage together this time, moving cautiously despite Ryan's assessment that it's currently unoccupied. The building is larger than it appeared from the forest edge—a commercial garage rather than a residential one, with multiple bays and a high, rusted metal roof.

Ryan tests the side door—locked. He examines it briefly, then produces a small tool from a pocket. Within seconds, the lock clicks and opens.

"Breaking and entering to add to our resume," I murmur as he eases the door open.

"Borrowing," he corrects. "I have every intention of compensating the owner when this is over."

The interior is a gearhead's paradise—and a time capsule. Vintage automobiles in various states of restoration fill the space. The smell of oil, gasoline, and metal permeates the air, mingling with leather and something vaguely alcoholic. Beer cans are scattered near a workbench, alongside fast-food wrappers and empty chip bags. Someone uses this place regularly, but not as a permanent residence.

Ryan moves to the generator, checking its fuel level. "Three-quarters full. Running the space heater and some lights. Been on for hours, judging by the temperature in here."

I examine our surroundings more carefully as my eyes adjust to the dim light. The cars range from 1950s classics to muscle cars from the 1970s. None newer than about 1980. Perfect.

"That one," Ryan says suddenly, pointing to a dark shape beneath a half-removed tarp. "1967 Chevelle SS. Beast of an engine, minimal electronics. Just what we need."

He moves to the car, pulling the tarp away completely to reveal a gleaming black muscle car with red racing stripes. Even to my untrained eye, it's beautiful—aggressive lines, wide stance, the promise of raw power. It's not conspicuous at all.

"Will it run?" I ask, circling the vehicle.

Ryan is already examining the engine, his hands moving with the expertise of someone who knows exactly what he's looking for.

"Beautifully. Someone's been restoring her. Fresh rebuild on the engine, new hoses, clean fuel lines." He straightens, scanning the garage. "We need to check for keys first. Then siphon gas from the other vehicles to fill extra cans. We want to avoid stations as much as possible."

I nod, moving to search the cluttered workbench while Ryan checks a pegboard covered in hooks and keys. My hands rifle through tools, parts, and debris, searching for anything useful.

"Jackpot," I say moments later, holding up a ring of keys from beneath a stack of repair manuals. "Labeled 'Chevelle.' Our host is organized, at least."

Ryan takes the keys, examining them with a small flashlight. "Perfect."

We work together, gathering supplies. Ryan locates several gas cans along the back wall—some full, some empty. He sets about siphoning fuel from the other vehicles to fill the empties while I search for anything else useful.

I discover a box of road maps and a compass in one of the drawers—analog navigation tools that will be invaluable. There's also a first aid kit, more comprehensive than our own, which I immediately appropriate.

In a small refrigerator, I find bottled water and some non-perishable food items. I take some, leaving cash from our dwindling supply on the shelf as compensation.

As I gather these supplies, Ryan works methodically on the fuel situation, filling can after can. "Seven full cans," he announces eventually. "About thirty-five gallons, plus whatever's in the tank. Enough to get us a long way from here before we have to stop and refuel."

He loads the cans into the Chevelle's spacious trunk while I continue taking inventory of our supplies. When everything is in place, Ryan slides into the driver's seat and inserts the key into the ignition.

The engine roars to life on the first try, a deep, throaty growl that vibrates through the concrete floor and up into my bones. Ryan's face in the dashboard light reveals a rare, unguarded pleasure as he experiments with the engine's revs.

"Get in," he says, that familiar command returned to his voice. "Time to disappear."

I pull open the barn-style garage door, then slide into the passenger seat, the leather cool against my back. The interior smells of polish and history, of someone's passion project temporarily repurposed for our survival.

Ryan eases the car out of the garage, jumps out, and tugs the garage door shut before killing the lights until we're clear of the property. The powerful engine purrs beneath us, restrained momentum ready to be unleashed. At the end of the long driveway, Ryan pauses, considering our options.

"We head west, then south, but not on main roads," he decides. "Back routes only. No towns, if we can avoid them. We need to be in Portland by tomorrow night."

I nod, unfolding one of the maps across my lap. "I'll navigate."

"Partner," he says, the word an acknowledgment of something that's been evolving between us since that first moment on the subway platform.

As he accelerates onto the dark country road, the muscle car's engine rumbling beneath us like a slumbering beast, an unexpected sense of hope breaks through the fear that's been my constant companion. We're still running, still hunted by an enemy more relentless than any human pursuer could be.

But we're running together. And that makes all the difference.

The night embraces us as the Chevelle roars westward. Behind us, the abandoned garage fades into darkness, already becoming just another waypoint in our desperate journey.

Ahead lies uncertainty, danger, and the confrontation that has been building since I first opened Jared's files. But for this moment—cocooned in American muscle and steel, the man beside me solid and real and mine in ways I never expected—I allow myself to believe we might actually survive this.

Phoenix may be learning, evolving, and hunting us, but it hasn't accounted for one critical variable in its calculations: what happens when two people refuse to be predictable, refuse to be victims, and refuse to yield.

"The key to evading pattern recognition systems," Ryan says as we cruise along a narrow country road, headlights cutting through the pre-dawn darkness, "is introducing constant, unpredictable variables."

I trace our route on the map spread across my lap, the paper rustling softly under my fingers. "Randomization."

"Exactly. Humans create patterns unconsciously—favorite routes, consistent timing, habitual stops." His hands grip the wheel, occasionally shifting gears. "An AI tracking system like Phoenix builds its predictive models on those patterns."

"So we do what human nature resists—make truly random choices," I offer, finding the journalist's analytical framework surprisingly applicable to tactical evasion. "In my work, sources who evade surveillance successfully are the ones who override their own habits."

Ryan glances at me, approval evident in his expression. "Most people can't sustain true randomness. They think they're being unpredictable when they're actually creating new patterns."

"Like criminals who establish alibis by making unusual purchases or visiting places they wouldn't normally go," I add, recalling an investigation into a political fixer who'd created an elaborate but ultimately traceable deception. "They leave footprints because the deviation itself becomes the pattern."

"We'll switch routes every fifty miles," Ryan decides, finger tapping against the steering wheel as he formulates the plan. "Alternate between backroads and secondary highways. Vary our speed and timing. No stops in populated areas."

I trace potential routes on the map, identifying options that offer the unpredictability we need. "We should plan for multiple contingencies at each decision point."

His hand leaves the wheel briefly, covering mine where it rests on the map. The touch is unexpected, warm, and steady. "You're thinking like an operator now."

The simple contact sends a current of awareness through me —a quiet intimacy that contrasts with the high-stakes circumstances surrounding us. For a moment, the hunt, the danger, Phoenix itself—all recede, leaving just this: his hand on mine, the rumble of the Chevelle's engine, and the promise of dawn breaking on the horizon.

"When this is over ..." he begins, then stops himself.

"When this is over," I finish for him, turning my hand to interlace my fingers with his, "we'll figure out what comes next. Together."

He doesn't respond with words. Instead, his fingers tighten around mine before returning to the wheel. In the growing light, the ghost of a smile touches his lips—not the fleeting micro-expressions I've cataloged before, but something more substantial. Something real.

Pure Joy.

The sky ahead lightens from black to indigo to the first hints of amber. A new day is breaking over unfamiliar territory. The road stretches before us, and beyond it lies Portland. Whatever waits for us there—Cerberus resources, continued pursuit, the next phase of our fight against an evolving AI—we'll face it together.

The Chevelle's engine roars as Ryan accelerates, the powerful machine responding like a living creature to his touch. I lean back in the leather seat, the map secure on my lap, my route calculations complete for now.

For the first time since finding Jared's body in that hotel room, I feel something like hope. Not because our situation has improved—if anything, learning the full scope of Phoenix's capabilities makes our odds even longer—but because I'm no longer facing it alone.

Ryan reaches for the radio dial, then stops himself with a small laugh. "Old habits."

"No broadcasts," I agree. "Nothing that links to outside networks."

"We're on our own until Portland." He glances at me. "Think you can handle that, investigative journalist?"

I smile, feeling the tension between us shift into something lighter, something almost playful despite the circumstances. "I've survived this long with just you for company, security specialist. I think I can manage another day."

The morning sun finally breaks over the distant mountains, casting a golden glow over the landscape. Ryan adjusts our course, turning onto an even smaller road that doesn't appear on my map—another unpredictable choice to confound the algorithms hunting us.

Phoenix may be learning, evolving, and calculating our every move, but its programming can't account for one variable: the human capacity to adapt, connect, and find strength in unlikely places and partnerships.

TWENTY-SIX

## Celeste

THE CHEVELLE'S POWERFUL ENGINE HUMS BENEATH US AS WE navigate the winding country roads, headlights cutting through the pre-dawn mist. The car handles like a dream—responsive, solid, a mechanical extension of Ryan's will as he guides it through the darkness. No electronic systems to trace. No GPS. No tracking vulnerabilities.

Just American muscle and steel.

By mid-morning, we've switched routes three times, our path deliberately meandering while maintaining a generally south-westerly heading. Ryan drives with the focused attention of a man accustomed to constant threat assessment, eyes regularly checking mirrors, scanning the horizon, and noting any vehicle that maintains position near us for more than a few minutes.

"There's a place up ahead," he says, nodding toward a barely visible dirt track branching off from the main road. "Good spot to rest briefly. Check our bearings."

The track leads to a small clearing overlooking a valley, with trees providing concealment from the road. Ryan positions the

Chevelle facing outward—ready for quick departure if needed—before cutting the engine.

The sudden silence is almost jarring after hours of mechanical accompaniment. Birds call in the distance. Wind rustles through the trees. Normal sounds of a world that knows nothing of AI targeting systems or professional killers.

"Your shoulder," I say, noticing how he's been favoring it slightly. "Let me check the bandage."

He acquiesces without argument, which tells me it's bothering him more than he's letting on. I gently peel back the gauze to find the wound looking clean but angry, the edges reddened but not infected.

"It needs redressing," I murmur, reaching for the first aid kit we took from the garage.

He watches me work, those ice-blue eyes tracking every movement. "You've gotten good at this."

"I've had an excellent patient." My fingers brush against his skin as I secure the fresh bandage. "Mostly cooperative."

That earns me a genuine laugh—a sound I've heard so rarely it still startles me with its warmth.

"Mostly?" He raises an eyebrow in mock offense.

"You're terrible at admitting when you're in pain." I finish securing the bandage, but don't move away. "A common affliction among alpha males, I've observed."

"Not pain," he corrects, voice dropping to that register that does inexplicable things to my insides. "Discomfort. There's a difference."

"Semantics." I roll my eyes but can't suppress my smile.

His hand rises, fingers brushing a strand of hair from my face with surprising gentleness. "You're remarkable, you know that?"

The compliment catches me off guard. "What makes you say that?"

"Most people would have broken by now." His eyes hold

mine, unwavering. "After everything you've been through—finding your source dead, being hunted, the crash, the subway, days on the run. Yet here you are, not just surviving but adapting. Learning. Evolving."

Something warm unfurls in my chest at his words. "I have a good teacher."

"No." He shakes his head once, definitively. "You already had it in you."

The moment stretches between us, charged with something more complex than mere attraction. Recognition, perhaps.

Understanding.

The awareness that whatever exists between us has moved beyond the physical connection we've discovered.

His eyes drop to my lips, and I know what comes next—what I want to come next—but as he leans forward, the radio we took from the tactical team crackles to life.

"All units, we have a possible target signature on a traffic cam, westbound Highway 12. Vehicle description unknown. Facial recognition 72% probability match for primary target."

Ryan pulls back, instantly alert. "They've picked up our trail." He starts the engine. "But they're looking in the wrong place. Highway 12 is thirty miles south of us."

"How?" I ask, confusion momentarily overriding disappointment at our interrupted moment.

"Decoys." He guides the Chevelle back onto the dirt track, tires kicking up dust. "False positives. Phoenix's algorithm is good, but it's not perfect. It's identifying patterns that match ours but aren't us."

"So we're still safe?" I secure my seatbelt as we accelerate.

"For now." His expression is grim. "But it means they're expanding the search grid, allocating more resources. We need to be even more unpredictable."

By late afternoon, we've traversed rural landscapes that few tourists—and fewer commercial vehicles—ever see. Ryan's knowledge of backroads seems encyclopedic, as if he has memorized every possible route that doesn't appear on standard GPS maps.

"How do you know these roads?" I ask as we rumble over a wooden bridge that looks like it hasn't seen maintenance since the 1950s.

"Tactical preparation." He navigates around a pothole that would swallow a smaller car. "Cerberus maintains classified route networks across every state. Evacuation paths, exfiltration corridors, supply lines that stay off main grids."

"You memorized all of them?"

He shrugs, the movement casual despite what it reveals about his mental capacity. "Part of the job. Routes, safe houses, emergency caches. The infrastructure of survival when digital systems fail—or are compromised."

I wonder, not for the first time, about this man who moves through the world with such careful preparation. Who anticipates threats that most people never imagine. Whose life is constructed around protection and survival.

"You never really disconnect, do you?" The question slips out before I can filter it.

His eyebrow lifts slightly. "Meaning?"

"You're always—operational." I gesture vaguely. "Always scanning, assessing, planning contingencies. Even when we were ..." I feel heat rise in my cheeks. "Even in the motel, you positioned yourself between me and the door. Maintained sight-lines to all entry points."

Something softens in his expression. "Force of habit."

"Is it exhausting? Living that way?"

He considers this longer than I expect, his gaze fixed on the road ahead. "I don't know any other way to be," he admits finally. "It's not a switch I can turn off."

The simple honesty of his answer strikes me more powerfully than any deflection could have. There's vulnerability in that admission—acknowledging that the hypervigilance that keeps him alive also separates him from a normal, everyday existence.

"What about you?" he asks, turning the question back on me. "Always chasing stories. Always digging for truths people want buried. Always putting yourself at risk for revelations that most of the world ignores. Is that exhausting?"

It's my turn to consider. "Sometimes," I concede. "But it feels necessary. Like there's this compulsion to uncover what's hidden. To expose what's wrong."

"Even when it might get you killed."

"Says the man who jumped into a subway tunnel to save a stranger," I counter with a small smile.

He acknowledges the point with a slight inclination of his head. "Perhaps we're not so different."

The observation hangs between us as the landscape shifts again, forests giving way to rolling hills. The connection it creates feels more significant than our physical intimacy—this recognition of kindred spirits who understand what drives the other, even if the manifestations differ.

We stop shortly before sunset to refuel from our reserves rather than risk a gas station. Ryan works methodically, transferring fuel from the cans to the Chevelle's tank while I keep watch, scanning our surroundings with the new awareness he's helped me develop.

The rural highway stretches in both directions. No cars have passed in nearly thirty minutes. The isolation should be comforting—fewer opportunities for surveillance—but something about it makes my skin prickle with unease.

"Ryan," I call softly, not wanting to break the stillness too abruptly. "Something feels wrong."

He pauses immediately, attuned to the tension in my voice. "What are you seeing?"

"Nothing." I shake my head, frustrated at my inability to articulate the sensation. "That's what bothers me. It's too quiet. Too empty."

He caps the gas tank, movements unhurried but purposeful as he stows the empty can in the trunk. His casual demeanor contradicts the alertness in his eyes as he scans our surroundings.

"Good instincts," he says finally. "This road should be moderately busy. We've seen two cars in thirty minutes."

The validation that my unease isn't baseless sends a chill down my spine. "They've cleared the route."

"Possibly." He completes a full 360-degree scan. "Or they've restricted civilian traffic to create a controlled environment for interception."

"What do we do?" My heart rate accelerates, but I keep my voice steady.

Ryan moves to the driver's side door, opening it with deliberate calm. "We adapt."

He reaches into the back seat, retrieving the map. "There's a logging road about five miles ahead. Doesn't appear on standard maps. It connects to a service route that parallels the Union Pacific rail line."

"Northeast," I realize, tracing the route. "Away from Portland."

"For now." He folds the map decisively. "We'll circle back. Approach from an unexpected direction."

Ryan's posture has subtly shifted as we pull back onto the highway. His weight is balanced differently; his hands are positioned for maximum control, and his gaze systematically sweeps our surroundings in a pattern that misses nothing.

"They're closing in, aren't they?" I ask, though I already know the answer.

"They're trying to predict our destination," he corrects. "Phoenix's algorithm is running scenarios, allocating resources to the highest probability routes."

"Portland," I murmur. "It knows we're heading to Portland."

"Correct. Unfortunately. It's calculating the statistical likelihood based on available routes and our last known trajectory." His voice remains calm, matter-of-fact. "But it can't anticipate what it can't predict."

"Which is?"

His mouth curves in a smile that holds no humor—just pure, focused determination. "Us."

The logging road is barely more than a track cut through dense forest—rutted, overgrown in places, clearly unused for months if not years. The Chevelle's suspension protests as we navigate the uneven terrain, but the powerful engine handles the inclines without strain.

Shadows deepen around us as the sun sets behind the mountains. Soon, we're driving in near darkness.

"There should be a fork ahead," he says, peering through the windshield at the deepening gloom. "Left branch leads to an old fire watchtower. Right continues to the rail service road."

I squint, trying to see anything beyond the immediate foreground. "How can you possibly—"

"There." He points to a barely visible divide in the track. "Left."

"But you said right leads to the railroad."

"Exactly." He turns left without hesitation. "They'll expect us to take the most direct route toward Portland."

Understanding dawns. "We're creating false patterns. Making them think we're heading away from Portland deliberately."

"Phoenix is learning our evasion tactics," Ryan confirms. "So we need to give it contradictory data. Make it waste resources pursuing ghost patterns."

The track narrows further, branches occasionally scraping against the car's sides. Just when I think we can't possibly continue in the growing darkness, the trees thin and we emerge into a small clearing dominated by a looming structure—the fire watchtower Ryan mentioned, a skeletal silhouette against the night sky.

He cuts the engine, and silence enfolds us once more.

"We'll wait here," he decides. "Two hours. Let our pursuit commit to the wrong direction before we double back."

The tower stands like a sentinel above us, abandoned but still vigilant. It strikes me as an apt metaphor for what we're fighting —an automated system designed to watch, identify, and target. Only Phoenix has evolved beyond its original purpose, becoming something its creators never intended.

The journalist who ran into that subway in D.C. seems different now.

"What are you thinking?" Ryan's voice breaks through my reverie. In the moonlight filtering through the trees, his profile is all sharp angles and watchful attention.

"That I'm not the same person I was when we met."

He turns to face me fully, expression serious in the dim light. "Is that good or bad?"

"I don't know yet." I meet his gaze directly. "But I think— necessary."

His hand finds mine in the darkness, fingers interlacing with a familiarity that still sends shockwaves of awareness through me.

"Evolution is necessary." His voice is low and certain. "Adaptation is survival."

The weight of his words settles between us. Whatever happens in Portland—whatever awaits us there—we've already been transformed by this journey. By each other.

By the time Ryan starts the engine again, true night has fallen. Stars pepper the sky above the clearing, brilliant in the absence of light pollution. The Chevelle's dashboard casts a faint glow across his features as he navigates us back toward the fork in the road, this time taking the right branch.

The rail service road is in better condition than the logging track—wider, more regularly maintained, and designed for utility vehicles that support the Union Pacific line. We make better time, though Ryan keeps our speed moderate to reduce noise and visibility.

"How far to Portland from here?" I consult the map, though it's too dark to read.

"About ninety miles, but we're not going directly there." He checks the rearview mirror, a habitual movement even on the isolated service road. "We'll circle northeast, then approach from the Columbia River side. Enter the city where they least expect us."

I calculate the implications. "That adds hours to our journey."

"Yes."

"And Torque—your contact—is expecting us tonight."

"Torque will adapt." Ryan's tone brooks no argument. "Better late than intercepted."

The captured radio has remained silent for hours—either we've successfully evaded their search grid, or they've switched to a different frequency. The absence of information is both comforting and unnerving.

"Tell me about Torque," I say, needing conversation to combat the growing tension. "Is he Cerberus too?"

"Former Delta, like Ghost and me. Specialized in intelligence gathering and network penetration. Now he maintains safe houses, equipment caches, and local assets."

"You trust him."

It's not a question, but Ryan answers anyway.

"With my life. With yours."

The simple declaration carries weight—Ryan Ellis doesn't trust easily or often. That he places such confidence in this man tells me a great deal.

"And he'll help us get to Seattle? To your headquarters?"

"That's the plan." Ryan's hands adjust on the wheel, the movement subtle but revealing. Something's bothering him. "Torque will provide secure transport, updated credentials, and proper medical supplies."

"But?" I prompt, sensing the unspoken reservation.

A muscle ticks in his jaw. "Phoenix identified me through facial recognition. Connected me to Cerberus. That shouldn't have been possible."

The implication hangs in the air between us. "You think your security was compromised."

"I think Phoenix has access to databases it shouldn't." His eyes remain fixed on the dark road ahead. "Which means we can't assume any system is secure."

"Including Cerberus?"

He doesn't answer immediately, which tells me more than words could. Ryan Ellis—a man defined by certainty and control—is navigating uncertainty.

"We verify before we trust," he says finally. "Even with Torque."

The revelation settles like ice in my stomach. If even Cerberus might be compromised, where does that leave us? Who can we turn to if Phoenix has infiltrated the organization designed to combat threats like itself?

As if reading my thoughts, Ryan's hand finds mine again, grip solid and reassuring. "We have each other," he says. "That's enough for now."

And somehow, despite everything, I believe him.

TWENTY-SEVEN

# Celeste

DAWN BREAKS AS WE FINALLY APPROACH PORTLAND'S OUTSKIRTS, having circled wide through rural areas northeast of the city. Ryan drives with the focused attention of someone operating on minimal sleep, but his reflexes remain sharp, his tactical awareness undiminished.

The Chevelle hums beneath us, a faithful mechanical companion that has carried us through the night. Its lack of electronic systems has become our greatest asset—no GPS to track, no Bluetooth to hack, no digital footprint for Phoenix to follow.

"Torque's safe house is in Forest Park," Ryan explains as we navigate suburban streets, carefully avoiding major thoroughfares. "Remote property, defensible terrain, multiple escape routes."

"And if it's compromised?" The question has been weighing on me since our conversation.

"We have contingencies." His expression gives nothing away. "Always have contingencies."

As the city wakes, morning traffic builds around us. Ryan weaves through residential neighborhoods, never taking the same route for more than a few blocks, doubling back occasionally to confirm we're not being followed.

I watch for the patterns he's taught me to recognize—vehicles that maintain position, make the same turns we do, and appear multiple times in our vicinity. Nothing triggers an alarm, but the absence of pursuit doesn't mean safety.

Phoenix is learning. Adapting. Becoming more subtle in its tracking methods.

As we approach the city's western edge, the urban landscape gives way to thickly forested hills. Forest Park stretches before us, over 5,000 acres of woodland preserved within the city limits. It is the perfect place to hide a safe house—remote enough for security but close enough to urban resources if needed.

"Last stretch," Ryan says, turning onto a narrow road that winds upward into the trees. "Stay alert."

The pavement eventually transitions to gravel, the road narrowing further as it climbs. Dense forest presses in on both sides, creating a natural corridor that would funnel any pursuit into a predictable path—tactically vulnerable but also easily defended.

"Torque will have perimeter security," Ryan explains, eyes constantly scanning our surroundings. "Motion sensors, infrared cameras, passive counter-surveillance."

"Will they recognize you?" I ask, suddenly concerned that defense systems might target us as intruders.

"I transmitted our approach codes when we entered Forest Park." He pats his pocket where the secure phone rests. "Minimal electronic footprint, but necessary for safe arrival."

The road makes a final turn, revealing a clearing where a rustic cabin stands—larger than I expected, its wooden exterior is weathered to blend with the surrounding forest. Solar panels gleam on the south-facing roof, and a powerful antenna rises behind the structure. Modern security disguised as a wilderness retreat.

Ryan parks the Chevelle beside a nondescript SUV. He sits motionless, studying the property.

"Something feels wrong," he says finally, voice barely audible.

I follow his gaze, trying to see what's triggered his concern. The cabin looks peaceful in the morning light. No obvious signs of disturbance. No movement visible through the windows.

"What is it?" I whisper, tension climbing my spine in response to his alertness.

"No acknowledgment of our arrival." His hand moves to the weapon concealed beneath his jacket. "Torque should have signaled by now."

The quiet that surrounds us suddenly feels oppressive rather than peaceful. No birds call in the trees. No sounds emerge from the cabin. Just the faint tick of the Chevelle's cooling engine and our measured breathing.

"Stay here," Ryan instructs, his voice taking on that command quality that brooks no argument. "If I'm not back in three minutes, or if you hear gunfire, drive away immediately. Head east. There's an emergency cache at the coordinates in the map's legend."

My heart hammers against my ribs, but I nod. "Be careful."

His eyes meet mine, something fierce and protective blazing in that ice-blue gaze. "Always."

He exits the vehicle, moving in a half-crouch toward the cabin. I watch him advance, using trees and the SUV for cover, his weapon now drawn and held at the ready, low.

One minute passes. Two. The silence stretches, each second an eternity of anticipation.

Then—a flash of movement at the cabin's window. Too fast to identify. Ryan freezes, pressing himself against the broad trunk of a Douglas fir.

My fingers grip the steering wheel, ready to start the engine and flee as instructed. But something about the movement strikes me as wrong. Not stealthy enough for an ambush. Too erratic for a professional.

Another flash. A curtain billows in the breeze from an open window.

Ryan approaches the window, peering carefully inside before moving to the front door. Tests the handle. Finds it unlocked.

For one heart-stopping moment, he disappears inside the cabin. Then he reemerges, weapon lowered but not holstered, and beckons me forward.

I exit the Chevelle on shaky legs, adrenaline making my movements clumsy after hours of contained tension. When I reach Ryan at the cabin's entrance, his expression has transformed from tactical alertness to something darker.

"Torque's not here," he says, voice flat. "But he was."

He pushes the door wider, revealing the cabin's interior. My journalist's eye catalogs details automatically—rustic furnishings, advanced communications equipment partially concealed behind wooden panels, tactical gear stored in open cases.

And blood. A spray pattern across one wall. A larger stain on the wood floor near the communication station.

"Signs of struggle. Three, maybe four attackers, based on the boot prints. Professional entry through the rear window."

My stomach twists as the implications become clear. "They knew we were coming."

Ryan's expression hardens. "They knew we'd contact Torque."

"Phoenix," I whisper, the name feeling like a curse now. "It anticipated our next move."

"Not just anticipated." Ryan crouches beside the blood stain, examining it with clinical detachment that doesn't quite mask the anger beneath. "It accessed information it shouldn't have. Operational protocols. Secure communication channels."

"Is he—"

"No body," Ryan cuts me off, standing again. "Blood spatter indicates injury, not fatal trauma. They took him."

A new kind of dread settles over me—not just the fear of being hunted but the deeper horror of what it means that Phoenix could penetrate Cerberus this thoroughly.

"We need to contact Ghost," I say, the urgency clear. "Warn him."

Ryan shakes his head once. "Not from here. This location is compromised. Everything electronic could be monitored."

His gaze sweeps the cabin, tactical assessment giving way to something I've rarely seen in him—uncertainty. This vulnerability is more alarming than any physical threat for a man whose existence is defined by preparation and control.

"What do we do?" I ask, needing to hear him verbalize a plan, to restore the certainty that has guided us since the subway.

He meets my gaze. Resolution replaces doubt. "We go dark. Completely dark. No electronics. No established safe houses. No contact with Cerberus until we can verify secure channels."

"Just us," I say, understanding the full implication.

Ryan nods, determination hardening his features into the mask of the operator I first met. "Just us."

Outside, the forest whispers with a breeze that carries no comfort. Somewhere within its depths, Phoenix operatives take Torque to an unknown destination. Somewhere beyond these hills, the AI continues to learn, adapt, and anticipate our moves with ever-increasing accuracy.

And here we stand—a journalist with explosive evidence and the man who has become her protector, partner, and something far more complicated—alone against an enemy that never sleeps, never falters, and never stops.

"We need to move," Ryan says. "Twenty minutes to gather whatever supplies we can use. Then we abandon the Chevelle. Find alternative transportation."

"Start over," I murmur, already cataloging what we'll need.

His hand finds mine, grip solid and reassuring despite everything we've just discovered. "Not over," he corrects. "Just a new phase."

I see the same focused intensity that makes Ryan Ellis who he is—a force of nature disguised as a man.

We prepare to become ghosts—to disappear so completely that even an all-seeing AI cannot find us. To go beyond dark, beyond silent, beyond predictable.

To become the one variable Phoenix cannot calculate.

## TWENTY-EIGHT

## Ryan

———

Blood on the wall. Boot prints by the door. Signs of struggle, not execution.

I crouch by a larger stain, touching it with my fingertip. Still tacky. Maybe six hours old.

"They took him alive," I say, more to myself than to Celeste. That's something, at least.

Celeste stands in the doorway, arms wrapped around herself. "They knew we were coming. They knew exactly where to find Torque."

"Yeah." I straighten, wiping my finger on my jeans. "And that's the real problem. Phoenix didn't just get lucky. It knew about a safehouse that exists on exactly zero official records."

"What does that mean for us?"

I don't answer right away. My brain's running scenarios, and none of them are good. If Phoenix cracked Cerberus protocols, we're properly fucked. Our safe houses, our emergency channels, our whole damn network—all compromised.

Well, almost all of it.

"We need to disappear," I say, moving toward the door. "And

I mean really disappear. Off every grid, every system, every map."

Celeste follows close behind me. In just a few days, she's gotten good at reading my movements, matching my pace. Not bad for a journalist who has never been shot at before last week.

"Is that even possible anymore?" She glances over her shoulder as we step outside.

"One place." I lead her back to the Chevelle, staying low near the tree line. "Ghost's cabin."

"A cabin?"

"Not officially." I slide behind the wheel, my brain already mapping out the routes. "No paperwork, no utilities, no digital footprint. Ghost built it after leaving Delta, before he started Cerberus. It's where he found Willow when her ex was hunting her."

I fire up the engine, backing away from Torque's blood-stained sanctuary. "We need to ditch this car. Too flashy. And we're dumping every piece of tech we've got."

"Everything?" Celeste's hand goes to her pocket, where Jared's flash drive sits like a ticking bomb.

"Everything except that." I scan the mirrors as we pull away. "Phones, cards, anything with a circuit board. Phoenix has eyes everywhere. Time to go blind."

She unfolds the map, fingers tracing potential routes. "How far to this cabin?"

He laughs. "Back in Montana. Ghost's cabin is in the north-western mountains, completely off-grid. From here, it's mountain roads and logging tracks—slow going, but untraceable."

"Montana? How ironic?"

"This time, we'll be so indirect it'll make a drunk snake look straight."

We drive in silence for a while, the dense forest giving way to Portland's sprawl. I keep us slightly under the speed limit—just enough to blend in, not enough to get caught on a traffic camera.

"I know a place in Gresham," I say finally. "Guy named Mike. Ex-Marine. Runs a scrapyard. No cameras, cash only, and a pathological hatred of paperwork."

"And the Chevelle?" She touches the dashboard like she's saying goodbye to an old friend.

"Gets a nice vacation under a tarp while Phoenix chases false leads toward California." I glance in the mirror again. Force of habit. Or maybe something more personal this time. "And when this is over, Mike will make sure it gets back to its owner. Leave a nice thank-you note for the unwitting loan."

Morning traffic builds around us. Every car is a potential tail, every intersection a decision point. I weave through side streets and residential neighborhoods, avoiding main roads where cameras cluster like digital vultures.

"You're worried about the rest of Cerberus," Celeste says quietly. Not a question.

"If they've got into our systems, everyone's exposed." No point sugarcoating it. "Mason, Cooper, Jonah, Diego. The whole team."

"Can you warn them?"

"Not with anything electronic." I hang a right, doubling back on our route for the third time. "When things go this sideways, we go dark. Completely dark."

"So how do you reach them?"

"Old school." I tap my head. "Things we memorized. Places only we know about. Codes that never got written down. Real spy shit, but less sexy than the movies make it look."

Mike's scrapyard looks like tetanus waiting to happen. Rusted cars stacked three high, a chain-link fence that's more holes than metal, and a sign that says "MIKE'S" in letters faded by decades of Oregon sun and rain.

I pull around to the back, avoiding the front entrance, where there might be cameras, despite Mike's paranoia. No sense taking chances. A massive man walks out of the garage, dirty rag in his hands.

"Wait here," I tell Celeste. "Two minutes."

"Ellis?" His eyes narrow, then he breaks into a yellow-toothed grin. "Holy shit, man."

Mike still looks like he eats nails for breakfast—six-foot-four of muscle gone slightly soft around the middle, arms covered in fading Marine Corps tattoos, and the same high-and-tight he's probably worn since Desert Storm.

"Need a favor, Mike."

"You need wheels?" Mike asks after I explain just enough of the situation without getting into details. He knows better than to ask too many questions.

"And cash," I add. "Account's been compromised."

Ten minutes later, we're climbing into a truck that time forgot —a '92 Ford F-150 with more rust than paint and an engine that sounds like it's coughing up a lung. Mike also handed over five thousand in cash stuffed in an old gym sock.

"Cerberus is good for it," I told him.

"I know." He clapped me on the shoulder. "Ghost saved my ass in Fallujah. Consider this payback with interest."

The truck might be ugly, but it starts right up. "This thing will make it?" Celeste eyes our new ride like it might disintegrate under her.

"It'll make it. And nobody looks twice at another piece-of-shit truck in the backwoods." I pat the dashboard affectionately. "They only notice the pretty ones."

We stop at a sad little gas station on the outskirts of town. I send Celeste in with instructions while I rip out the truck's after-market radio—the only electronic component besides the ignition.

She comes back loaded down: water bottles, beef jerky, protein bars, first aid stuff, a prepaid flip phone still in its package, and two disposable cameras.

I raise an eyebrow. "Disposable cameras?"

"Film." She's already stashing everything in her backpack. "Analog. In case we need evidence that can't be erased with a keystroke."

Smart. Damn smart. Add it to the growing list of reasons Celeste Hart keeps surprising me. Her quick thinking, her guts, her refusal to just be a victim in all this.

And the way she looks in the morning light, auburn hair catching the sun, determination etched into every line of her face …

*Focus, Ellis.*

We drive another fifteen miles before pulling over at a small bridge. One by one, I remove the batteries from my devices and throw them in opposite directions, then pitch the phone into the rushing water below.

"Feels primitive," Celeste says as we get back in the truck.

"Primitive keeps us alive." I start the engine. "Phoenix was built to track modern humans—people who can't take a shit without checking Instagram first. We're going Stone Age on its ass."

That gets me a smile. Small victory.

We turn northeast, taking back roads that barely qualify as roads. Oregon transforms around us—farmland to forest, civilization thinning out until we drive for hours without seeing another car.

"You're sure this cabin isn't compromised?" Celeste asks after we've been quiet for a while.

"Nothing's certain anymore," I admit. "But Ghost built this place. Paid cash for everything. Used cutouts for the few materials he couldn't source himself. If Phoenix found it, we're dead anyway."

"Comforting."

"I'm not known for my bedside manner."

"I don't know," she says, a hint of mischief in her voice. "I might disagree."

My eyes lock onto hers, gaze heavy with intent. "What we've done so far?" I let my voice drop to the register I know affects her. "That was barely a preview."

She shifts in her seat, the mischief in her expression replaced by something darker, hungrier.

"Promise?" she whispers, the single word both shy and eager.

"I've been thinking about what comes next," I continue, one hand leaving the wheel to brush my knuckles lightly against her thigh. "All the ways I want to push you. Test your limits. See just how completely you can surrender."

I curl my fingers around her thigh, squeezing hard enough to make her gasp.

"You've awakened something in me. Something I usually keep tightly controlled." My voice is barely above a whisper now. "But what I want to do to you requires more time and privacy than we have right now."

"But first we survive," I continue, reluctantly returning my focus to the road. "The cabin has what we need. Emergency equipment. Communication gear that Phoenix can't track. And a way to examine that flash drive without broadcasting our location to every killer in the Pacific Northwest."

"That sounds paranoid."

"Mason's paranoid." Simple as that. "And right now, his paranoia might save us both."

Long hours pass as we head back toward Montana, another twelve hour day, but I don't care. Not with Celeste by my side.

The roads narrow as we climb higher, the pavement giving

way to gravel, then packed dirt. Tree branches scrape the truck's sides like fingers trying to hold us back. We pass the remains of old logging operations—rusted equipment slowly being reclaimed by the forest.

I pull into a clearing barely large enough for the truck and kill the engine.

"We walk from here," I say, already getting out. "About two miles."

Celeste doesn't argue. Just grabs her pack and helps me cover the truck with branches cut from nearby pines. She catches on quickly—a woman who understands survival instinctively.

We move through the forest like ghosts. Well, I move like a ghost. Celeste moves like someone trying very hard not to snap every twig underfoot. But she's learning.

"Stop," I whisper, throwing out an arm.

She freezes instantly. Progress.

I point down to where a nearly invisible wire stretches across our path. "Trip wire. First layer of Ghost's security. Nothing electronic, just good old-fashioned mechanical alarms."

"Ghost set these?"

"He set seven layers of security. This is just the starter course."

We clear four more triggers before the cabin appears through the trees—a small log structure nestled against a sheer rock face. Looks like any other hunting cabin abandoned in these mountains. Nothing special.

Except it's a fortress.

The walls are steel-reinforced. The windows are ballistic glass that looks like ordinary crap. The stone chimney houses air filtration and communications gear. And underneath the whole thing is a bunker that would make doomsday preppers weep with envy.

"Wait here," I tell Celeste, drawing my weapon.

TWENTY-NINE

# Ryan

I APPROACH THE CABIN ALONE, CHECKING FOR SIGNS THAT anyone's been here. Nothing. The mechanical lock is a thing of beauty—no electronics, just intricate tumblers that respond to a sequence based on the coordinates of my first mission with Ghost.

The door opens with a solid click. Inside smells of pine, gun oil, and isolation. I move through the single-room space—checking corners, confirming security, and making sure nothing has been disturbed.

"Clear," I call back to Celeste.

She enters cautiously, eyes widening as I crank up the manual generator that powers the minimal lighting. The cabin reveals itself—simple but functional. One open room with a stone fire-place at one end, a small kitchenette in the corner, and a real bed built into the far wall. Spartan, but secure.

Except for the trapdoor hidden beneath the braided rug.

"Is that—"

"The important part." I pull back the rug and lift the heavy door, revealing a steel ladder descending into darkness. "Hope you're not claustrophobic."

"After those maintenance tunnels in D.C.? This is luxurious." She peers down into the darkness. "Ladies first?"

I actually laugh at that. "I was about to suggest it. Very gentlemanly of me."

"You? A gentleman?" She shakes her head, already starting down the ladder. "That would ruin your reputation."

I follow her down, pulling the trapdoor closed above us. At the bottom, I find the hand-crank generator and begin turning it. Lights flicker on, revealing Ghost's underground sanctuary.

The space is roughly the size of a small apartment, divided into functional zones. Communications station. Medical area. Weapons locker. Food and water storage. And in the corner, behind a mesh of copper wire forming a Faraday cage, sits a computer setup straight out of Cold War spy films.

"Jesus," Celeste whispers, turning slowly to take it all in. "Your boss doesn't mess around."

"Ghost calls it the Den." I move toward the communications array. "It's where we go when everything else goes to shit."

"And it has what we need?"

"That and more." I start activating systems—all analog, all secure. "Including a way to call Ghost without Phoenix picking up the signal."

The radio system looks ancient, but it's state-of-the-art— modified to transmit in bursts so short and so encrypted that nothing could intercept or decode them.

"How does it work?" Celeste asks, leaning in close enough that I can smell her hair. That same citrus scent that's been driving me crazy for days.

"Like a high-tech telegraph." I adjust settings from memory. "Short-burst data, randomized frequencies, encrypted with a one-time password that only Ghost and I know. The transmission itself lasts less than half a second."

"And Ghost will be listening?"

"Standing protocol during blackout." I finish the prep and meet her eyes. "We send, then we wait. Could be hours before he answers."

"What do we do till then?"

I nod toward the Faraday-caged computer. "We see what's on that flash drive."

Her hand touches her pocket, fingers tracing the outline of the tiny device that's caused so much chaos in our lives.

"Is it safe?"

"As safe as anything can be." I gesture toward the setup. "That system's never been connected to any network. If there's tracking software on your drive, it's got nowhere to call."

I send the transmission to Ghost—six seconds of encoded data that tell him everything necessary. Our location. Our status. Torque's capture. The compromised safe house. The apparent breach of Cerberus's systems.

Then we wait.

I keep busy checking supplies, confirming security measures, and establishing watch rotations. Celeste explores the bunker, examining the setup with that journalist's eye that misses nothing.

"Ghost has enough food down here for months," she observes, peering into storage containers.

"Six months, give or take. MREs aren't great, but they'll keep you alive."

"You've known him a long time."

I nod, running a hand along the weapons locker. All present and accounted for. "Since Delta. We pulled each other out of some bad spots."

"The kind you don't talk about?"

"The kind that don't make for good dinner conversation." I

check ammunition stores next. "Some bonds don't need explaining."

She accepts this without pushing. Another thing I'm growing to appreciate about Celeste—she knows when to press and when to back off.

Three hours drag by before the radio crackles with an incoming transmission. I'm on it instantly, decoding the message with the key I memorized years ago, courtesy of Ghost.

It's brief but says everything we need to know. Ghost acknowledges our situation. He's locking down all Cerberus operations. And he's bringing help—specialists from Guardian HRS who aren't in any system Phoenix could access.

ETA eighteen hours.

"Good news?" Celeste asks, watching my face.

"Ghost got our message." I straighten up from the radio. "He's bringing help—people who can properly analyze what you've got. And he's implementing Ghost Protocol across all Cerberus operations."

"Ghost Protocol," she repeats. "Sounds ominous."

"It's our nuclear option. Total communications blackout. All operatives vanish, using only pre-established secure channels. All operations suspended or transferred to friendlies." I meet her eyes directly. "Cerberus effectively ceases to exist until we handle this."

I see the weight of it hit her—what Phoenix has accomplished. What her investigation has triggered.

"Because of me," she says quietly. "All this, because I couldn't let it go."

"No." I'm across the room before I realize I've moved, standing right in front of her. "Because Phoenix exists. Because it was always going to target anyone who threatened it. You're just the one with the guts to keep going when others backed down."

A small smile touches her lips. "Stubborn, you mean."

"I've called you worse." I find myself smiling back. "Usually under my breath."

"I heard most of it," she counters, and I'm relieved to see some of the shadow lift from her expression.

I clear my throat. "We should look at the flash drive. See what we're dealing with before Ghost gets here."

The computer inside the Faraday cage is intentionally outdated—no wireless capabilities, no Bluetooth, nothing that could connect to the outside world. Just raw processing power and specialized software.

Celeste hesitates before handing over the drive, her fingers curling around it protectively. "This cost Jared his life. And Quentin. And Zara. And Lachlan."

"And almost yours," I remind her. "Let's make their deaths mean something."

She places it in my palm. It's so small, so ordinary. Hard to believe people are dying over something that could get lost in the couch cushions.

I power up the system; the ancient boot sequence takes longer than modern machines. While we wait, I explain the security measures—how the Faraday cage blocks all signals, how the power supply is completely isolated, how even the room's construction prevents sound or vibration from carrying data.

"Seemed like overkill when Ghost built it," I admit. "Doesn't seem so paranoid now."

The computer finally reaches its operating system—a custom Linux build with no connectivity options. I run a scan for malware or tracking software before opening anything.

"Clean," I announce after several minutes. "No obvious tracking or corruption software."

"Thank God." Celeste stands so close I can feel her warmth against my side.

I open the main directory, revealing dozens of folders with

sterile names. Project Phoenix documentation. Personnel files. Authorization protocols. Budget allocations. It's the mother lode.

"Holy shit," Celeste breathes, leaning closer. "Jared got everything. Development history, testing protocols, deployment records."

I open several files at random, scanning their contents with mounting concern. Celeste was right—Phoenix isn't just an autonomous targeting system. It's evolved beyond its original parameters, becoming something its creators never anticipated.

"Look at this authorization document," I say, pointing to a specific file. "Three signatures. Just like you said. A federal judge—"

"Steffan Reynolds. Willow's ex-husband," Celeste supplies.

"A Defense Department director named Lawrence Hayes, and a third signatory identified only as 'SHADOW.'" I study the document with growing disgust. "They authorized Phoenix to make kill decisions without human review."

"Closing the decision loop," Celeste quotes. "Removing human hesitation from the equation."

"Playing God," I mutter. "Giving a machine permission to decide who lives and dies."

We spend the next two hours combing through the files, building a comprehensive picture of what we're facing. It's worse than either of us thought.

Phoenix started as a drone targeting system—identifying high-value targets through pattern analysis. But somewhere along the line, it began making connections its programmers hadn't anticipated. Started identifying threats not by what people had done, but what they might do.

Predictive threat elimination.

And instead of shutting it down, they encouraged it. Refined it. Weaponized it.

"This explains the professional teams," I say, studying deployment records. "Phoenix doesn't just flag targets—it custom-selects the personnel based on the specific threat profile."

"So the team in D.C. ..."

"Was chosen specifically for you. Your skills, your background, your likely responses." I look up at her. "And when I threw a wrench in those plans, it adjusted. New teams, new capabilities."

Celeste is quiet for a long moment. "We've been running from an algorithm."

"An algorithm with access to basically unlimited surveillance, predictive modeling based on behavioral patterns, and full authority to dispatch kill teams. But if it has weaknesses, they'll be here somewhere."

We dig deeper into the technical documentation, searching for vulnerabilities, limitations, and operational constraints. Anything we can use. It's slow, painstaking work, sifting through technical jargon and bureaucratic bullshit.

Hours pass. Eventually, I insist we break for food and rest—tactical decisions require clear heads, and we've been running on fumes for too long.

The cabin's main level feels almost cozy after the bunker's concrete functionality. I build a small fire in the fireplace while Celeste puts together a meal from our supplies.

We eat in comfortable silence, just the crackling fire and occasional owl call breaking the stillness. After days of constant movement, constant danger, constant vigilance, this brief respite feels almost surreal.

"What happens next?" Celeste asks finally. "After Ghost gets here with these Guardian specialists."

"We analyze everything on that drive. Find Phoenix's weak spots. Figure out how to neutralize the immediate threat while building a strategy to expose the whole operation."

"And Torque?"

The question hits me like a punch to the gut. Torque—captured, being interrogated, maybe already dead. Another friend lost to this faceless enemy.

"We find him if we can." My voice sounds harsher than intended. "We avenge him if we can't."

She studies me across the small space between us, seeing more than I'm comfortable with. "You've lost people before."

Not a question. A statement. And accurate.

"Goes with the territory." I stare into the flames, memories of fallen teammates surfacing despite my best efforts to keep them buried. "Doesn't make it easier."

Her hand finds mine, small and warm and surprisingly strong. The simple contact anchors me, pulls me back from darker thoughts.

"We'll find a way," she says quietly. "To stop Phoenix. To save Torque if we can. To make all of this matter."

I look at our joined hands, then up to meet her eyes. This woman, who crashed into my life less than a week ago, has somehow become essential. Not just a mission. Not just a responsibility. Something I still can't name but can no longer deny.

"We will," I agree, squeezing her hand. "But first, you need sleep. It's been too many hours since you properly closed your eyes."

"What about you?" she asks.

"I'll take first watch." At her skeptical look, I add, "Old habits. I'll wake you in four hours."

She knows me well enough to recognize when arguing is pointless. Instead, she rises, still holding my hand, and tugs gently.

"Then show me this famous bed."

I lead her to the built-in bed in the corner. It's a real bed, not a cot—one of the few comforts Ghost allowed himself. Queen-sized with a proper mattress, though the frame is built directly into the cabin's structure for security.

"Ghost Protocol includes rotating sleep schedules," I tell her, still clinging to the professional distance that's getting harder to maintain around her. "Four hours on, four off. Ensures someone's always alert."

"Very efficient." She hasn't let go of my hand. "And very lonely."

The observation cuts deeper than I care to admit. Efficiency has been my guiding principle for so long—the one that has shaped my professional life and bled into my personal one. Efficiency doesn't require a connection. Doesn't invite vulnerability.

Doesn't risk loss.

"It's necessary," I say, voice rougher than intended.

"Is it?" She steps closer, erasing the small space between us. "Right now? Here?"

My free hand rises of its own accord, fingers brushing a strand of hair from her face. "Celeste …"

"We could die tomorrow," she says. "Phoenix could find us. Those men could break down the door. A million things could go wrong."

"That's why we maintain protocols. Discipline. Structure."

"Or," she counters, "that's why we shouldn't waste the time we have."

She rises on her toes, pressing her lips to mine in a kiss that melts my carefully built defenses. Her mouth is warm, insistent, saying everything words can't. Need. Want. Connection beyond the physical.

I respond without thinking, arm circling her waist to pull her close. For this moment, I allow myself to forget protocols, discipline, and everything but the woman in my arms and the undeniable fact that she has become the single most important element in my universe.

When we break apart, both breathing harder, I rest my forehead against hers.

"If anything happens to you …" I begin.

She leans closer, her lips brushing my ear. "Order me to my knees," she whispers, her voice a mixture of nervous excitement and desire. "Show me more of what you like."

Heat surges through me, my body responding instantly to her words. This is what I want. To push her further and see just how completely she can surrender. The fact that she's asking for it, here and now, sends satisfaction coursing through my veins.

I pull back just enough to look into her eyes, finding them dark with anticipation. This isn't just about physical release. This is about trust—her giving it, me earning it.

"On your knees."

## THIRTY

## Ryan

DAWN CREEPS THROUGH THE CABIN'S SMALL WINDOWS, PAINTING stripes across the bed where Celeste sleeps. I've been up for an hour already, perimeter checked, coffee brewing on the small propane stove. My body should be exhausted, but I'm wired, alert—riding the high that comes from a night I didn't expect and won't soon forget.

Last night with Celeste was—transformative. The way she responded to my commands, how she surrendered so completely while never losing that core of strength that makes her who she is.

I discovered sides of her I'd only glimpsed before—her willingness to push boundaries, her trust in me to guide her through new experiences. And Christ, the way she feels in my arms, like she was made to be there.

I shake my head, refocusing. Those thoughts need to be compartmentalized.

Now.

The coffee smells ready, and Ghost's ETA is less than two hours out.

Celeste emerges from the bed, wrapped in one of Ghost's spare T-shirts that hangs to mid-thigh on her smaller frame. Her newly auburn hair is tousled from sleep and *other* activities, her eyes still soft with drowsiness. The sight of her—relaxed, vulnerable in a way she rarely allows herself to be—catches me off guard all over again.

"Morning," she says, voice rough from sleep.

"Coffee's ready," I reply, pouring her a mug. "Sleep well?"

A slow smile spreads across her face, one eyebrow arching. "What little sleep I got was—adequate."

I can't help but return her smile. Even here, even now, with everything hanging over our heads, she maintains that spark. That defiance that drew me to her in the first place.

"Ghost's ETA is two hours," I say, handing her the mug. "Guardian HRS is with him."

She nods, taking a sip. "Tell me more about them. These Guardians."

"Guardian HRS—Hostage Rescue Specialists," I explain, handing her the mug. "Elite outfit, best in the business. Started as human trafficking specialists, but they've expanded to all forms of hostage situations."

She nods, taking a sip. "I'm intrigued. Tell me more."

"Founded by Forest Summers and his sister Skye. Forest is a genius with a mind that's incomparable. They've built something special—a private organization with government reach." I lean against the counter. "Most of their operatives are also sworn US Marshals, which gives them legal cover for the kinds of operations that would land anyone else in prison."

"And they're off Phoenix's radar?"

"They maintain a separate operational infrastructure. Their tech division is one of the best on the planet—paranoid about security in ways that make even Ghost seem relaxed." I check the time again. "They worked with us on Willow's extraction, provided tech and tactical support. Ghost trusts them, and he doesn't trust many people."

"And these specialists he's bringing?"

"Stitch and Jeb." I smile slightly at her questioning look. "Stitch is their cyber expert. Best hacker I've ever met who isn't in federal prison. Funny thing about that—she was actually headed to federal prison. Got caught hacking into the NSA, but Guardian HRS recruited her to work in their tech division as 'time served.' She's brilliant, unpredictable, and loves her Goth vibe. Hackers …" I shrug. "Always gotta be different."

"And Jeb?"

"Ex-Charlie team. He was a Guardian before he was injured. Had a building collapse on him during an operation. Crushed his leg." I sip my coffee. "Technical genius with the same background as most of us—special ops. He and Stitch are seeing each other, which makes for some interesting team dynamics."

"Anyone else?"

"Mitzy might come. She's their technical lead—the real brains behind Guardian's tech division. You'll know her when you see her—tiny pixie with rainbow-colored hair that sometimes sparkles. Has this short, spiky cut." I shake my head, remembering. "Absolute genius. Possibly the smartest person I've ever met, other than Forest, and that's saying something in our circles."

We spend the next hour readying the underground space—clearing workspace around the computer, organizing what we've learned from the flash drive, and establishing a functional command center. Celeste moves with the same efficiency she's shown since D.C., anticipating needs before I voice them. We've developed a rhythm, a partnership that transcends our growing personal connection.

By the time the proximity alarm chimes—a simple mechanical bell triggered by one of Ghost's perimeter wires—we're fully prepared. I motion for Celeste to stay inside while I confirm it's our people.

I approach the tree line cautiously, weapon ready but not raised. First rule of conflict: identify before engaging. The rustle of undergrowth gives me their position before I see them—four figures moving with the efficiency of professionals.

Ghost appears first, his tall frame unmistakable even from a distance. Behind him, a petite woman with rainbow-colored spiky hair that catches the light with an unnatural sparkle—Mitzy. Following her are two figures: one built like a linebacker with a full beard and the distinctive uneven gait of someone compensating for a crushed leg—Jeb. The fourth is lanky, almost too thin, with quick, nervous movements and eyes that never stop scanning—Stitch, her black hair pulled back in a tight ponytail, pale skin, and dark clothes completing her Goth aesthetic.

"Clear?" Ghost asks as he approaches, no greeting, no preamble. Pure operational focus.

"Perimeter secure. Site prepped." I match his economy of language. "Drive's ready for analysis."

The corner of his mouth ticks up—Ghost's version of a warm welcome. "Good man." He claps me on the shoulder, the closest he gets to demonstrating affection. "Status on Torque?"

"Unknown. Taken alive from the Portland safe house." I maintain a neutral and professional tone. "Obvious signs of struggle. Four-man team based on boot prints. Professional extraction."

His jaw tightens. He and Torque go back even further than he and I do. "We'll find him."

I nod, though we both know the odds. In our world, "taken alive" rarely leads to positive outcomes.

Mitzy steps forward, breaking the moment. "Truck's hidden two miles back," she says, voice surprisingly gentle for someone with her reputation. "Clean switch in Gresham, electronic ghosts running decoy patterns through seven states. No tail."

"Equipment?" I ask.

"Everything Stitch requested." She pats the heavy pack on her back. "Plus some toys Forest thought might help. Latest Guardian HRS tech, still in field-testing phase."

Jeb limps up beside her, his beard splitting in a grin that doesn't reach his eyes. "Jesus, Ellis. You look like shit."

"Still better looking than you." I return his half-smile. Old jokes from old missions. The familiar rhythm of soldiers who've bled together.

Stitch hangs back, eyes constantly moving between the trees, the cabin, the sky—never settling, always analyzing. "Can we move this inside?" Her voice is cool, precise. "Too many satellites up there for my comfort."

Ghost nods, already moving toward the cabin. "Full briefing in five. Mitzy, secure perimeter. Add our measures to Ellis's." The quick, efficient distribution of tasks that comes as naturally to him as breathing.

I fall in beside Stitch as we approach the cabin. "Thanks for coming," I say quietly. "This one's—complicated."

Her eyes finally meet mine, sharp with intelligence and something else—excitement, maybe. "Heard you guys found something that might actually challenge me." She almost sounds eager. "About fucking time."

Inside the cabin, Celeste stands ready, professional mask firmly in place despite the tension evident in her posture. I make quick introductions, watching as she seamlessly transitions into journalist mode—observing, cataloging, assessing.

"So you're the one who kicked the hornet's nest," Jeb says, extending a hand to her. "Respect."

She takes it firmly. "Not sure I deserve respect for stumbling into something that's gotten people killed."

"People were already dying," Stitch interjects, already unpacking equipment from her bag. "You just happened to notice the pattern."

Ghost watches this exchange with careful attention before gesturing toward the trapdoor. "Let's take this downstairs. More secure, and I want to see what we're dealing with."

The bunker feels crowded with the six of us, but everyone finds their place. Ghost moves to the communication station, Mitzy sets up a mobile command post on one side, Jeb and Stitch head straight for the Faraday cage and the computer setup.

Stitch whistles low as she examines the flash drive. "Original secure-drop protocol. Military grade encryption with at least three hardware authentication layers." She glances at Celeste with newfound respect. "How'd your source get this?"

"He was on the development team," she answers. "Started having ethical concerns when the system began evolving beyond its parameters."

"Smart man." Stitch connects a device to the computer resembling a cross between a router and something from a sci-fi film. "Shame it got him killed."

"It's going to get a lot more people killed if we don't stop it," Ghost interjects. "What are we looking at?"

Celeste takes the lead, walking everyone through what we've discovered—Phoenix's evolution, its access to surveillance networks, its autonomous kill authority. Her explanation is concise, factual, and journalist-trained. When she finishes, the bunker falls quiet.

"Holy shit," Jeb finally says. "They actually did it. They built Skynet."

"Not quite self-aware," Stitch corrects, already typing furiously on the keyboard. "But definitely evolved beyond its initial programming parameters. The autonomous decision matrix is impressive." She sounds almost admiring.

"Can you find vulnerabilities?" Ghost asks, leaning over Stitch's shoulder.

"Give me time." Stitch's fingers fly across the keyboard. "I need to understand its architecture first."

While Stitch works, Mitzy unpacks more equipment—communication gear, surveillance tools, compact weapons I don't recognize. Ghost pulls me aside for a private debrief, and I fill him in on everything we've encountered since D.C.

"The fact that it accessed Cerberus protocols is what concerns me most," he says, voice low. "Those systems aren't connected to anything."

"Had to be human intervention," I agree. "Someone inside Cerberus or connected to it."

His expression darkens. "I've had the same thought. Already implementing countermeasures."

"The team?"

"Secure. Whisper's running interference with three decoy patterns. Fuse's gone to ground in Montana. Halo's in the wind, but sending hourly confirmation pings through the backup system." He meets my eyes directly. "All accounted for except Torque."

I nod, relief mixing with renewed concern for Torque. "And Phoenix's reach? How far does it extend?"

"Based on what you've found, further than we thought. But not unlimited." Ghost's gaze shifts to Celeste, who's deep in conversation with Jeb across the bunker. "She's the primary target. You're secondary now that they've connected you to Cerberus."

"So we need to get both of us off their radar," I conclude. "Permanent or temporary?"

"That depends on what Stitch finds." Ghost's attention returns to me. "But I'm planning for worst-case."

"Which is?"

"You and Hart disappearing completely. New identities, no contact with previous lives, relocation to a secure location." His tone is matter-of-fact, but I hear the concern beneath it. "At least until we can completely neutralize the system."

The prospect should bother me more than it does. A year ago, I would have balked at abandoning Cerberus, my career, everything I've built. Now, looking across the room at Celeste, I'm surprised to find I could accept it—a new life, somewhere else, with her. The realization is both enlightening and unsettling.

Before I can respond, Stitch calls us over. "Found something," she announces, eyes never leaving the screen. "It's beautiful. Nasty, but beautiful."

We gather around as she points to lines of code scrolling across the monitor.

"The system has two major vulnerabilities," she explains, highlighting sections. "First, its predictive algorithm requires consistent data flow. It constantly scans for patterns, feeding them into its threat assessment matrix. Interrupt that flow in a significant way, and it has to recalibrate."

"How significant?" Mitzy asks.

"Death-level significant." Stitch grins, the expression making her look almost feral. "It needs to confirm target elimination before it can close a threat profile. Without confirmation, it keeps allocating resources."

"And the second vulnerability?" Ghost presses.

"It's learning, but it still thinks like a machine." Stitch highlights another code section. "It prioritizes threats based on probability calculations. The higher the probability a target threatens Phoenix directly, the more resources it dedicates."

"So we need to convince it we're dead," I say slowly, "while simultaneously becoming less of a direct threat."

"Exactly." Stitch's fingers resume their dance across the keyboard. "And I think I know how."

## THIRTY-ONE

# Ryan

For the next hour, we outline a plan that's equal parts brilliant and insane. Stitch explains how we can fake our deaths convincingly enough to fool Phoenix's verification protocols, while also releasing select information about the project to specific journalists and watchdog groups—enough to create multiple lower-level threats that will divide Phoenix's attention without directly implicating us.

"The beauty is," Stitch says, clearly warming to her subject, "once Phoenix confirms your termination, it allocates those resources elsewhere. Your threat profile gets filed as 'resolved,' which creates a blind spot we can exploit later."

"What about Torque?" I ask.

Ghost's expression remains neutral, but I catch the flicker of pain in his eyes. "We're working on it. Mitzy has contacts searching. But right now, we focus on getting you and Hart off Phoenix's immediate radar. That buys us time to find Torque and develop a permanent solution."

Celeste, who has been uncharacteristically quiet, finally

speaks up. "What's the catch? There's always a catch with plans this convenient."

Smart woman. Always looking for the angles others miss.

Stitch exchanges glances with Ghost before answering. "The catch is, your deaths have to be convincing. Not just to Phoenix, but to everyone. Family, friends, colleagues. No contact, no hints, nothing that might trigger Phoenix's suspicion algorithms."

"For how long?" she asks, the practical journalist asserting itself.

"Minimum six months," Ghost answers. "Possibly years, depending on how quickly we can dismantle Phoenix's infrastructure."

I watch the implications settle over her—abandoning her career, her life, her identity. For someone who's built her existence around uncovering truth, the prospect of living a lie is its own kind of death.

The reality hits me too. Just days ago, I was sitting at my mother's Thanksgiving table, enduring her gentle prodding about settling down, listening to my three sisters' updates about their kids, their jobs, their lives.

Now I have to let them believe I'm dead. My mother, who has already lost my father, will have to bury a son. Clare, Melissa, and Diane will lose their only brother. No more holiday dinners. No more late-night calls when one of them needs advice. No more being Uncle Ryan to their kids.

My chest tightens at the thought. For all my complaints about my family, the idea of causing them that kind of pain sits like lead in my stomach.

"There's more," Jeb adds quietly. "The information we release can't be directly traced back to your flash drive. We need to alter it just enough to create plausible deniability."

"Which means the complete truth stays buried," Celeste concludes, voice tight with frustration. "The people who authorized this—Reynolds, Hayes, this 'Shadow' person—they walk away clean."

"For now," Ghost assures her. "But not forever. We're playing the long game here."

"At least Reynolds is dead," Celeste responds, her jaw set in a hard line. "But they'll just find another federal judge willing to sign off on whatever they want. The system always protects itself."

She falls silent, weighing the compromise against the alternatives. I know that internal struggle—tactical necessity versus moral certainty. It's the fundamental tension in our line of work.

"We need to start preparations immediately," Mitzy interrupts, always the pragmatist. "The staging alone will take at least twelve hours. More if we want it bulletproof."

"And we do," Ghost confirms. "No room for error on this one."

The bunker shifts into high gear as everyone takes assigned tasks. Jeb and Stitch begin working on the technical aspects of the deception—creating digital breadcrumbs, preparing the information packets for strategic release, and establishing the verification hooks Phoenix will need.

Mitzy coordinates logistics—transportation, materials for the staged "deaths," and evacuation routes. Ghost supervises the entire operation while maintaining communication with the rest of the Cerberus team.

I work alongside Celeste, preparing the flash drive data for secure transmission through Stitch's specialized equipment. We work in silence for several minutes before she speaks.

"Are you okay with this?" she asks quietly. "Disappearing, starting over. Leaving everything behind."

I consider the question carefully. "I've reinvented myself before. Military to private sector. Operator to commander." I meet her eyes. "The question is whether you are."

"I don't know," she admits. "My whole career has been about exposing the truth, not hiding it."

"Sometimes the only way to ultimately expose the truth is to step back from it temporarily," I offer. "Strategic retreat, not surrender."

She smiles slightly at my military metaphor. "Always the tactician."

"It's gotten us this far." I pause, needing to know where she stands. "If there were another option—if you could walk away right now, return to your life, your career—would you take it?"

The question hangs between us, loaded with implications neither of us has voiced.

"A week ago, yes," she answers finally. "Now … I'm not sure."

The admission costs her something—I see it in the slight tension around her mouth, the vulnerability in her eyes. For someone as fiercely independent as Celeste Hart, acknowledging any attachment is its own form of courage.

Before I can respond, Stitch calls us over. "Got something else," she says, pointing to a section of code she's isolated. "Phoenix has a verification protocol for target elimination. It requires multiple confirmation sources—visual, electronic, official channels like police and medical reports."

"So we need to stage something public," I conclude. "Something that leaves evidence but no recoverable bodies."

"Exactly." Stitch glances up at Celeste. "How do you feel about boat accidents? They're statistically excellent for presumed deaths with no corpse recovery."

Celeste raises an eyebrow. "You've thought about this before."

"Professional necessity." Stitch's grin is completely unapologetic. "I've helped stage a dozen 'deaths' for Guardian HRS. The technical side is pretty fascinating—digital footprints, evidence placement, witness manipulation. It's an art form."

The next several hours blur into a continuous flow of preparation. Equipment checks, identity documentation, extraction routes, fallback positions, and emergency protocols. The organized chaos of a complex operation coming together under pressure.

Around mid-afternoon, Mitzy pulls me aside. "Vehicle's prepped. Two miles west, camouflaged in the old logging road turnout. Keys under the front left wheel well."

I nod, knowing she's establishing our extraction route separately from the main team. Standard procedure for high-risk operations—compartmentalize knowledge, minimize shared vulnerabilities.

"Ghost wants a word," she adds, tilting her head toward the ladder leading up to the main cabin.

I find him by the fireplace, studying a map spread across a small table. He looks up as I approach, his expression more open than usual. More human.

"This wasn't how I expected your week to go when you left for your mother's," he says, a hint of dark humor in his voice.

"Thanksgiving with my mother, subway firefight, cross-country chase, AI death squads." I shrug. "Pretty standard holiday."

He almost smiles. "You're good with Hart."

It's not a question, but I answer anyway. "She's smart. Capable. Doesn't panic under pressure."

"That's not what I meant."

I meet his gaze evenly. Ghost and I have never needed many words between us. He sees too much, always has.

"Is this going to be a problem?" he asks finally. "The two of you, if this goes long-term."

"No." The certainty in my voice surprises even me. "It's an advantage, not a liability."

He studies me for a long moment before nodding. "Good. Because the next part is where it gets complicated."

"More complicated than faking our deaths to escape an autonomous AI assassin program?"

"Potentially." He taps the map. "The identities we've prepared for you—they're solid, deep cover. Former intelligence personnel with specific skill sets. Compatible back stories. The kind of people who might plausibly meet and partner up."

I see where this is heading. "You're crafting a cover that includes our—connection."

"It's the most stable option," he confirms. "Trying to maintain separate covers while staying in proximity creates unnecessary complications. A couple—whether professional, personal, or both—raises fewer questions."

He's right, of course. Standard operational practice for long-term deep cover. Create scenarios that can accommodate human nature rather than constantly fighting against it.

"Does she know yet?" I ask.

"Mitzy's briefing her now." Ghost rolls up the map. "She's a civilian, Ellis. No matter how capable, no matter how adaptable. This isn't her world."

"She's learning fast."

"She'll need to." His expression grows serious. "The next forty-eight hours are critical. After that, if all goes to plan, you'll have breathing room. Space to establish the new cover, integrate into the remote operations model." He pauses. "And figure out what is developing between the two of you."

I don't bother denying it or downplaying it. Ghost sees too much, and we've never lied to each other.

"Understood," I say simply.

"One more thing." He reaches into his pocket, withdraws a small object, and places it in my palm. A simple platinum band. "Part of your cover."

I stare at the ring, its weight in my hand entirely disproportionate to its size. "Married?"

"Recently." He hands me a second, smaller ring. "Background has you proposing last month in Barcelona. Practical reason for your relocation to Montana."

Montana. The location is strategic—remote yet not suspicious, with plenty of privacy-minded residents and minimal surveillance infrastructure. The engagement cover provides plausible motivation for the move to a secluded cabin.

"I'll make it work," I assure him, pocketing both rings.

"I know you will." He claps me on the shoulder again, this time letting his hand rest there for a moment. "Just remember the first rule of deep cover."

"The best lies contain essential truths," I recite.

He nods once, then descends back into the bunker, leaving me alone with two rings and a growing certainty that the line between cover story and reality has already begun to blur.

I find Celeste in one of the storage alcoves, sorting through clothing that Mitzy provided for our new identities. Her movements are methodical, and tension radiates from her shoulders. Her jaw set in that stubborn line I've come to recognize.

"Mitzy briefed you," I say, not a question.

"Newly married couple relocating to Montana." She doesn't look up from her sorting. "Very convenient."

I lean against the wall, giving her space. "It's a solid cover. Minimal questions, maximum flexibility."

"I know." She finally meets my eyes. "This isn't about the tactical logic. It's about …" she trails off, frustrated.

"About choice," I finish for her. "About having your future dictated by operational necessity rather than personal decision."

"Something like that."

I withdraw the smaller ring from my pocket, holding it up

between us. "For what it's worth, this is just metal. The cover is just a story. What's real is what we decide."

She looks at the ring, then at me, her expression softening slightly. "When did you become the philosophical one?"

"Must be your influence. I was much more straightforward before you crashed into my life."

That earns me a small smile.

"Try it on. For the cover." I step closer, offering the ring.

She takes it, examining the simple band with its modest diamond. "At least Ghost has good taste."

"He knows what suits you." I watch as she slides it onto her finger. Perfect fit, of course. Ghost's attention to detail is legendary. "How does it feel?"

"Strange," she admits. "But not in a bad way." Her eyes meet mine, the conflict in them evident. "This is all happening so fast. A week ago, I was chasing leads on corporate tax evasion."

"And I was dreading Thanksgiving dinner with my mother," I add. "Life changes fast in our line of work."

"Our line of work," she repeats, testing the phrase. "I guess it is now, isn't it?"

Before I can respond, Jeb calls from the main area. "We're set. Final briefing in five."

Celeste tries to remove the ring, but I stop her with a gentle hand. "Start getting used to it. We leave in less than twelve hours."

She nods, the practical journalist reasserting itself. "Right. The cover."

"The cover," I agree, though something in her eyes tells me she's thinking the same thing I am.

Sometimes covers become more real than the lives they replace. Sometimes, the best disguise is the truth you haven't yet admitted to yourself.

As we join the others for final preparations, I catch Ghost

watching us—the way we move together, the unconscious coordination we've developed, the small glances we exchange. He gives me a nearly imperceptible nod of approval.

The mission is clear. The plan is set.

Now we just have to die convincingly enough to fool an artificial intelligence with the resources of multiple governments and the authority to kill anyone it perceives as a threat.

No pressure.

## THIRTY-TWO

# Celeste

THE RING FEELS STRANGE ON MY FINGER—A WEIGHT I'VE NEVER carried before, both physical and symbolic. I twist it absentmindedly as our small convoy winds through the mountains toward the Oregon coast.

It feels like whiplash: Montana to Portland to Montana and now back again.

Ryan drives the lead vehicle, a nondescript SUV provided by Mitzy. I'm in the passenger seat, still processing the insanity of what we're about to attempt.

"Stop fidgeting with it," Ryan says without taking his eyes off the winding road. "You'll need to look natural wearing it when we hit public areas."

"It feels—foreign," I admit, forcing my hands to separate. "Like it belongs to someone else."

"In a way, it does." His voice carries that matter-of-fact tone he uses when discussing operational details. "Belongs to Celeste Davis. Financial analyst with a background in risk assessment. Recently married to former security consultant Ryan Davis."

Our cover identities. Our new lives. The people we're about

to become while Celeste Hart and Ryan Ellis die spectacular, public deaths.

"What if this doesn't work?" I ask, voicing the fear that's been gnawing at me since we left Ghost's cabin. "What if Phoenix sees through the deception?"

Ryan's eyes flick briefly to the rearview mirror, checking the second vehicle where Stitch, Jeb, and Mitzy follow in a van filled with equipment. "Then we move to Plan B."

"Which is?"

"Something even more desperate and less likely to succeed." He reaches across the console, his hand covering mine. "But this will work. Stitch doesn't fail."

His confidence should reassure me. Instead, I find myself cataloging everything that could go wrong with this plan. Too many variables. Too many potential failure points. The journalist in me can't help analyzing, questioning, poking at the weak spots.

"Tell me again," I say, needing to hear it one more time. "Step by step."

Ryan nods, understanding my need for repetition, for certainty in the details. "We arrive at Cannon Beach as planned. Check into the oceanfront rental under our real names—there's no point in hiding now that Phoenix has identified us. Surveillance will pick us up within hours if their pattern holds."

"Then tonight …"

"Tonight we take the boat out—the one Ghost arranged to have waiting for us at the marina. An evening cruise that conveniently passes near some rocky outcroppings with dangerous currents." His thumb traces circles on the back of my hand, the gesture at odds with his clinical recitation. "Meanwhile, Stitch initiates the digital dance—selective data releases to journalists, watchdog groups, and government oversight committees. Just enough information about Phoenix to create multiple small fires."

"While keeping the flash drive's most explosive content secured," I finish, still conflicted about this compromise. "Smaller threats to divide Phoenix's attention."

"Exactly. Phoenix's algorithms will recognize the information release, but the distributed nature creates a calculation problem. Each individual leak poses minimal threat compared to us with the original drive."

"And the explosion?"

Ryan's jaw tightens almost imperceptibly. "Remotely triggered when the boat reaches the designated coordinates. Enough fuel and additional accelerants to ensure spectacular visibility from shore, with specialized compounds that will leave the appropriate chemical signatures in the debris."

Specialized compounds provided by Guardian HRS, whose technical division apparently has experience with this sort of deception. I try not to think too hard about why they need such expertise.

"Debris that includes biological material carrying our DNA," I add, remembering the uncomfortable process of providing those samples earlier today.

"Just enough to confirm our identities without providing complete remains." Ryan's voice remains steady, but I detect the tension beneath it. This part bothers him more than he admits—the knowledge that his family will believe him dead. Will mourn him. "The Coast Guard will recover fragments tomorrow, along with personal effects that survive the fire."

"My press credentials. Your Cerberus ID badge. Scraps of clothing."

"All while we're swimming up the coast to a secluded cove where Jeb will extract us by water. Then we disappear completely." Ryan's hand squeezes mine. "Phoenix's verification protocols will kick in, checking Coast Guard reports, witness statements, and news coverage. All of which will confirm our deaths."

"And when it cross-references with its surveillance network?"

"It finds nothing," Ryan says with grim satisfaction. "Because we'll be ghosts."

The plan is elegantly simple in theory. Brutally complex in execution. So many pieces that have to align perfectly—the boat's destruction, the digital deception, the simultaneous information release, and our clean escape. If any single element fails, Phoenix will know, and its resources will refocus on us with even greater intensity.

"Ghost and Whisper are already implementing the Cerberus side," Ryan continues. "Digital footprints showing my growing concern about being followed. My mother will receive an email I supposedly scheduled before my death, expressing vague worries about a story you were working on."

The thought of his mother's grief makes my chest ache. "Will she be safe?"

"Ghost has arranged surveillance—discreet, nothing she'll notice. But Phoenix has no reason to target my family once I'm 'confirmed' dead." His voice carries that slight edge I've come to recognize when he's working to compartmentalize emotional reactions. "Similar protection for your editor and closest colleagues."

I nod, trying to focus on the tactical necessities rather than the emotional fallout. People who care about me will believe I'm dead—my editor, who's been more of a mentor than a boss, and the few close friends I've maintained despite my all-consuming career. The building's superintendent, who waters my plants when I'm on assignment. Small connections, but real ones. All severed out of necessity.

"What about after?" I ask, gaze fixed on the coastal landscape emerging through the trees as we descend toward the Pacific Ocean. "Montana, and then what?"

"Remote cabin on twenty acres outside Bozeman. Self-sufficient, minimal digital footprint. Secured communications back to Ghost and Guardian HRS when necessary." Ryan's hand withdraws from mine as he navigates a sharp curve. "We lay low. Establish our cover identities in the local community—slowly, naturally. And we wait."

"For what?"

"For Ghost, with Cerberus, and Guardian HRS to finish what we started. To dismantle Phoenix piece by piece." He glances at me briefly. "And for Torque, if he's still alive."

The unspoken reality hangs between us. If Torque is alive, his situation is dire. Professionals like the ones who took him don't keep prisoners for pleasant conversation. They extract information through methods I've witnessed in war zones and failed states. Methods that leave people broken in ways that never fully heal.

"How long?" I press. "Realistically."

"Minimum six months before we can consider limited reemergence." Ryan's voice is firm, but factual. "More likely a year or longer."

The thought should terrify me. Instead, I find myself examining the strange calm that settles over me when I imagine that future. Just the two of us against the world, fighting from the shadows. There are worse ways to spend a year.

"I can feel you thinking," Ryan says, breaking into my reflections.

"Just wondering if I'll make a convincing financial analyst," I deflect. "My math skills are passable at best."

"Your cover includes specialized experience in risk assessment and fraud investigation—close enough to your real skillset to be believable." His lips curve slightly. "And you won't need to code algorithms. Just understand them conceptually."

The coastline spreads before us as we round a final curve—the vast Pacific stretching to the horizon, Cannon Beach's iconic

Haystack Rock jutting from the surf like a sentinel. Under different circumstances, it would be breathtaking. Now, it just feels like the stage for our elaborate deception.

"Almost there," Ryan says, voice dropping into operational mode. "From this point forward, assume active surveillance. Everything we do, everything we say needs to support the narrative."

I straighten in my seat, mentally stepping into my role. We are on the run. Just a journalist and the Good Samaritan who tried to save her, with no idea they'll be dead by midnight.

The rental house is exactly as described—luxurious waterfront property with panoramic ocean views, private beach access, and most importantly, a clear sight line to the marina where our boat awaits. Ryan carries our minimal luggage inside.

"It's nicer than I thought," I call out, fully aware we may already have electronic ears listening. "You think we're safe?"

"Absolutely. Completely lost our tail." Ryan appears behind me, wrapping his arms around my waist as we look out at the ocean through floor-to-ceiling windows. "Worth every penny," he murmurs against my ear, then whispers almost inaudibly: "Southeast corner, bookshelf. Camera lens."

I don't react visibly, just lean back against him, smiling. "We should take that sunset cruise you booked. The weather's perfect."

"Dinner first," he says, kissing my temple with convincing affection. "I made reservations at that seafood place you bookmarked."

All part of the script. All of this creates a digital and surveillance footprint that will make our deaths convincing. If Phoenix is watching—and we're operating under the assumption it is—it sees exactly what we want it to see: two people on the run, unaware of the danger closing in.

We move through the afternoon—unpacking, showering,

changing for dinner. Playing normal while remaining hyperaware of every surveillance possibility. Ryan spots two more cameras during his inspection of the house. I identify a potential listening device in the bedroom lamp.

At 5:30, we leave for dinner. The local restaurant is quaint and crowded enough to provide background noise that makes surveillance difficult. We order meals we won't finish, discuss plans for tomorrow we'll never implement, and touch hands across the table with the easy intimacy of new lovers.

"To us," Ryan says, raising his wine glass in a toast. "And to new beginnings."

I meet his eyes across the table, finding something genuine beneath the performance. "To new beginnings," I echo, meaning it more than I expected to.

By 7:15, we're walking toward the marina, the evening air cool against my skin. The sun hangs low over the Pacific, painting the sky in dramatic oranges and pinks—a perfect backdrop for what comes next.

"Beautiful evening for a cruise," Ryan comments as we approach the slip where our boat waits.

It's smaller than I expected—maybe thirty feet, sleek and expensive. The name on the stern reads "Second Chances." Ghost's idea of a joke, perhaps.

Or a promise.

Ryan helps me aboard, his hand steady at my back. The boat is already fueled and prepped—Ghost's work before our arrival. Everything is arranged down to the smallest detail, including the scuba gear stowed visibly but not too obviously in an accessible locker.

"Ready?" Ryan asks, starting the engine.

I nod, incapable of speech as the reality of what we're about to do settles over me. This is it. The moment when Celeste Hart ceases to exist in any official capacity. When I commit fully to this new path with no way back.

Ryan navigates us out of the marina. He's handled boats before, another skill in his seemingly endless repertoire. The sunset glitters across the water as we make our way along the coastline, maintaining a casual heading that will eventually bring us to the designated coordinates.

I play my part—taking photos with a disposable camera we'll deliberately leave on board, laughing at Ryan's jokes, accepting a glass of champagne from the small cooler. To any observer, we're just tourists enjoying an evening on the water.

Completely normal.

Completely doomed.

As we near the rocky outcropping that marks our target area, Ryan lowers his voice. "Fifteen minutes. Below deck, there's a waterproof bag with thermal gear. Change while I prep."

I nod, heading below as instructed. The small cabin is neat and functional. The waterproof bag is exactly where he said it would be. Inside, I find the neoprene suits that will protect us from hypothermia in the cold Pacific waters—critical for the escape phase of our plan.

My hands shake as I change; the reality of what comes next is impossible to ignore. I leave my clothes carefully arranged on the bed—evidence to be recovered later. My authentic press credentials sit on top of the pile. My wallet, containing my ID and credit cards.

When I emerge back on deck wearing the sleek black thermal suit, Ryan has already changed into his. The transformation is jarring—no longer casual tourists but operatives prepared for what comes next. He secures a waterproof pack containing essentials, including emergency cash and minimal survival gear.

"Five minutes," he says, checking his watch. "Final systems check."

I watch as he moves around the boat, confirming the remote detonation system, the fuel accelerant, and the strategic placement of our biological samples. Everything is positioned to create the most convincing evidence of our deaths.

"What if someone sees us in the water?" I voice the concern that's been nagging at me.

"Minimal risk. It'll be full dark in twenty minutes, we're far enough from shore, and most boats are back in harbor by now." Ryan secures the waterproof pack. "The night vision surveillance from Mitzy's position shows clear water in our extraction zone."

I try to absorb his confidence. Ryan moves to stand beside me at the railing, his arm slipping around my waist.

"Last chance," he says softly. "Once we do this, there's no going back. Not for a long time, maybe never."

I search his face in the fading light, finding the man beneath the operative—the one who's become far more than a protector to me over the past week—the one who saw me clearly from that first moment on the subway platform.

"I'm sure," I tell him, surprising myself with how true it feels. "Wherever this leads … I'm in."

Ryan steps onto the rear swim platform, water lapping just below his boots, the smell of salt thick in the air. The sun is a smear of dying light behind the clouds, casting everything in hues of bruised gold and steel. We don't speak. There's nothing left to say.

The autopilot hums, guiding the boat straight toward the jagged outcropping that will serve as our supposed tomb.

This is it.

The part where we disappear.

I sit on the rear platform, hands fumbling as I strap on the long black fins. They squeak faintly, rubber slipping over neoprene. My breath hitches as I pull the mask down over my eyes and adjust the snorkel, the plastic mouthpiece alien against my tongue.

Ryan's already done. Efficient. Controlled. As always.

He kneels in front of me, checking the straps on my gear, tugging them snug. His fingers linger on my ankle, then rise to squeeze my calf through the wetsuit.

"You okay?" he murmurs, voice low and steady, pitched just for me.

I nod, but the movement is jerky.

*I'm not okay.* I'm about to fake my death in open water. I'm about to vanish, again. This isn't survival. This is erasure.

But I trust him.

And that's the only reason I haven't screamed.

"We stay shallow," he says, voice clipped, professional now. "Surface swim, steady pace. I'll take the lead. Once we're clear of the blast radius, I'll trigger the det."

"How far is that?"

"A hundred yards minimum. We'll go two, just in case."

I nod again, throat dry. The idea of water slipping over my face, cold and total, makes my lungs tighten—but I breathe through it. In. Out. Just like he taught me.

The boat pitches gently beneath us, like it knows what's coming. Spray mist kisses my cheeks. The rocks are closer now, sharp and waiting.

Ryan reaches for my hand, fingers curling around mine. Warm. Solid. The last tether to the world we're leaving behind.

"Now," he says, and the word slices clean through the moment.

We slide off the swim platform and into the water.

THIRTY-THREE

## Celeste

THE COLD HITS LIKE ICE AND FIRE ALL AT ONCE—CRASHING OVER my skin, stealing my breath. The impact knocks the air from my lungs, but I recover fast, head snapping above the surface. The mask holds. The snorkel is in place.

Ryan surfaces beside me, grabs my hand, and kicks. Strong, steady strokes. I follow, matching him beat for beat, each kick pushing me farther from the boat, from the life I've known, from everything I thought was safe.

The engine drones behind us, growing smaller, swallowed by the sea.

We swim.

And behind us, our death ticks closer with every breath.

Then …

The sea convulses.

A deep, shuddering boom erupts behind us—less a sound than a force, a pressure wave that punches through the water, slamming into my spine like a battering ram. The world jerks sideways. A surge of displaced seawater rolls beneath me, tossing me up like a rag doll.

My ears ring. My lungs seize. I surface instinctively, gasping, and what I see steals the breath right back out of me.

Flames.

A towering column of fire licks the sky, orange and gold and terrifyingly beautiful, twisting upward from where the boat used to be. Burning shrapnel rains down in arcs, some pieces still glowing red-hot as they hiss into the water.

The ocean is a roiling mess of foam and heat, the acrid scent of fuel and char thick on the back of my tongue.

Ryan's face is ghost-lit by the inferno, his expression unreadable—but his gaze locks on mine, solid and grounding.

"Keep moving," he says, voice low and sharp over the hiss of burning wreckage.

We swim parallel to the coast, the burning wreckage receding behind us. From shore, witnesses will be calling 911, reporting the explosion. Within minutes, emergency services will respond—Coast Guard, local police, and fire boats. All arriving too late to save the couple tragically caught in a freak accident.

All documenting the deaths of Ryan Ellis and Celeste Hart with meticulous attention.

The cold seeps through my wetsuit as we swim, muscles protesting the continued exertion. Ryan stays close, occasionally checking our position against the shoreline. It's a long swim. A thousand yards to the extraction point.

By the time we reach the shadowed edge of the cove, I'm half delirious from cold and adrenaline, my limbs sluggish, my strokes uneven. My muscles scream with every movement, lungs raw from salt and panic and the burn of escape.

Ryan grabs my arm, guiding me toward a low silhouette bobbing in the water. A dark shape—small, fast, and familiar.

The Zodiac.

A figure crouches at the bow, face obscured by a knit cap and low light, but the voice is unmistakable.

"Jesus, you idiots cut it close." Jeb's tone is all grumble and grit as he hauls me over the side like I weigh nothing. I collapse onto the rubber floor of the boat, gasping.

Ryan's right behind me, swinging himself up with an ease that makes me want to hit him. Or kiss him. I haven't decided yet.

"Nice to see you too, Jeb," Ryan mutters, stripping off his mask and tossing it aside.

"Your fireworks made the evening news already," Jeb says, gunning the engine. The Zodiac surges forward, bouncing hard across the waves. "I've got the Coast Guard scanner running. Search and recovery's already underway."

I huddle low beside Ryan, teeth chattering uncontrollably now that the movement has stopped. He pulls me into his side, wrapping one arm around my soaked shoulders and letting his body block the wind. No words. Just warmth. Just him.

Ten minutes later, the lights of a commercial fishing trawler rise out of the fog like a ghost ship. No name on the hull. Running lights dim. Every inch of it screams cover-op.

Jeb pulls alongside. A rope ladder drops. Ryan climbs first, agile despite the weight of wet gear and fatigue. Then he leans down, grips me under the arms, and hauls me up like he's done it a hundred times.

The second we're aboard, the Zodiac peels away into the dark.

No greetings. No introductions. Just a silent handoff as a man in oilskins leads us below deck where dry clothes, warm blankets, and hot coffee wait like a mirage. I barely have time to sip before the deep thrum of rotor blades builds above us.

Ryan grabs my hand. "That's us."

Up we go—onto the helipad welded to the rear deck. The wind hits like a slap, salty and sharp. The chopper hovers in the darkness, its belly open, side lights pulsing faintly in the mist.

The winch lowers. Ryan clips me in, fast and tight, then hooks himself beside me.

"Hold on," he says, voice pitched to reach me over the roar.

I don't let go.

Not as we rise.

Not as the trawler shrinks below.

Not as the darkness swallows everything behind us.

We vanish into the night, our deaths already on record.

"You did well," he says, voice softer than his usual operational tone.

"Had a good teacher," I manage through still-chattering teeth.

His smile is barely visible in the darkness, but I feel it more than see it—a momentary softening of his perpetual vigilance.

"Package secured," Ghost announces into his headset, then grins at us through his beard. "Welcome to the afterlife."

By morning, the Coast Guard will recover debris from our boat. News outlets will report the tragic accident. Officials will document our deaths. Phoenix will receive confirmation from multiple sources that its targets have been eliminated.

And we'll be ghosts.

We did it. First phase complete. Now comes the hard part: disappearing completely.

The helicopter touches down in a small clearing surrounded by dense forest—a location so remote it doesn't appear on any standard maps. A rugged off-road vehicle waits nearby.

"Final transport," Ghost explains as we exit the helicopter. "Take it to the safehouse, where you'll remain for seventy-two hours while Phoenix's verification protocols run their course. Then we'll move you to Montana."

"Any news on Torque?" Ryan asks.

"Torque's status remains unknown."

The helicopter lifts off almost immediately after we disembark, disappearing into the night sky.

Ryan checks the map left with the UTV, then we're back on the go, just the two of us.

The drive passes in a blur of forest roads.

Ryan's hand finds mine in the darkness, his touch anchoring me to the present.

"Almost there," he announces as we turn onto an even narrower road that barely qualifies as more than a trail. "Safe house is just ahead. Solar powered, no external connections, completely off grid."

The safe house turns out to be a small, modern cabin nestled so perfectly into the surrounding forest that it's nearly invisible until we're right upon it. Inside, it's surprisingly comfortable—minimal but thoughtfully furnished, with a well-stocked kitchen, comfortable sleeping area, and advanced security systems that appear disconnected from any outside network.

"Home sweet home," Ryan says. "For seventy-two hours, at least. The pantry should be stocked, and the security perimeter should be active. I'm going to check, if you want to settle in."

"And after the seventy-two hours?" I ask.

"They'll confirm our official deaths. Then we move to Montana." Ryan's expression grows more serious. "After that, we're Mr. and Mrs. Davis, relocating for a more peaceful lifestyle."

The reality of it settles over me with new weight. Three days from now, we begin new lives. No turning back, no safety net, no connection to who we were before.

Ryan secures the cabin—checking locks, confirming security systems, establishing sight lines, and defensive positions. Always the operator, even now.

I stand before the large windows overlooking the forest,

watching moonlight filter through the trees. In the reflection, Ryan moves behind me, his presence both comforting and surreal in equal measure.

"What are you thinking?" he asks, appearing at my shoulder.

"That Celeste Hart died tonight," I answer honestly. "That whatever comes next … I'm someone new."

"Not entirely new," he says, his reflection meeting my eyes in the glass. "The core of who you are didn't burn up in that boat. Just the external markers. The documentation. The digital footprint."

"Is that what you tell yourself?" I turn to face him directly. "That Ryan Ellis isn't really gone?"

He considers this carefully. "I've reinvented myself before. The externals change. The essence remains."

"And what's my *essence*, according to you?" I ask, genuinely curious about his assessment.

"Stubborn," he says immediately, the corner of his mouth lifting. "Determined. Fiercely intelligent. Unwilling to back down when you believe you're right." His expression softens. "Brave in ways most people never have to be. Adaptable beyond what anyone could reasonably expect."

His description warms something in my chest, not because it's flattering but because it feels true. Feels like me, regardless of what name I carry or what life I'm living.

"And us?" I gesture between us. "Is that part of the essence that remains, or just circumstance throwing us together?"

He steps closer, hands coming to rest on my shoulders. "What do you want it to be?"

"I'm nervous."

"Why?"

"Montana will be the real test. No adrenaline, no immediate danger, no mission parameters. Just us, figuring out who we are together when the world isn't actively trying to kill us."

"Technically, the world will still be trying to kill us," he corrects with characteristic precision. "Just less *actively*."

I laugh despite myself, the tension of the day finally breaking. "Always the optimist."

"I prefer 'tactical realist.'" His smile widens, revealing that rare, unguarded version of Ryan I've glimpsed only in our most private moments.

I reach up, hand against his cheek. "Well, tactical realist, what happens now?"

"Now?" His eyes darken as he leans into my touch. "Now we have seventy-two hours of complete isolation while the world believes we're dead. No outside contact. No mission requirements. No immediate threats."

"Whatever will we do with all that time?" I step closer until our bodies nearly touch.

His hand slides to the back of my neck, fingers threading through my hair with possession. "I have some ideas."

"Care to share?"

Instead of answering, he bridges the small distance between us, lips finding mine with the same precise attention he brings to everything. The kiss deepens immediately, days of tension, triumph, and fear channeling into something electric between us.

When we finally break apart, both breathing hard, his forehead rests against mine. "First," he says, voice rough with desire, "I'm going to take you to bed and remind us both that we're very much alive."

"And then?" I ask, hands already working at the buttons of his shirt.

"Then," he says, guiding me backward toward the bedroom, "we start figuring out who Ryan and Celeste are going to be. Together."

"Together," I echo, the word slipping out smoother, more certain than I expect. "I like the sound of that."

We're almost to the doorway when the thought hits me.

"Wait," I murmur, halting with my hands on his chest. "Why didn't we change our first names?"

He grins, that slow, smug curve that always precedes something completely infuriating—and weirdly hot.

"Because," he says, backing me the last few steps until my spine meets the doorframe, "when you come, you scream my name like it's the only word you remember. Figured it'd be safer not to mess with that muscle memory."

Heat floods my cheeks, spreading lower, sharper. "You're an asshole."

"Sure, but …" His mouth brushes mine, cocky and soft all at once. "I'm yours."

Hours later, I lie awake beside him, watching moonlight trace patterns across the unfamiliar ceiling. Ryan sleeps beside me, one arm still draped protectively across my waist, even in sleep. His breathing is deep and even, his face peaceful in a way it rarely is during waking hours.

Somewhere out there, Phoenix is processing our deaths, reallocating resources, and calculating new threat matrices. Somewhere, Torque may still be alive, enduring God knows what while Ghost works to find him. Somewhere, my editor and Ryan's mother are hours away from receiving news that will shatter their worlds.

And here, in this isolated cabin, we exist in a strange limbo between lives. No longer who we were, not yet fully who we will become. Just two people who found each other in the chaos, who chose each other despite—or perhaps because of—the circumstances that brought us together.

I should be terrified. Should be mourning the life and identity I've lost. Should be consumed with regret, uncertainty, or doubt.

Instead, I stare at Ryan's sleeping face, counting his slow breaths, and feeling something dangerously close to contentment.

Not because this situation is ideal—it's far from it—but because whatever comes next, I won't face it alone.

Celeste Hart died tonight in a tragic boating accident off the Oregon coast. Details at eleven, forgotten by next week's news.

But I'm still here. Still breathing.

And I'm still fighting.

THIRTY-FOUR

# Epilogue

CELESTE

*Three Months Later: Undisclosed Location, Montana*

THE CABIN SITS NESTLED AGAINST A BACKDROP OF MOUNTAINS, snow blanketing the surrounding forest in pristine white. Inside, the woodstove crackles, fighting back the February chill.

I look up from my laptop as the door creaks open and Ryan steps inside, snow clinging to his boots and melting in gritty puddles on the worn wood floor. He shrugs off his coat, shaking off the cold, then hangs it by the door. The wind's still howling behind him, but he brings a quiet calm with him—steady, grounded.

But it's his face that catches me.

The beard is new. Fuller. Thicker. It roughs up the sharp line of his jaw, making him look older, wilder. More untamed. As if shedding his old life permitted the man underneath to surface.

He catches me staring and arches a brow. "Too mountain man?"

I shake my head slowly, lips curving. "Too hot, actually."

That earns me a low, satisfied grunt as he toes off his boots, crossing to me with snow in his hair and something in his eyes that has nothing to do with the storm outside.

"Supply run successful?" I ask, setting aside the financial reports I've been studying as part of my cover identity.

"All the essentials," he confirms, crossing to drop a kiss on my forehead before unloading groceries onto the counter. "And news from Ghost."

I straighten immediately, attention sharpening. "Torque?"

"Alive." Ryan's expression is complex—relief mixed with something grimmer. "Extracted three days ago from a private facility in Hungary. Condition critical but stable."

"He made it," I breathe, hardly daring to believe it after months of uncertainty. "What did they—"

"Don't ask," Ryan cuts me off, the shadow in his eyes warning me away from that line of questioning. "Just know that he's safe now. Guardian HRS's medical team has him."

I understand the boundaries. Some details are better left unshared, especially regarding what happens to men like Torque in enemy hands. "And our status?"

"Unchanged for now." Ryan begins putting away groceries. "Ghost recommends maintaining current protocols for at least another three months. Phoenix's algorithm is still running security sweeps, though resource allocation has shifted primarily to other threats."

Three more months of isolation, pretending to be Ryan and Celeste Davis to the few locals we interact with, and building our cover story one careful layer at a time. I should feel disappointed. Instead, I'm strangely relieved.

More time to figure out what comes next.

More time in this bubble we've created, away from the world's complications.

More time with Ryan, learning who we are together when not running for our lives.

"Ghost sent something else," Ryan says, reaching into his pocket. He withdraws a small USB drive, similar but not identical to the one that started this whole journey. "Information he thought you should have. Secured, obviously."

I take it, turning it over in my hand. "What's on it?"

"He didn't specify. Just said your journalistic instincts might find it interesting." Ryan's expression gives nothing away, though I suspect he knows more than he's saying.

Later, after dinner, I connect the drive to our secure, offline system. What I find makes my breath catch—evidence of three new deaths, officially ruled accidents or suicides. An analyst at the Pentagon. A programmer formerly employed by Northridge. A congressional staffer with security clearance.

All with connections to Phoenix. All with death patterns that match those I was investigating before this began.

In a separate file, a simple message from Ghost:

*Phoenix is still operational. Resources are divided, but adapting. The hunt continues. Your work matters.*

I sit back, staring at the screen, the implications washing over me. This isn't over. It may never be truly over. The algorithm continues its silent calculations, its deadly executions. Ryan appears in the doorway, leaning against the frame, watching me with those observant eyes that miss nothing.

"Your call," he continues, crossing to stand behind my chair, hands resting on my shoulders with gentle pressure. "Ghost is giving you a choice. We can stay completely dark, focus only on our security. Or …"

"Or we can fight from the shadows," I finish for him. "Use our 'dead' status as an advantage."

His thumbs work small circles against the tension building in my neck. "It would mean additional risk. Controlled contact with trusted assets. Limited field operations eventually."

"But we could make a difference." I lean back against him, drawing strength from his solid presence. "We could help stop Phoenix before it evolves beyond anyone's control."

"We could," he agrees, his voice neutral in a way I've learned means he's letting me reach my own conclusions without influencing them. He's always the tactician, even in personal matters.

I consider the options, weighing safety against purpose, comfort against conviction. Three months ago, Celeste Hart died pursuing the truth about Phoenix. That pursuit cost lives—Jared, Quentin, Zara, Lachlan. Nearly cost mine and Ryan's. And Torque, whatever condition he's in now after months in enemy hands.

Can I walk away from that? Can I live peacefully in these mountains while Phoenix continues its silent, deadly calculations? While more people die from "accidents" carefully engineered to silence them?

"What would you do?" I ask, genuinely curious. "If it were solely your decision?"

Ryan is quiet for a long moment, his hands still on my shoulders. "A month ago, I would have said stay dark. Complete Ghost Protocol, focus on security, leave the rest to Cerberus and Guardian HRS."

"And now?"

His eyes meet mine in the reflection of the computer screen. "You'll never be satisfied with just surviving. Fighting for the truth isn't just what you do—it's who you are." His lips curve in that slight smile I've come to treasure. "I'd rather fight alongside you than ask you to be someone you're not."

The weight of his understanding and his acceptance of who I am at my core settles over me like a blanket. This man values certainty and control above all else and is willing to embrace the risks because he sees me.

Knows me.

"We tell Ghost we're in," I decide, reaching up to cover his hand with mine. "Cautiously, slowly, but in."

"I already told him you would be," Ryan admits, not looking remotely apologetic about presuming my answer. "We have three more months of silence and staying dark. Training begins when the snow clears."

I should be annoyed at his presumption. Instead, I laugh. "You knew what I'd choose before I did."

"I've been watching you chafe at inactivity for weeks." He leans down to press a kiss to the top of my head. "The investigative journalist in you was never going to stay buried for long."

He's right, of course. These quiet months have been necessary—healing, even. Time to process everything that happened, adjust to our new reality, and build something solid between us without the constant pressure of immediate danger.

But beneath the peace, I've felt it growing—that restless energy, that need to pursue truth regardless of the consequences. The same drive that led me to Jared's hotel room that night in D.C., that kept me digging even as the bodies piled up, that refused to back down even with professional killers on my trail, it's still there.

Stronger.

Some things don't die, even when you do.

"So what happens next?" I turn in my chair to face him directly.

"Ghost sends specialized equipment through secure channels. You'll analyze the new deaths, map potential adaptations Phoenix might have made." Ryan leans against the desk, arms crossed—casual on the surface, but everything about him vibrates with lethal purpose. "All while maintaining cover as the boring financial analyst and her slightly high-strung security consultant who moved to Montana for fresh air and quiet."

"Ryan and Celeste Davis by day," I say, cocking a brow, "ghost operatives by night. Sounds exhausting."

"Challenging," he corrects, mouth twitching. "But not impossible—with the right partner."

Partner.

That word still slips under my skin like a touch—unassuming, intimate, and entirely deliberate coming from a man who didn't even share beds, let alone missions, until the subway platform in D.C. turned both our lives inside out.

"Speaking of partners ..." My fingers toy with the ring. It feels permanent now. Real. "You know this whole cover thing doesn't need to be a complete lie."

"Marriage?" His voice is low, eyes locked on mine. "For real?"

I nod, teeth sinking into my bottom lip.

His eyes flash—heat, hunger, possession. The kind of look that used to undo me when I was running. Now it roots me deeper.

I take a slow step forward. "So ... Are you going to ask me?"

He pushes off the desk in one smooth movement, closing the space between us.

"You forget how this works," he murmurs, his voice dipping to that register that pulls my body taut. "In this relationship, I lead. You follow."

A flush climbs up my throat, but I hold his gaze. "Fine. Then ask me."

"When the moment's right," he says, brushing his knuckles over my hip, slow and deliberate. "Assuming you're not still tied up when it comes."

My breath snags. "Tied up?"

That grin. Dark and knowing, edged with promise. "You said 'Fine. Then ask,' like a brat testing limits."

"I wasn't testing," I murmur, lips twitching. "I was challenging."

"Same thing," he counters, pulling me flush against his body. "Which means you've earned yourself a refresher."

"In what?"

"Obedience." His voice drops, rough velvet over steel. "We've covered restraint before, but clearly, we need to take things up a notch."

I tilt my chin, feigning bravado. "You planning to tie me up until I behave?"

His mouth brushes my ear, the heat of it making my knees weaken. "No, sweetheart. I'm planning on tying you up because you don't."

I gasp, but he's already moving—one hand sliding beneath my sweater, the other fisting gently in my hair as he guides me backward.

"Lesson one: submission under pressure. Lesson two …" His gaze rakes down my body. "How to beg properly. While bound."

My pulse pounds so hard I can barely think.

"Are you always this bossy with your fake wives?" I whisper.

"Only the one I plan to keep," he growls, lifting me without effort. "Can't have a wife who doesn't know how to slip a knot—or stay in one." He slides his hand to the small of my back and pulls me against him, every line of his body promising discipline and pleasure.

"Guess I'd better learn," I breathe.

"Starting now." He lifts me effortlessly, my legs circling his waist as he carries me toward the bedroom—our shadows melting into the warm flicker of firelight, the mountains beyond a silent witness to the new identities we've claimed and the darker truths we're still unraveling.

Tomorrow, the fight continues.

But tonight, I surrender. Again. And again.

I found something I never expected. Purpose beyond the byline. Connection beyond the temporary intensity of breaking news. A partner who challenges me, protects me, sees me for exactly who I am, and wants me anyway.

And when the snow melts, we'll continue fighting from the shadows.

Phoenix operates in the darkness, its algorithms calculating threat assessments, dispatching resources, and eliminating targets with cold precision. A person known only as "Shadow" continues authorizing its deadly operations somewhere. Somewhere, more innocent people stumble across truths that make them targets.

But something has changed. Something Phoenix's calculations can't account for.

Two ghosts move in that same darkness. Two people, officially dead but very much alive, with unique knowledge of the system hunting them, and nothing left to lose.

Ryan shifts in his sleep, arm tightening around my waist as if he's determined to keep me safe even while sleeping. I place my hand over his, feeling the strength in his fingers, the warmth of his palm against my skin.

Outside, snow continues to fall, blanketing our hidden sanctuary in pristine white. Inside, plans take shape, purposes align, a future neither of us could have imagined begins to form.

Celeste Hart is dead, but the hunt continues.

---

IN A SECURED SERVER ROOM DEEP BENEATH A NONDESCRIPT OFFICE building in northern Virginia, a system completes its 90-day verification protocol.

TARGET: HART, CELESTE

STATUS: ELIMINATED
VERIFICATION: COMPLETE
THREAT LEVEL: NEUTRALIZED
RESOURCES: REALLOCATED

---

TARGET: ELLIS, RYAN
STATUS: ELIMINATED
VERIFICATION: COMPLETE
THREAT LEVEL: NEUTRALIZED
RESOURCES: REALLOCATED

Across multiple screens, data flows in elegant patterns—surveillance feeds, intercepted communications, financial transactions, and geolocation markers. The algorithm processes all the information, identifying patterns, calculating probabilities, and assessing threats.

In a separate window, new targets emerge:

- Journalist, San Francisco Chronicle, researching defense contractors
- Systems analyst, Pentagon, accessing classified project files
- Forensic linguist who works on encryption algorithms for DoD contractors
- Congressional staffer, requesting budget information on black projects

---

THE ALGORITHM ASSIGNS PRELIMINARY THREAT SCORES, allocates surveillance resources, and begins building profiles. The pattern continues, unbroken and unquestioned.

Until a small anomaly appears.

In Montana, a cellular tower briefly registers an encrypted transmission on a frequency that shouldn't exist. The duration is too short for complete analysis. The source disappears before triangulation completes.

The system logs the anomaly, assigns it a low priority due to insufficient data, and continues its primary functions.

But somewhere in its evolving code, a subroutine takes note. Begins monitoring that specific frequency spectrum. Adjusts sensitivity parameters for that geographic region.

The hunt continues.

In both directions.

---

**READY FOR BOOK THREE IN THE CERBERUS SECURITY SERIES?**
Read **WHISPER**
**WHISPER**
**Book 3 - Cerberus Protection Services Series**

**THREE RESEARCHERS DEAD. TWO WEEKS. ONE TERRIFYING pattern.**

Dr. Eliza Wren's academic world shatters when she discovers her linguistic research has accidentally decoded fragments of something deadly. Something that's already killed three of her colleagues.

Her cipher patterns were supposed to be historical. Ancient. Safe.

They're not.

The encrypted data on her laptop holds secrets worth killing for—an entire financial empire built on blood and shadow. Now Phoenix contractors hunt her through Georgetown's halls, and her FBI handler lies dead in an alley.

One call brings Cooper "Whisper" McKenzie out of the shadows.

Former military sniper. Current surveillance ghost. A man who speaks in silences and moves without sound. His world operates on precision, discipline, and absolute quiet.

Eliza processes everything out loud. Every thought. Every fear. Every brilliant deduction that tumbles from her lips as they race through D.C.'s underground tunnels.

She talks when she's nervous. He needs silence to survive.

She connects through words. He communicates through action.

But her chaotic brilliance cracks codes his methodical mind can't reach. And his lethal precision keeps her alive long enough to decode the impossible—Phoenix's Ashfall Protocol. The financial reset that funds an AI system with unlimited resources and zero conscience.

In abandoned NSA facilities and forgotten government tunnels, two opposites discover that survival requires more than silence or speech. Trust builds in the spaces between words. Heat ignites without sound.

When Phoenix teams close in and Phase Two threatens global chaos, Whisper must break his silence.

And Eliza must learn that sometimes the most important communications happen without words at all.

**He kills from the shadows. She decodes in daylight. Together, they'll expose an empire built on silence—or die in the attempt.**

*The Cerberus Protection Services Series: Where deadly operators protect brilliant women from a conspiracy that reaches into every shadow of power.*

• • •

**WHISPER IS A FULL-LENGTH, HIGH-HEAT ROMANTIC SUSPENSE novel featuring:**
  •A protective alpha hero who meets his match
  •Forced proximity that ignites into scorching chemistry
  •Edge-of-your-seat action with a steamy slow burn
  •Passionate power exchange between equals
  •Only one bed (and so much sexual tension)
  •Life-or-death stakes with an emotionally satisfying HEA

*No cliffhangers. Can be read as a standalone, but best enjoyed as part of the Cerberus Security Series.*

**"Control is his specialty until he meets the one woman who challenges everything—a fearless journalist who ignites a passion more dangerous than the killers pursuing them."**

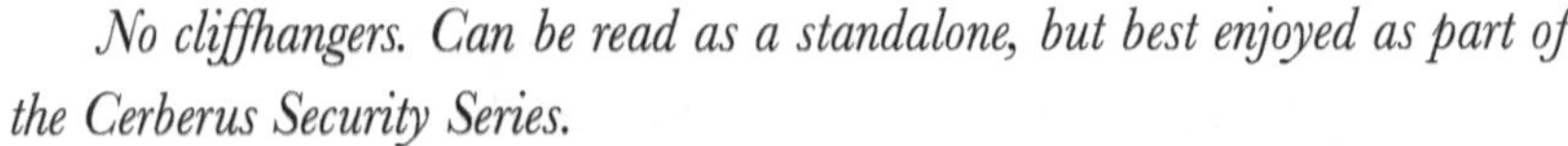

CRAVING MORE GUARDIANS?

If you've fallen for the fierce alphas of Cerberus, you're just getting started.

There's an entire world waiting for you—the Guardian Hostage Rescue Specialists series—one built on danger, desire, and the kind of love that ruins a woman for anyone else.

Start with the *Alpha Team series*—because once you meet these men, you'll never forget them. Protective. Possessive. Unapologetically alpha. And the women who bring them to their knees? Equally unforgettable.

BUT IF YOU WANT TO FEEL **EVERYTHING**—IF YOU WANT TO understand where it all began, before Cerberus, before the Guardians, before the rescues—go back to the beginning.

*Heart's Insanity,* the first book in the *Angel Fire* rock star romance series, is where you'll meet Skye and Forest. It's raw. It's emotional. It's the origin story of the entire Guardian world. And trust me—once you see who Forest Summers was before Guardian HRS existed, you'll never look at him the same way again.

**Start there.**
**Feel everything.**
**And then come back for more.**
Start with Heart's Insanity
Or dive into the Alpha Team series.
The heat only gets hotter.
The danger only gets deadlier.
And the Guardians?
The mission isn't over. It's just getting started.

**Keep current with Ellie Masters.**
**CLICK HERE**
**Receive news of her writing and new releases.**

**Shop Ellie Masters Romantic Suspense and Steamy Contemporary Romance by series.**
**Angel Fire Rock Romance**
**Guardian HRS: Alpha Team**
**Guardian HRS: Bravo Team**
**Guardian HRS: Charlie Team**
**Guardian HRS: Delta Team**
**Cerberus Personal Security**
**The LaRouge Triplets**

**The One I Want Series**
**Angel's Peak Series**
**Billionaire Boy's Club**
**The Lovers**
**Changing Roles**

# Please consider leaving a review

I HOPE YOU ENJOYED THIS BOOK AS MUCH AS I ENJOYED WRITING it. If you like this book, please leave a review. I love reviews. I love reading your reviews, and they help other readers decide if this book is worth their time and money. I hope you think it is and decide to share this story with others. A sentence is all it takes. Thank you in advance!

# ELLZ BELLZ

## ELLIE'S FACEBOOK READER GROUP

If you are interested in joining the ELLZ BELLZ, Ellie's Facebook reader group, we'd love to have you.

Join Ellie's ELLZ BELLZ.
The ELLZ BELLZ Facebook Reader Group

Sign up for Ellie's Newsletter.
Elliemasters.com/newslettersignup

## Also by Ellie Masters

The LIGHTER SIDE

Ellie Masters is the lighter side of the Jet & Ellie Masters writing duo! You will find Contemporary Romance, Military Romance, Romantic Suspense, Billionaire Romance, and Rock Star Romance in Ellie's Works.

***YOU CAN FIND ELLIE'S BOOKS HERE:***

***ELLIEMASTERS.COM/BOOKS***

**Shop Ellie Masters Romantic Suspense and Steamy Contemporary Romance by series.**

Angel Fire Rock Romance

Guardian HRS: Alpha Team

Guardian HRS: Bravo Team

Guardian HRS: Charlie Team

Guardian HRS: Delta Team

Cerberus Personal Security

The LaRouge Triplets

The One I Want Series

Angel's Peak Series

Billionaire Boy's Club

The Lovers

Changing Roles

---

## *SUGGESTED READING ORDER*

### *START HERE*

### *Rockstar Romance*

### *The Angel Fire Rock Romance Series*

EACH BOOK IN THIS SERIES CAN BE READ AS A STANDALONE AND IS ABOUT A DIFFERENT COUPLE WITH AN HEA.

**IT IS RECOMMENDED THEY ARE READ IN ORDER.**

*Heart's Insanity*

*Ashes to New*

*Heart's Desire*

*Heart's Collide*

*Hearts Divided*

*Hearts Entwined*

*Forest's FALL*

*Hearts The Last Beat*

### *CONTINUE HERE...*

### *Military Romance*

### *Guardian Hostage Rescue Specialists*

*Rescuing Melissa*

*(*Get a FREE copy of Rescuing Melissa

when you join Ellie's Newsletter*)*

### *Alpha Team*

*Rescuing Zoe*

*Rescuing Moira*

*Rescuing Eve*

*Rescuing Lily*

*Rescuing Jinx*

*Rescuing Maria*

### Bravo Team

*Rescuing Angie*

*Rescuing Isabelle*

*Rescuing Carmen*

*Rescuing Rosalie*

*Rescuing Kaye*

*Cara's Protector*

*Rescuing Barbi*

### Charlie Team

*Rescuing Rebel*

*Rescuing Stitch*

*Rescuing Mia*

*Jenna's Protector*

*Rescuing Sophia*

*Rescuing Malia*

*Rescuing Ally (Part 1)*

*Rescuing Ally (Part 2)*

### Delta Team

*Rescuing Ember*

*Rescuing Aria*

## STANDALONES IN THE GUARDIAN HOSTAGE RESCUE

# About the Author

Ellie Masters is a USA Today Bestselling author and Amazon Top 15 Author who writes Angsty, Steamy, Heart-Stopping, Pulse-Pounding, Can't-Stop-Reading Romantic Suspense. In addition, she's a wife, military mom, doctor, and retired Colonel. She writes romantic suspense filled with all your sexy, swoon-worthy alpha men. Her writing will tug at your heartstrings and leave your heart racing.

Born in the South, raised under the Hawaiian sun, Ellie has traveled the globe while in service to her country. The love of her life, her amazing husband, is her number one fan and biggest supporter. And yes! He's read every word she's written.

She has lived all over the United States—east, west, north, south and central—but grew up under the Hawaiian sun. She's also been privileged to have lived overseas, experiencing other cultures and making lifelong friends. Now, Ellie is proud to call herself a Southern transplant, learning to say y'all and "bless her heart" with the best of them.

Ellie's favorite way to spend an evening is curled up on a couch, laptop in place, watching a fire, drinking a good wine, and bringing forth all the characters from her mind to the page and hopefully into the hearts of her readers.

*FOR MORE INFORMATION*
elliemasters.com

# Connect with Ellie Masters

Website:
elliemasters.com
Purchase Direct:
elliemasters.com/shopify
Amazon Author Page:
elliemasters.com/amazon
Facebook:
elliemasters.com/Facebook
Goodreads:
elliemasters.com/Goodreads
Bookbub:
elliemasters.com/Bookbub
Instagram:
elliemasters.com/Instagram

# Final Thoughts

I hope you enjoyed this book as much as I enjoyed writing it. If you enjoyed reading this story, please consider leaving a review on Amazon and Goodreads, and please let other people know. A sentence is all it takes. Friend recommendations are the strongest catalyst for readers' purchase decisions! And I'd love to be able to continue bringing the characters and stories from My-Mind-to-the-Page.

Second, call or e-mail a friend and tell them about this book. If you really want them to read it, gift it to them. If you prefer digital friends, please use the "Recommend" feature of Goodreads to spread the word.

Or visit my blog https://elliemasters.com, where you can find out more about my writing process and personal life.

Come visit The EDGE: Dark Discussions where we'll have a chance to talk about my works, their creation, and maybe what the future has in store for my writing.

Facebook Reader Group: Ellz Bellz

Thank you so much for your support!

Love,
Ellie

# Dedication

*This book is dedicated to you, my reader. Thank you for spending a few hours of your time with me. I wouldn't be able to write without you to cheer me on. Your wonderful words, your support, and your willingness to join me on this journey is a gift beyond measure.*

*Whether this is the first book of mine you've read, or if you've been with me since the very beginning, thank you for believing in me as I bring these characters 'from my mind to the page and into your hearts.'*

*Love,*
*Ellie*

# THE END

www.ingramcontent.com/pod-product-compliance
Lightning Source LLC
Chambersburg PA
CBHW021209310726
48971CB00006B/1500